MOONLIGHT AND MISTLETOE AT THE CHRISTMAS WEDDING

BOOK 6 IN THE NEW YORK EVER AFTER SERIES

HELEN ROLFE

Boldwood

First published in 2020. This edition first published in Great Britain in 2022 by Boldwood Books Ltd.

Cover Design by CC Book Design

Cover Photography: Shutterstock

A CIP catalogue record for this book is available from the British Library.

Paperback ISBN 978-1-80415-656-8

Large Print ISBN 978-1-80415-657-5

Hardback ISBN 978-1-80415-655-1

Ebook ISBN 978-1-80415-658-2

Kindle ISBN 978-1-80415-659-9

Audio CD ISBN 978-1-80415-650-6

MP3 CD ISBN 978-1-80415-651-3

Digital audio download ISBN 978-1-80415-653-7

Boldwood Books Ltd
23 Bowerdean Street
London SW6 3TN

For my husband who makes me lunch every day so that I can get more writing done!

1

KAISHA

Kaisha was on her way to join friends at the Inglenook Inn for Thanksgiving and she loved being here in Manhattan again, flooded with memories of her days as a New York University student whose only worries had been whether her art history essay was too verbose or whether she'd be able to stay awake in lectures after a big night out. She wondered if, one day, she might call the city home again. Could she ever be brave enough to take the leap and go after what she truly wanted? To do that she'd have to gain back the confidence she'd once had in herself and that wasn't easy when those she was closest to had abused her trust and hurt her beyond belief.

As she walked, the cold November air mingled with the aroma of fresh coffee and doughnuts drifting from a nearby café and wrapped around her along with the banter of groups passing by, the mayhem that this time of the year brought with it. She had come into the city from Connecticut nice and early so she could somehow catch a glimpse of the Macy's Thanksgiving Day Parade and, as usual, the event had drawn millions of spectators, all keen to be a part of New York's marking of another holiday season, cheering along performers, celebrating amongst oversized balloons that bobbed along, marching bands, floats, and a feeling of merriment that Kaisha couldn't quite muster this year. Because last Christmas she'd been full of hope; she thought she knew what her future held and all she'd have to do was make the break and move forwards, but now she had no faith in herself, no belief in her own judgement, let alone her ability. And she'd told nobody about what really happened between her and her sister, Bree. Until now, she'd simply put a smile on her face in front of family and in front of friends, including Cleo who was there at the door to the Inglenook Inn when Kaisha arrived at the brownstone in Greenwich Village.

'Come in out of the cold,' Cleo urged. Not only was Cleo Kaisha's boss, but she'd become a good friend too.

Kaisha hugged Cleo hello and stepped inside to the warmth of the inn. 'How you ever gave birth to two children with a figure like that is beyond me.' She looked at her friend, who was wearing the dress Kaisha had made for her, a ruby-red, crushed-velvet piece that flattered her curves perfectly. Her wavy, dark-blonde hair hung loose and just a touch of make-up around her blue eyes made Cleo look gorgeous as ever.

Kaisha used the mirror in the hallway to run a hand through cropped wavy hair and check her own appearance. 'It's windy out there, I feel like I've got Manhattan debris everywhere.' But at least the wind hadn't disturbed the mascara or eyeliner surrounding her hazel eyes, or the coral lip gloss she'd chosen to put on tonight. 'I can't check the back,' she pleaded, looking to Cleo.

'Crouch down, let me.' Kaisha's height in comparison to Cleo's often came in handy when they were working at the Little Knitting Box in Inglenook Falls, because Kaisha could reach the yarns on the uppermost shelves when Cleo struggled. When Kaisha crouched down now, as instructed, Cleo checked and confirmed, 'You're all clear and looking gorgeous tonight, so stop fretting.'

Darcy was next along the corridor with a glass of eggnog balanced in her palm, ice-blue eyes glittering with all the mischief of the season and the excitement of being back at the inn even though she owned and ran her own place out in Inglenook Falls now. 'Kaisha, welcome!'

'It's as though you still work here,' Kaisha hugged her hello. 'Where's Sofia?' Sofia was the business owner and she and Darcy had been a good partnership for a long time until Darcy decided to make her own way.

'Her daughter is in town so she's having a big Thanksgiving with the in-laws. I offered to manage guests here at the inn at the same time as hosting our own Thanksgiving.'

'You always were good at multitasking,' Cleo complimented.

'Says the woman with more things on the go than Santa Claus,' Darcy joked, her chestnut hair shimmering beneath the lights in the hallway.

Kaisha watched the exchange, glad to be a part of this group Cleo had drawn her into gradually over the years they'd known one another. There was a trust built up between Darcy and Cleo, a strong friendship between them and others, and Kaisha doubted anyone would ever abuse that. She'd give anything to feel that secure, knowing friends and family had her back, that they'd be there for her no matter what.

Once Kaisha had hung her coat on one of the hooks near the entrance, she followed the others into the cosy lounge with the Christmas tree visible from the street. Sparkling and festive, it instilled a sense of peace without really trying. 'How's it going at the Inglenook Lodge?' she asked as Darcy ladled out a measure of eggnog for her. Last Christmas Darcy and her husband Myles had announced they'd bought the former Chestnut Lodge in Inglenook Falls, Connecticut, renamed it the Inglenook Lodge with Sofia's blessing given this very place had a similar name, and slowly it was beginning to take in guests.

'We're open for business,' Darcy beamed. 'But not for Thanksgiving this year; the dining room is still undergoing renovations and we've shut that off from the rest of the place, so next year will be our first big Thanksgiving event for guests.'

'You'll have a full house soon when Cleo's wedding guests arrive.'

'I can't wait; the more visitors the better. You know me, I get a thrill with it all.'

'Loving your job is the way to be happy,' Kaisha smiled. She really did live by the mantra that life was too short to do something you didn't love, although sometimes she was guilty of sitting back and falling into the usual routine when, really, it was time she made a change.

'Cheers to that.' Cleo took another mouthful of eggnog before setting down her glass to go and use the restroom.

Kaisha sipped the creamy, luxurious mixture. 'This is really good.'

'Made to Cleo's recipe,' said Darcy, reciting the ingredients from memory. 'Actually, while I've got you on your own for a minute, I wanted to ask how she is.'

'Cleo?'

'Is she coping with the wedding plans?'

'She's more excited than anything else.' Between them they kept a close eye on their friend for signs of stress, overworking, both of which Cleo wasn't a stranger to but could catch her out when she least expected.

'Not too busy?'

'Well, you know Cleo. She's busy, but at least very organised.'

'Good to hear.'

They watched as their friend came back down the hall chatting with Rupert, the chef at the Inn who Darcy had paid to put on a full Thanksgiving dinner for them all this evening before he went off to join his own friends and family.

'The dress you made her is gorgeous by the way,' said Darcy. 'You have a real talent.'

'I'm not sure about that.'

'Don't sell yourself short.' Darcy, dressed in heels and a deep-green kimono wrap dress and with her hair hanging loose around her shoulders rather than in the work-day chignon she usually favoured, saw to a guest who had come down the stairs and needed directions to the Rockefeller Center.

'It must be nice to be back here in the city,' said Kaisha when Darcy was free again.

'It's lovely to visit.'

'The Inglenook Lodge is stunning though and it must be wonderful to have your own place.'

'It feels right, you know?' she beamed. 'When Myles and I agreed to buy the lodge I knew we'd made a good decision.' She crossed her fingers on both hands. 'Let's hope it's a booming business in years to come.'

'I'm sure it will be.' Kaisha had witnessed both Darcy and Myles cope with strenuous workloads, overheard enough conversations to know that it had been a source of much stress for them. Not that running your own business was any less pressure. 'Is Myles happy to be out of the rat race?'

'More than I thought he would be. I thought he'd miss it, but so far he's so busy turning his hand to help with renovations, working with Dylan to do a new snazzy website, keeping the paperwork for the business in order, that I don't think he's had a chance to miss the world of investment banking. And the time we spend together... well, it's priceless.'

Kaisha had a pang of sorrow because once upon a time she'd spoken about her former boyfriend Cory in the same way as Darcy was talking about her husband now. Last Christmas she'd glowed like Darcy; like Cleo, too, with her upcoming nuptials with Dylan. But this year, Kaisha's smile was in place for one reason and one reason only: so that she didn't have to admit the truth to anyone.

* * *

'Is that one of your trees too?' Kaisha asked Mitch as they all gathered in the dining room of the inn to take their seats for Thanksgiving dinner. In the corner was a seven-foot-tall pine tree, its branches full and laden with silver and ice-blue baubles, lights winding round and round from top to bottom.

'Sure is.' Mitch ran the Christmas tree farm in Inglenook Falls and had been a recluse in the not-so-distant past, but this group of people had rallied around him and supported him at a time when he needed it the most. The handsome, part-shaven man pulled out a chair for his partner, Holly, before sitting down himself.

'It's a beauty,' Kaisha complimented. 'And the smell is wonderful.'

'Let's hope it lasts,' said Holly, auburn curls bouncy around her shoulders. 'Although I'm almost immune to the scent now, living in the log cabin in the woods surrounded by pines and cedar trees.'

'You don't miss your city apartment?' Kaisha wondered, never quite having managed to shake off the thrill of Manhattan.

'I occasionally miss the freedom of strolling around the city taking photographs, or grabbing takeout at weird hours of the night if I'm out late, but there's so much to see wherever you are. You adjust, I guess, and I love Inglenook Falls.'

'It's my favourite town too, but I do miss the city.'

'Think you'll ever move back?'

She wanted to be careful what she said in front of Cleo. 'Maybe one day, who knows.'

Candles stood proudly down the centre of an enormous Thanksgiving table draped with a red tablecloth. Glistening silver rings hugged festive green napkins in cigar shapes, rectangular, silver, straw placemats were framed with gleaming, heavy silver cutlery, and a range of glasses shone at each position. A centrepiece of holly and ivy adorned with red berries and snow-dusted pine cones was moved to one end by Darcy to make room for the food and the whole room was as welcoming as a big family gathering.

Kaisha gulped at the thought of her own family strewn across the miles this year, that sense of togetherness shattered. But for now, among friends, she put her smile back in place, determined to let her worries seep away if only for tonight.

Myles was next to arrive and Kaisha soon found herself surrounded by happy couples – Cleo and Dylan who were tying the knot before the end of the year, Darcy and Myles who seemed to be so in sync with each other these days, and Holly and Mitch who behaved like a couple of newlyweds, which was hardly surprising given the log cabin in the woods filled with Christmas trees. It couldn't get much more idyllic than that.

'Did you watch the parade?' Cleo asked Kaisha as she made her way around the table pouring champagne into awaiting glasses.

'I did. I came to the city early especially,' Kaisha admitted. She and her sister had watched the parade on television as kids, then when they were older their parents had brought them to Manhattan for the unique atmosphere and Kaisha had continued to come every year as an adult when she could, something Bree could never understand. To Bree it was the same old rituals, jostling crowds, the same streets, and Bree had never been one to be content with what she had. She'd always wanted more.

'Ruby and Jacob went with Prue this year,' said Dylan, passing Cleo another bottle of champagne he'd popped the cork on. His ex-wife had never been reliable when it came to the kids and Kaisha was glad to see things appeared to be settling down.

'I'll bet they loved it even though the crowds were a challenge.' Despite her lack of festive cheer, Kaisha had enjoyed sharing time and space with so many New Yorkers and visitors excited for the holidays. It was a good tonic to distract her mind from the approaching Christmas without her loved ones.

Cleo started off with the Thanksgiving toasts. 'I'm thankful for babysitters so Dylan and I can be kid-free this one night.'

'I would have to second that,' Dylan grinned, green eyes shimmering with love every time he looked in his wife-to-be's direction.

Darcy was next. 'I'd like to give thanks that Myles and I have survived going into business together. I've heard it can be the making or breaking of some couples.'

Myles agreed. 'I'm thankful for my wife's patience,' he told everyone.

'Holly, you're next,' Cleo prompted.

'I'm thankful for another year with this wonderful man.' She touched a hand to Mitch's cheek. 'And for how much firewood he chops to keep the log cabin so nice and warm.'

'And I'm thankful for you,' he batted back, 'and for first impressions that didn't last.' Everyone laughed then because when Holly first met Mitch she'd run away from him, scared by his rugged appearance, the matted hair and beard, a loner in the woods who'd surprised them all.

'Kaisha?' Cleo and everyone else looked her way.

Kaisha beamed a smile around the room. 'I am thankful for friends, all of you, and how much you all mean to me.'

The clinking of glasses echoed in accompaniment to the Christmas carols playing through a speaker set up at the side of the room. The waft of turkey, salty gravy, and candied yams drifted closer and closer until Rupert and Myles between them delivered the main platters for the feast.

'Should we wait?' asked Cleo.

'For what?' Kaisha's tummy rumbled in anticipation.

'Dylan's friend, his best man.'

Ah, the infamous best man Dylan had said very little about apart from that he was a childhood friend, they'd been out of touch for a long while, but that he was the only person suited to the job.

'He should be here by now.' Dylan shook his head. 'I'm sure he won't be long – I know he's in town already. But we can't let this feast go cold. Rupert, you've done a mighty fine job.'

'It all looks amazing,' Kaisha agreed. 'And there'll be plenty to go round, so if Finn is late I don't think it'll matter,' she reassured Cleo, although she was secretly fuming inside at this person she had never met, already letting the side down. She didn't know much about Finn but Kaisha had noticed that every time his name was mentioned, Cleo seemed to tense as though she were wondering whether this was the part of their wedding that would cause the most trouble. And if his timekeeping skills were anything to go by, she could be right.

Rupert served the turkey. The platter of vegetables made its way round, Kaisha exchanged the dish of yams for the parsnips and honey-glazed carrots, and the gravy boat was passed from person to person.

A tear threatened to trickle from the corner of Kaisha's eye, partly from unhappiness at what had gone on in the last twelve months, the other part because she really was thankful for what she still had. Here tonight, with true friends, she knew that she'd never let anybody around this table down, not ever.

The sound of cutlery against plates, laughter, and merriment filled the room as they ate. Cleo looked at her watch yet again, no doubt fretting about Finn.

His absence hadn't escaped Dylan's notice either and he was frowning, checking his phone again. 'I don't know what's keeping him. He's local, staying with his grandad, so he should've been here a lot earlier than the rest of us.'

'I hope he's more reliable on your wedding day,' Myles joked.

'He will be,' Cleo smiled, as though reassuring herself rather than anyone else.

'How long have you guys been friends?' Mitch directed his question to Dylan.

'Since we were kids. He spent a lot of time at our place, almost like a brother in many ways. He had a bit of a tough time over the years, doesn't really like to talk about it.'

'Sounds like someone else,' Holly smiled at Mitch. 'Although we coaxed you out of your shell eventually. Maybe that's all Finn needs.'

Dylan ran a hand across his smooth-shaven chin. 'I wouldn't go there if I were you. Even I don't broach the subject of his childhood with him, and as long as we don't, we're all good.'

Kaisha had grown closer to Cleo over time, they often joked they were like sisters, and unlike Kaisha's biological sister, Cleo deserved to be happy and not have this Finn character ruin her big day. Kaisha wasn't so sure about having such a loose cannon as part of the wedding. Wasn't it asking for trouble?

'What does Finn do for work?' Darcy scooped out some more yams and smiled in thanks to Myles for pouring more gravy onto her plate. They seemed to know each other's ways so well and it was cute to watch.

'He's between jobs,' was Dylan's reply.

Kaisha knew what that meant, it was code for being unemployed and bumming around. Her sister had been doing that for years as she travelled around, then again when she returned to Connecticut.

Deciding she'd heard enough about Finn for now, Kaisha changed topic. 'Your big day is getting so close,' she smiled to Cleo.

'Everything is on track too.' Cleo crossed the fingers of her free hand after she passed the bowl of glazed carrots in Kaisha's direction.

Kaisha declined and she set them down on the table. Like every other Thanksgiving, the feast was enormous and they still had dessert to go yet. Knowing Rupert, who had made an equally sumptuous spread for the Fourth of July barbecue here at the inn, dessert would likely be something irresistible and moreish and Kaisha wanted to save at least a little bit of room.

'You've picked an amazing location for the wedding,' Holly smiled, sipping her champagne. 'The Bampton Lodge is stunning, it'll be the most perfect day.'

Cleo's shoulders relaxed, but that could've been the champagne she was knocking back given the novelty of kid-free time tonight. 'I'm beginning to get excited now it's all falling into place. The reception room is wonderful, the archway we'll get married beneath is gorgeous.'

'A great venue in any season,' Darcy added.

'I still can't believe you didn't get a wedding planner,' said Myles. 'It's a lot to organise on your own.'

'You know me, I wouldn't trust anyone else to do it as well as I could, and there's not too much to do now, we're almost there.'

'Remember I'm on hand to ask,' said Kaisha, 'whatever you need.'

'You're a good friend, Kaisha.'

'After everything you've done for me, I can't repay you enough.'

'Don't ever feel indebted to me,' Cleo insisted. 'I won't have friends feeling that way.'

But Kaisha did. Not only was she renting the apartment above the Little Knitting Box in Inglenook Falls at a ridiculously cheap rate, she had a job she enjoyed with a flexibility that allowed her to flit between the store and the markets. And even though she hadn't shared what happened over the last year with Cleo, her friend had always been there in the background in case she needed to talk. She was just too embarrassed to tell anyone how she'd been so gullible and hurt all in one go by those who should never have betrayed her.

'Your wedding will be nothing short of magical,' Holly put in, 'and I can't wait to take the photographs.'

Cleo's eyes sparkled. 'Up until now I've been doing my utmost not to get carried away.'

'But it's your wedding day,' Kaisha urged. 'Getting carried away is all part of it.'

Holly leaned in and whispered to Kaisha, 'She's been catastrophising.'

'I have not,' Cleo insisted, but one nibble of the end of a carrot and she confessed, 'well, maybe I have, just a bit.'

Darcy took hold of her friend's hand. 'As long as you and Dylan both turn up, then whatever else happens, rain, hail, or shine, if your dress gets trashed, the cake dropped, you say the wrong name – as if – then so what?'

Kaisha began to laugh. 'Don't listen to her, Cleo.'

'She knows I'm humouring her,' said Darcy, who had had enough things go wrong before her own wedding and somehow still made it down the aisle to marry Myles.

Cleo lifted a glass. 'Here's to fate doing whatever the hell it likes.'

'Bold statement,' Kaisha giggled.

When Dylan passed behind their chairs it was clear he'd over-heard the tail end of their conversation. He gave his wife-to-be a kiss of reassurance. 'I'm going into the lounge for some quiet so I can call Finn before he misses out on the entire evening.'

Once he'd left, Kaisha couldn't help herself. 'How reliable is this Finn? I mean, really? Because so far he's not looking like he is at all.'

'I don't know much about him. All I do know is that his family aren't particularly close, and he was Dylan's best mate growing up. He's never really been on the scene, Dylan didn't mention him much before we got engaged, but as soon as we agreed the wedding date Dylan was insistent Finn was his best man. There was no ques-tion, no suggestion it would ever be anyone else. And I had no reason to worry, until now.'

'You're worried?' Kaisha knew it; this Finn was going to be trouble.

'I get the feeling it wouldn't take much to upset this guy, from what Dylan has said.'

'Dylan is a pretty good judge of character,' said Darcy. 'I'm sure he's made a good choice.'

Dylan came back to join them. 'He's almost here; got lost apparently.'

'Easily done,' said Mitch, 'these streets all look the same in the dark.'

Dylan looked worried but Kaisha didn't mention it, although ten minutes later she knew exactly why he had that look of concern on his face.

'Everyone, this is Finn.' Dylan had answered the door and after murmured voices seemed reluctant to let Finn join the crowd even though he'd been anxious to get his friend here for the past hour.

Tall, blond, and decidedly dishevelled, bundled up in a winter coat with checked scarf, Finn's cute smile surrounded by stubble did little to deflect from the fact he must've hit the bar – or bars, plural – before coming to the Inglenook Inn.

'Great to meet you all.' Finn made an effort to sound as though he wasn't inebriated in the slightest but, stumbling into the table and then finding a chair more by luck than judgement gave the game away.

'Let me take your things.' Darcy, ever the hostess, took the charcoal parka from Finn after he'd wrestled it off. He didn't seem to realise that it would've been far easier to stand up and push his chair away from the table before he tried to get undressed.

Everyone rallied without too many questions to make Finn a part of this evening, and soon his plate was filled with a feast he couldn't ignore. Probably a good job – eating would keep him busy, sober him up, while they all thought about the right way to handle this. He looked Kaisha's way once, electric-blue eyes finding hers until the warning stare she sent back made him focus on nothing but his meal.

Dylan had tactfully filled up everyone's glass of water to the brim from a jug Rupert brought through, including Finn's, rather than singling his friend out and instructing him to hydrate and not ruin Thanksgiving. And talk soon turned to the wedding again.

'Could be grotty weather at Christmas,' Finn put in. Kaisha supposed she should be happy he was at least talking reasonably well.

With the warmth of the inside he removed his sweater, whipping it off so fast Kaisha caught a glimpse of a body that was no stranger to physical workout. Toned and manly, a scar on one side above his waist, a tattoo that looked strangely like a bumblebee on his upper left arm. But she only saw a flash of both before he covered up and got on with shovelling an overly generous portion of yams into his mouth.

'Or it could be beautiful,' Kaisha retaliated, turning her attention back to Cleo and Dylan. 'There could be a glistening frost sparkling on the trees or a light fall of snow outside as you say your vows. It would make it even more magical.'

Eyes on his plate, fork spearing the remaining piece of turkey, Finn batted back, 'Or the white snow could've turned to filthy mush that gets everywhere, all over white dresses, making the wedding party look like a scene out of a dark horror movie...'

Holly took the reins. 'We'll deal with whatever the day throws at us; I for one can't wait.'

Finn looked up at the various faces watching him as though he were an imposter. He shrugged. 'Fair enough, I was just saying.'

'We're getting married at the Bampton Lodge. Do you know it?' Cleo attempted to engage Finn in further conversation.

'Can't say I do, no.'

'Why don't we have a break before dessert?' Darcy suggested after Finn had dragged the last piece of yam through the gravy on his plate and pushed it into his mouth. Others took the cue and started stacking plates so between them they could clear the table.

Kaisha wasn't sure whether to be annoyed that Finn wasn't helping or glad he was staying put and not getting in the way. 'Top-up?' she asked Cleo after finding another bottle of champagne doing the rounds.

'Go on then,' she grinned. 'Grandpa Joe has the kids tonight. He and Maggie have set them up in their living room on airbeds like a campsite. They'll have a lot of fun but I dread to think how much sugar they're being fed.'

'Grandparents are the best,' said Finn, studying his glass of water and not looking up. 'The very best,' he muttered again, almost to himself.

'You all right there, buddy?' Dylan sat beside Finn.

Kaisha and Cleo were doing their best to leave them to it although Kaisha couldn't get out of her seat very easily with Finn's chair blocking the way. She was doing her best to squeeze past without having to ask him to move.

'Parents are in town,' said Finn.

'Oh.' Dylan reacted as though Finn's explanation answered all of his questions.

Cleo had taken one pile of plates away and came back to grab the bowl that had nothing left but one lonely roast potato, which Finn plucked with his fingers before she could disappear out to the kitchen again.

'You're crazy to get married,' Finn declared after Cleo had taken the empty bowl away. He was holding the golden potato ready to shovel it down with the rest of his food.

Kaisha stopped trying to squeeze past Finn's chair and froze on the spot.

'I'll forgive you for saying that just this once.' Dylan's voice begged no argument. 'But I'm telling you, you're wrong.'

'All it'll bring is heartache,' Finn rambled on. 'Look at my parents. Look at Prue. Marriage is a waste of time.'

'Listen up, you.' Kaisha jabbed a finger in Finn's direction. She couldn't hold her tongue any longer when he finally looked at her, still behind him, still unable to get out. Ignoring the playful lips behind the stubble on his jaw, she told him, 'Just because you're messed up about something doesn't mean you can come in here and ruin things. Don't you dare say anything like that in front of Cleo.'

'You're feisty,' Finn said with an air of approval. 'I like that.'

Kaisha leaned closer. 'I am feisty, so watch out or I'll shove that potato somewhere rather uncomfortable.'

Finn began to laugh, Dylan looked shocked at the outburst, and all three of them pretended nothing at all was wrong when Cleo came back in the room. Finn had his first warning and Kaisha wouldn't be afraid to give him another.

And by the time they all resumed their seats to enjoy pumpkin pie cheesecake at least Finn had settled down a bit. But when he looked her way again, Kaisha glared at him to let him know she wouldn't stand for any fooling around or cutting remarks when it came to the wedding. Cleo and Dylan were getting married at the beautiful Bampton Lodge on Christmas Eve and nobody was going to ruin it for them.

2

FINN

Finn picked up the comforter that had fallen from the arm of the sofa onto the wooden floor. On the sofa itself were his pillows and the rolled-up camping mat that may as well have been a sheet of paper given he'd felt as though he were sleeping directly on the floor last night until he'd dragged the coffee table aside and laid the mat on top of the Persian rug.

His head ached from the liquor he'd consumed yesterday before heading on over to the Inglenook Inn and making a great first impression on Dylan's fiancée and friends. He winced at the memory now as he rested his head back, one arm keeping charge of the comforter so it didn't topple off the arm of the sofa again.

His grandad shuffled past and over to the wing-backed chair at the edge of the room. The long, narrow windows of this pre-war apartment allowed plenty of daylight to filter in, showing up the dust on nearly every surface. This was a common peril of living in the city, where pollution found its way inside no matter what, but Grandad was a proud man; it wouldn't be right to point it out. Instead, Finn would tell Beryl, the carer who came in every day to see to things like cleaning, cooking, and generally keeping John company. Finn's dad, Andy, had tried to put John Thompson in a home in Connecticut where he'd be with people his age, where wardens could keep an eye on him and so could he. But Finn could've told his dad how that suggestion would go down even before he tried it, and the compromise had been for a paid carer to come in every day. Finn was relieved Grandad had agreed, because as adamant as he was that he wasn't going anywhere, any fool could see the old man was lonely. And that in itself broke Finn's heart.

Looking up at the soaring ten-foot-high ceilings that made him, at six feet four, struggle when it came to changing a light bulb, Finn understood why his grandad loved this place. It was almost part of his identity – he'd lived here since before Finn was even born. The age-old, tatty, burgundy armchairs, taupe wing-backed chair and sofa with the patched repairs his grandma had made over the years she was alive were going nowhere, the dark-chestnut, solid-birch bureau sat in the same corner it always had, the doorway to the kitchen still had pencil marks denoting Finn's height changes. He wished Grandad would paint over the marks now so he no longer had to see them as a reminder of why they'd stopped the ritual all of a sudden.

Finn scraped a hand through his hair to try to get some life back in his system, and this time he abandoned the comforter when it fell to the floor yet again. 'Mom and Dad are freaking out that I'm staying here, imposing on you,' he told his grandad. They'd shown their disapproval yesterday – one of the many reasons he'd stopped at several bars on his way to Thanksgiving dinner.

'I told them I don't mind. And it's my choice, not theirs.' His grandad always had been unswerving when it came to having things his way; not a bad quality in Finn's book.

'When have either of them ever cared about what anyone thinks other than themselves?' he muttered.

Ignoring him, Grandad tilted his head in the direction of the kitchen. 'Make yourself useful...'

Finn grinned – he knew exactly what the request meant – and remembering that yesterday his mum and dad had both warned the ninety-six-year-old man not to have such strong coffee, he felt good to be doing something they rigidly censured. 'One coffee, extra strong, coming right up.'

'I'll enjoy it before Beryl gets here. That woman can't make a decent coffee. She serves me something more resembling dishwater than something I'd pay good money for.'

'Don't worry, I'll see to it.'

'And get rid of the smell before Beryl arrives.'

'Sure thing.'

Thank God for Beryl, who was a balm to his grandad's loneliness so much more than Finn had ever thought a carer would be. Finn would have loved nothing more than to keep his grandad company for longer, but he had to get out there and find work. He'd headed back this way to spend time with Grandad as well as for Dylan's wedding but he was no sponger; even though he didn't have much of a career direction, he'd take any job he could.

In the confined kitchen that at least had a window, even though it didn't look out to much other than someone else's window and fire escape, Finn put a generous amount of coffee into the machine, filled the water reservoir and set the machine to go. His body craved some kind of pick-me-up after yesterday. Thanksgiving had a lot to answer for and right now the only thanks he felt like giving were that his mum and dad weren't here again today. He wasn't sure he could handle them with a hangover.

Yesterday, his parents had put on the usual performance. They'd come to the apartment on the pretence of it being a special occasion of the year, a day that was all about family, when they barely were one of those any more. Finn's parents had divorced a long time ago and why they'd stayed together for so many years before they went their separate ways was anyone's guess. The second Finn moved out in his early twenties, they'd split up, and the only reaction Finn had had was to wish they'd done it sooner. Ever since he was a teenager and the family was faced with more pain than some saw in a lifetime, all Beverly and Andy Thompson had done was bitch and moan at each other. They'd fight, yell, they had so much anger inside of them, and on the fringes of that shocking advertisement for marriage was Finn, wondering what the hell type of family they were. Finn had got away as soon as he could. And he'd been running ever since. But family was family, and when Grandad had asked Finn to join them all yesterday for drinks on Thanksgiving – probably knowing full well that peace throughout a whole meal would be too much to expect – Finn couldn't refuse. He'd do anything for his Grandad.

Including making him a decent cup of coffee.

The strong brew flooded the apartment and Finn took the coffees through to the living room, where he stood by the window holding his own, looking down onto the street. 'It's getting colder.' He put the back of his hand against the glass. 'I love the change of seasons.' He loved change full stop. It kept him going. It was when he stood still for too long that he started to think too hard about the way his life might have been had things been different.

'I'm hoping for snow,' his grandad declared. 'It's not much for an old man to ask for, is it?' He slurped the coffee that Finn knew was way too hot. Knowing Grandad he'd be thinking of Beryl marching in here reprimanding him and wanted to get the beverage into him before she could take it away. 'Snow makes winter real, it makes Christmas. It's magical.'

He sounded like that girl at the inn last night. 'And the slush, and dirt, and the city grinding to a halt, people getting injured or worse with black ice... really magical.'

'I hope you weren't this miserable at the Thanksgiving gathering you went to. How is Dylan, by the way?'

Grandad had at least been in bed when Finn got home from the inn, although if he'd commented on the intoxication, Finn would've told him it was down to a rocking good time rather than anything else. 'He's good, business is going well, Cleo seems nice.'

'She's his fiancée, have I got that right?'

'Your mind is sharp as ever,' Finn smiled. 'And they're marrying on Christmas Eve.'

'Romantic.'

'Or stupid.'

'I hope you didn't tell them that.'

Finn's brow creased. 'You know, I think I might have mentioned something.'

'Marriage can be terrible if the fit isn't right. But your grandma and I had over fifty wonderful years together.'

'You never fought?'

'Of course we did, but the trick is to laugh together, to talk, and remember, never fight when you're hungry.'

'Why?' Finn perched on the edge of the window sill.

'Because being hungry makes you ratty. And besides, if you fight and you haven't eaten, you might not get any dinner at all. You know your grandma was the cook in the family, you got your talents from her.'

Finn ignored the hint of praise and gulped down more of his coffee, urging Grandad to do the same when the intercom buzzed, signalling Beryl's arrival.

'Don't you go letting your parents' behaviour and choices influence your life,' said Grandad for good measure.

'Bit late for that.' He pressed the button to answer the call and unlock the door downstairs.

'Damn.' Grandad took one more gulp of coffee. 'You'll have to get rid of the rest, I'll be in the emergency room with second-degree burns to my throat otherwise.'

Finn cleared away the evidence and put the cups in the slimline dishwasher before pulling open the door to the apartment. 'Hey, Beryl.' He kissed her on the cheek. Not only was she a carer, she also saw herself as a member of the family and Finn humoured her as much as he could. She meant well, she was reliable and chatty, and his grandad didn't resent her presence as many of his age perhaps would. 'Happy Thanksgiving for yesterday.'

'Happy Thanksgiving to you too.' She bustled in. 'Almost Christmas. John, you organised that tree yet?'

It always sounded weird when someone called Grandad by his actual name. Even his mum called him Dad half the time because they'd always got on famously. And after Finn's parents split up, Beverly had stayed in regular contact with Grandad.

'I'll pick one up this morning,' Finn assured her.

'See – all organised, Beryl,' Grandad insisted. 'Told you I'd get it done.'

'I smell coffee,' she detected, setting down her straw bag filled with goodness knows what and taking off a heavy wool coat that only just fitted on the last hook by the door.

'That'll be me,' Finn explained. 'Can't start the day without a cup.'

'Not too many of those a day for your grandad,' she warned, waving her hand in the air for effect. 'His blood pressure and nervous system will be all over the place.'

'I'm sitting right here,' said Grandad, 'and I haven't lost my marbles yet. No need to talk over me.'

When Beryl had got straight to work as she always did and tidied a pile of books on a side table before grabbing a cloth to wipe down the coffee table, Finn had a quick word in her ear about the dust. She assured him, discreetly, that she'd get right to it and as she fussed around the apartment, her dyed-black curls bounced as much as she did in rubber-soled shoes, her laughter hit the walls, rebounding off of them like a supersonic squash game. She was a jolly character and exactly what Grandad needed. Finn's parents had agreed that whoever they found via an agency shouldn't be someone too serious, and while Beryl had a no-nonsense manner, she was still friendly and could while away the hours with anyone. She was bossy too, but Finn had a feeling Grandad didn't mind that. It kept him on his toes, and he kept Beryl on hers.

'Remember, dental appointment at one o'clock,' Finn reminded her.

She sighed. 'I know his schedule better than you do.'

Finn smiled. Of course she did. 'Saw it in the diary, thought I'd mention it in case.'

She put her hand against Finn's arm briefly as a reassurance she had everything in hand, he could go off and be a thirty-four-year-old male without worrying. On a few occasions she'd got a front-row seat and seen what his parents were like when they were in a five-metre radius of each other. One time she'd witnessed them arguing over the choice of biscuits – his dad was supposed to pick up Grandad's favourite, double choc chip, and he'd got the wrong ones, oatmeal and raisin. A petty gripe from his mum had led to bickering over how Andy couldn't get the tiny details right, which had led to him accusing Beverly of needing to relax, and all of this done at a volume that crescendoed to an uncomfortable level.

Maybe it was sympathy that caused Beryl to confuse his hang-over with feelings of melancholy and sensitivity over his family. But he'd learnt how to distance himself from them a long time ago.

Beryl had started going through news headlines on her iPad, ready to discuss current affairs and no doubt get into a heated argument or two with Grandad. She still had a duster in her hand after wiping it over the photo frames lined up on the mantel, over the squirrel figurines his grandma had collected and his grandad would never part with, and Finn left them both to their banter while he set off in search of a Christmas tree.

He'd only made it to the end of the street when he got Dylan's text asking if they could meet up. He was in town on business, seeing a client to discuss their website, and suggested they meet at a café they'd been to before in Greenwich Village. Finn noted he didn't suggest a bar and hoped his behaviour yesterday wouldn't get him fired from the position of best man. So he didn't agree with marriage, everyone had their own opinion, but it didn't mean he wouldn't be supportive. Dylan had been like a brother to him growing up; his parents were the surrogate mum and dad he sometimes wished he'd had, feeding him dinner more times than Finn could remember, and they'd turn in their graves if they thought Finn was doing anything to stand in the way of their son's happiness. Finn knew he could be a loose cannon sometimes, but one thing he wasn't was disloyal and he sure wasn't ungrateful either.

Finn replied to the text and instead of walking around in search of a tree, he pushed his way through crowds all heading underground at the subway station and caught the train downtown to meet his friend.

At the café, Finn went for a full breakfast accompanied by a flat white and when they slid into one of the booths in the café, he apologised again for last night. 'I probably made a terrible impression with everyone, and I'm sorry, it was rude of me.'

'Doesn't matter, you'd had a few drinks.'

'Yeah, you could say that.'

'I take it things didn't go so smoothly with your parents.'

'Grandad's mad even putting them in the same room together, but it was Thanksgiving, I couldn't not show up.'

'Haven't they got any easier?' Dylan thanked the waitress for their coffees and cut up the hash browns on his breakfast plate. 'I thought they'd mellow as they got older, especially after the divorce.'

'When I talk to them on the phone individually it's bearable, but as soon as they come together they lose any ability to let the past go.' The challenges they'd faced as a family had broken them all in different ways. His parents had split up; Finn had become angry and resentful, unsure which way to turn. But most of the anger he harboured now was because they hadn't been there to help him through the tough times. This man opposite him now, him and his family, as well as Grandad, they'd been the ones to see Finn through his heartbreak. And he had no idea what he would've done without them.

Finn stabbed the last of the egg white that refused to stick to his fork. He could feel the temper that he'd pushed down yesterday rising up in a big bubble to the surface all over again. 'Grandad seemed to like seeing them both, I suppose, until they began to bicker.' Once upon a time Grandad would've threatened to knock their heads together if they couldn't sort it out, but this time he'd sat in his chair, less energy than usual, as though he'd had enough of it all and just couldn't be bothered any more.

'Are they still pressuring your grandad to go into a home outside the city?'

'They're wary of Beryl and whether we made the right choice having her rather than insisting Grandad moves out. Dad's probably getting impatient, wanting to hurry things along, get his hands on the apartment, sell it or whatever.' He trailed a piece of toast through the egg yolk that had spilled from the set white when he moved it across his plate.

'And how is your grandad? Well enough?'

'As far as I can see he's doing great,' Finn smiled, forever grateful to still have Grandad in his life. 'But he's ninety-six. He's getting more clumsy, his arthritis flares up on occasion and he's not so interested in getting out and about. He's sometimes forgetful too – called me Andy more than once.' Grandad's appetite seemed to have waned as well. After the argument about those biscuits he'd barely touched any of them and Finn knew he'd only eaten half the sandwich Beryl had made him for lunch.

'He's coping with you roughing it on his floor?'

'Just about. My parents are none too impressed but New York rentals are a killer. I don't have work yet and I don't even know how long I'll hang around. You know me.'

'I do.' Dylan cut a piece of toast and pushed it onto his fork. 'Would you go back to engineering when you look for work?'

Ah, the big career question. 'Would you go back to being in an office all day?'

Dylan smiled. 'Not a chance.'

'Exactly.'

'What's the plan then?'

At thirty-four Finn still felt like he was there in the treehouse in Dylan's back garden, asking his advice about school, girls, how to live a life when his family had disintegrated in front of him. 'Right now, it's about getting any work I can find – enough to keep me in the style I've become accustomed to,' he joked. 'And in the New Year... the world's my oyster.'

'Not tempted to settle down?'

'Never.' Although he was beginning to tire of moving around, he wasn't ready to admit it yet. And so he kept it quiet that part of this return to New York was to see Grandad, part was to be at the wedding, and the rest was to see if he could possibly fit in back here again. But he'd have to take it day by day, see what happened job-wise, see if he could survive here better than anywhere else. Occasionally it was as though demons were chasing him and he could only shake them off when he moved on. At this rate he'd be a lonely old man in his sixties or seventies with no place to call home.

Time for a change of subject – his mood was falling, rapidly. 'Hey, I meant to ask, who's that girl who was at the dinner last night? The one in the colourful clothes, short dark hair, fiery temper?'

'Ah, you're talking about Kaisha. And get that look off your face,' Dylan warned. 'I've seen that look, right before you go after your latest conquest. No Kaisha, okay?'

Finn held up his hands. 'I was just asking.'

'And I'm just telling. Not her.'

'She's a good friend?'

'She works for Cleo. She's dedicated to the job, always goes above and beyond and she's become a good friend. I don't think she's had the best road over the last year.'

She wasn't the only one who'd had a tough time, and rather than Dylan's words warning him off, it made Finn all the more interested. He chowed down on the remains of his hash brown as Dylan took a call from his other half. Finn tried not to eavesdrop but given the word choices, his friend had to be talking about the wedding cake.

'Sorry about that.' Dylan put his cutlery together having finished his breakfast. 'That was Cleo double-checking – well, quadruple I think is what we're up to by now – that we made the last payment on the cake. She's stressing. All I want is for this wedding to go smoothly, Finn. God knows it's taken me long enough to get her down the aisle.'

'You obviously don't have as much charm as you thought you did,' Finn teased. 'So everything is organised now?'

'Yup. The cake was one of the last things we did, took us ages to decide. Plenty of tasters though.'

'You would've enjoyed that.'

'Cleo was stressing about whether red velvet was a good choice, but I honestly don't care.'

'You can't lose with red velvet.'

'That's right, I forgot you used to bake.'

'Yeah, not any more.' He hadn't so much as glanced at a cake tin or mixing bowl since his teenage years. It had been a way of banishing painful memories.

'You still think your dad would disapprove?'

'I'm past caring what he thinks.' His dad had never seen baking as a worthwhile profession and he'd certainly let it be known, but that wasn't the only reason for Finn's reluctance, just that sometimes it was easier to think that was all it was instead of having to tell people, like Dylan, the truth. And so Finn carried on the pretence. 'Don't you remember me telling you about the parent-teacher conference at school, when a teacher mentioned to Dad that I should seriously consider pursuing baking as a career because I had talent and passion?' When Dylan didn't answer, his coffee cup still at his lips, Finn filled him in on the details. 'We got in the car and he said there was no way a son of his was going to put on an apron and make pretty things all day. I was better than that, apparently.'

'Why was he always so sure about it not being a valid career choice?'

'Because he's old-fashioned, mean and a stubborn son-of-a—'

'Can I get you anything else?' The waitress was beside the table again, pen and pad poised.

'No thank you,' Dylan smiled.

At least her appearance had broken the process of disseminating everything that was wrong with Finn's life. They'd be here all day if he wasn't careful and over the years Finn had got used to keeping things to himself unless he was talking to Grandad. But now, as far as he was concerned, he didn't particularly relish the thought of airing his dirty laundry in public. Even if Dylan was his best friend.

'Back to the topic of work,' said Dylan, reminding him of the subject they'd touched upon briefly before Finn began asking about Kaisha. Not that it had done him any good – she was off limits, well and truly. 'How do you feel about helping out on a Christmas tree farm?'

'You mean Mitch's place?'

'Ah, so you weren't so drunk last night that you can't remember the conversation we all had.'

'Actually, I've totally forgotten anything other than that he had the farm.' He pulled a face. 'Remind me.' He took out some notes from his wallet to make up his share for breakfast as Dylan recounted where the farm was, the job that was on offer.

'What do you say? Should I tell Mitch you're in?'

'Only problem is going to be the commute from here to Inglenook Falls... I don't mind doing it, but it depends on wages and whether it's worth my while.'

'Mitch will pay fairly.' Dylan shrugged on his coat and buttoned it up. 'Why don't we go see him? He's over at the Garland Street markets today.'

'We'll kill two birds with one stone then. I need a tree for Grandad's apartment.' Not that it would be easy to fit in, with his own sleeping arrangements being in the same room, but for Grandad he'd put up with anything, even snow and the havoc it would cause if that was what he wanted to see this year. Finn was determined this Christmas would be a good one for Grandad. He'd caught pneumonia last year and Finn had flown home from Denver, where he was working a casual job behind a bar. They'd thought it was the end, that it was goodbye, but Grandad had pulled through and surprised them all. Andy and Beverly had tried to move him into a home then, but Grandad had been together enough to tell them to shove it – those were his exact words, Finn remembered – and instead had returned to his New York apartment and his treasured memories of Finn's grandma, Esther, who had passed away in her sleep seven and a half years ago.

At the Garland Street markets, Mitch was busy wishing customers happy holidays and the netting machine was in constant use as a helper wrapped up a tree. Mitch's breath mingled with the cold and he turned up the collar of his coat before shaking hands with Dylan and then Finn.

'I brought Finn along to talk about work possibilities.' Dylan stepped out of the way of a couple trying to tackle the crowd with a Christmas tree, netted and being carried on its side. 'I'll leave you guys to chat and head over to see Cleo. She's got a stall here even after she vowed never again.' He patted Finn on the shoulder and left them to it.

Mitch hauled another tree over to the netting machine and it was clear their work talk would take place while he kept on going. Finn wondered if he should apologise for his behaviour last night but Mitch didn't seem bothered by much other than the reason he was here now. 'I need help out at the farm – felling trees, chopping wood, helping customers load up vehicles, maybe taking trees out to sell in nearby towns. So I guess my first question is whether you'd be happy to commute.'

'If the wages are right, then sure.'

Mitch confirmed the rate of pay and it was indeed favourable. 'You wouldn't believe the amount of firewood we've been selling lately. I can't keep up. Lord knows where they were all getting it from before I came along.'

'Online probably,' Finn suggested.

'I expect you're right, but folks in Inglenook Falls seem to enjoy being able to come pick out a bag themselves now. I deliver some, others load it into their trucks or cars and head on home.'

'How many hours can you give me per week?'

'To be honest I need someone up there every day until the

holiday season is over.'

Finn whistled through his teeth. 'I'm up for it.'

'There'll be a rota with some early starts, which are kind of special out in Inglenook Falls.'

Finn didn't think he'd be seeing it that way at all. Mitch was a rugged, outdoorsy type who lived in a log cabin in the woods and was used to life on the land. Finn had been doing odd jobs, not many of them outside, and this would take some getting used to.

'There'll be some late finishes too, but I'll try to vary it up so you're not exhausted.'

'Sounds good to me.' And a lot of hours would cover his travel costs as well as everyday expenses. 'Is there much accommodation out that way?' Maybe he could stretch to a hostel a few nights so he didn't have to do the commute every time. Sleeping on the hard floor after a day bumming around the city was one thing, but after a day of hard physical labour?

'There's a hostel in nearby Bampton; have a word with Dylan, he might know of something a bit closer to Inglenook Falls. One more question...' Mitch took payment for another tree and wished the customer happy holidays, and Finn hoped this wasn't going to relate to his drinking habits, which had been out of control yesterday. 'When can you start?' When Mitch smiled kindly, Finn got a sense that this man might have had problems of his own once upon a time, that he understood not everything was as black and white as it seemed.

Dylan came up behind him as he and Mitch shook hands on the new arrangement. 'You got the job?' He put a hand across his heart and pretended to shed a tear. 'I'm so proud of you.'

'Get lost,' Finn joked. 'Looks like I'd better start setting an alarm unless you can point me in the direction of a hostel out that way.'

'Actually, I might have an alternative solution for you,' Dylan told him when they moved out of the way of enthusiastic shoppers trying to bag the biggest, fullest, best tree. 'Although I'd need your word you'd be on your best behaviour.'

'It's living with you and babysitting your kids isn't it... walked into that one.'

'There's no way I can put you up. We're overrun as it is with in-laws arriving soon, the wedding fast approaching. I was thinking about the apartment above Cleo's store.'

'It's empty? That's great.'

'Slow down... it's not empty. Someone lives there at the moment.'

'Out with it, why are you holding back from telling me more?' he asked when Dylan didn't immediately share the details.

'That's because I might be making a stupid suggestion. The tenant right now is Kaisha.'

'Kaisha from last night? The one you warned me off?' He held up his hands. 'I promised didn't I, and when have I ever broken a promise to you?'

'You haven't. So you'll behave?'

'Of course I will. If I get a bed and it's close to the Christmas tree farm, I'm there. And I'll be too tired every day from the list of jobs Mitch has in mind to bother Kaisha.'

'Did I hear my name?' A voice came from behind and when Finn turned, it was to see the girl herself. Dressed in a bright-orange coat, a deep-mahogany scarf covering her neck exposed from short hair, she was balancing three takeout coffees, one on top of the other, in her gloved hands. The look she gave him wasn't particularly favourable either.

'Finn, you remember Kaisha?'

'Of course.' He also remembered his promise and tried to keep any thoughts strictly platonic. 'How are you doing?'

Her long eyelashes flicked up obediently. 'Have you sobered up yet?'

'I have, and I apologise if I was in any way annoying.'

She seemed taken aback by his expression of regret and passed out the coffees, one to Dylan, one to Mitch, and the third to Finn himself, although this begrudgingly. Clearly Dylan had requested the beverages and she'd had no idea who the third one was for until now.

'Do we have a problem?' Finn asked her when Mitch and Dylan were separated from them by a crowd of passing tourists all eager with selfie sticks to capture the markets in this unassuming corner of Greenwich Village.

'I don't have a problem,' she said in a manner that suggested of course she did.

'Something tells me you do.' He took a swig from the cup. 'Good coffee.'

That got under her skin even more. 'Let's just say I *will* have a problem if you make trouble for Cleo and Dylan.'

'Now why would I want to do that?'

'Just a feeling I get.'

'What are they to you anyway?'

'They're good friends, I don't want them hurt by some waster who flits in and out of town whenever he feels like it.'

'Wow. Harsh.' He almost wanted to carry on the arguing – it was kind of fun winding her up and she didn't seem to mind a bit of a squabble; she'd challenge him, and he liked that. His last girlfriend would've done anything for him and, to be honest, he'd got bored and it was part of the reason he'd ended things. But Kaisha, she was different.

Their conversation came to a halt when Dylan joined them and Mitch got back to work. Dylan put an arm around Kaisha's shoulders, his other cradling his coffee, and Finn suspected the move was to remind Finn of his warning over this good friend of his. 'Kaisha, remember how I just mentioned I needed a favour?'

Wary of Finn being any part of this conversation, she said, 'Anything, you know you only have to ask. And I'm happy to put guests up in the apartment for the wedding, to make it easier for you guys.'

'It's not really about a wedding guest, although, technically, perhaps it is,' Dylan admitted.

'Oh, is it a favour to do with organising the actual wedding?' she quizzed more excitedly. Typical woman getting all high-pitched and swirly when anyone mentioned the W word.

'Not the wedding, no. I need a favour for someone in need of a place to stay, someone who would love a bed rather than a floor and a sleeping bag.'

'Who's sleeping rough?' A softer side, a caring one, lingered for a moment.

'That'll be me,' Finn put in, amused by her immediate glare. 'Well not rough exactly, but on the floor, at my grandad's apartment. It's not the most comfortable.'

'And where might that apartment be?' Thick eyebrows almost joined in the middle with her frown.

'East 74th.'

Kaisha laughed and sipped her coffee. 'You want me to believe that living in a Manhattan apartment is in some way a terrible, terrible inconvenience. What, did your wallet bulge with too many bank notes, or are you fed up with living among the rich and famous?'

'My grandad is hardly famous. And his apartment is small, one bedroom, and I'm a little in the way. He's ninety-six. He's the best man in the world and I can't do it to him any longer.' It was more about losing the commute from Manhattan to Inglenook Falls, but in the back of his mind Finn never wanted his grandad to feel stuck in a position where he couldn't ask him to move on. It was up to Finn to take charge before they reached that point.

Kaisha looked almost accepting of his explanation and turned to Dylan. 'How can I help, exactly?'

'I wondered if you'd mind Finn moving into the tiny room in the apartment above the store.' He quickly added, 'It's only temporary, while he works at the Christmas tree farm.'

Rosebud lips fell open at the suggestion and already Finn suspected they had their answer but she said, 'Of course, not a problem. It'll be a squeeze, but I'm sure we'll manage just fine.'

With relief, Dylan told them both, 'You might not even see that much of each other. It sounds as though Mitch will be working Finn pretty hard and Kaisha, you put in a lot of hours too.'

Cleo had come to join them, catching the tail end of the conversation, and her face fell. She looked to Kaisha. 'Don't tell me he already asked you?'

'About sharing the apartment? Yep.'

'Dylan.' Cleo frowned. Finn didn't know her at all but she looked stressed out. He'd heard that happened with brides to be – yet another reason to avoid the whole marriage sham. 'Kaisha, I wanted to talk to you before he asked. But really, you don't have to do this, it's your place as long as you need, so please say if it's a problem.'

Finn wondered whether he should point out that he was standing right here, but maybe keeping quiet was the way to go.

'It's honestly not a problem,' Kaisha insisted. 'I'm paying next to nothing in rent, I owe you more favours than I can count, I'm happy to do it, and it's not for long anyway, right?'

'The farm is a year-round job,' Mitch put in when he had a moment between customers. 'Who knows, I might keep him on.'

'He's a good employer,' Cleo assured Finn, perhaps awkward that she'd just been ranting to Kaisha right in front of the very cause of her concern.

'And I'll be a good worker.' Finn thought it best to clarify because right now Cleo's only impression of him was the way he'd been at Thanksgiving. He wasn't sure but he thought he heard Kaisha harrumph and it tickled him that he'd got under her skin so much in less than twenty-four hours. He directed his next remark to her. 'I'll do my best to be a good house guest, and I'll pay half the rent.'

'You get the smaller room, it wouldn't be fair –'

'Half the rent, I'm not a charity case.'

'Fine. Your choice.'

Cleo returned to her market stall and Finn thought he might as well pick a tree from here and rope Dylan in to helping him carry it home. He perused the choices, some tall, some short, some fat, others thin, all smelling exactly like Christmas even out here on the New York streets with the aroma of food drifting on by, mingled with traffic fumes, in the air that had at least cleared after the dense early morning fog.

'See one you like?' Mitch asked.

Kaisha hadn't moved on and Finn sensed she wasn't finished with him yet. Maybe he was about to get a whole list of house rules. 'This one's good,' he told Mitch.

'Got far to go?'

'East 74th.'

'I'll net it and deliver at the end of the day if that suits better.'

'You're sure?'

'He's sure,' Dylan said, pleased to be escaping the task of helping negotiate streets and crowds with a seven-foot tree. 'You had to pick the biggest one.'

'My grandad would've picked the smallest but I figure he deserves this.'

Mitch netted the tree, Dylan left Finn paying for it while he went off to a second client meeting of the day, and Finn could see colourful Kaisha still hovering – the alliteration of this description for her seemed to fit and it tickled him to think of it – and you really couldn't miss her in the orange coat. It stood out a mile against the bleak skies, against the darker clothes most other people dressed in to withstand a long, harsh winter.

He moved away from Mitch's chalet to where Kaisha was standing. 'Why do I get the feeling you've got more to say?' He pushed his wallet into the inside pocket of his jacket. 'Is this about not upsetting Cleo and Dylan, or is it about the fact we're about to move in together?'

'We're not moving in together,' she bristled. 'And you can't blame me for being wary after the way you acted at the Inglenook Inn.'

He was about to reply but instead simmered. 'Look, in fairness, I was an ass.'

She began to smile. She looked totally different when she did. Hazel eyes looked more like smooth toffee, a slight crease in her right cheek hinted at a dimple if he could make her laugh enough. 'You were an ass.'

'And I apologise.' He pulled his scarf tighter as the Manhattan wind zipped down Garland Street. 'You could say relationships and family haven't made for entirely happy memories in the past, but I will try to rein in my opinions and play nice.' She seemed satisfied with that but still looked circumspect as she turned to go. 'Looking forward to sleeping in a bed at last,' he called after her.

She gave him a strange look and when a woman as old as his grandad threw him a cheeky wink he supposed he had just shouted out their private business down the street.

But he had work, he had a place to live for a while, and Kaisha was someone he wouldn't mind spending more time with even though he knew it was a hands-off situation after Dylan's warning.

Maybe being back in New York and having to go to a wedding wasn't going to be so bad after all.

3

KAISHA

'You got it?' Dylan asked as he passed another box to Kaisha. 'It's heavy.' They were in the room out back of the Little Knitting Box in Inglenook Falls that led up to the apartment above and they'd been finding out the Christmas decorations for the last hour.

'I'm stronger than you think,' she assured him, taking the weight. She set down the box at the same time as the bell tinkled above the entrance door in the store to announce Cleo's return.

When Kaisha went to see Cleo, she found her boss armed with three takeout mulled ciders. It was easy to go across the road to the fields beyond and all the festive cheer of the Inglenook Falls markets to bring back something to warm you up, such as the tempting spiced cider that was on sale there year after year.

'For you,' – Cleo handed her a cup – 'and for you,' – she held out a second cup to Dylan when he came through to join them after he'd brought down yet another box – 'and one for me.' She closed her eyes and took a sip.

'We need to replenish the mulberry worsted.' Kaisha indicated the almost-empty basket beside the ladder shelves that ran up one wall and had various shades and mixes of yarn hanging at intervals.

'I sold ten hanks this morning to a customer on holidays in Connecticut. First time she'd been here and she did ask where the decorations were.'

Cleo shook her head. 'I usually like to have them up for Thanksgiving. Just didn't happen this year.'

'Better late than never,' Dylan said softly, always there to have Cleo's back, the way a couple should be. Not that Kaisha had ever had any luck in that area. Trust was something she longed to find in a relationship, but it remained elusive.

All three of them took a break, warming up with the apple liquid laced with star anise, a hint of vanilla, and a burst of citrus from the oranges coming through. Surrounded by yarns in all colours and textures, it was a delight to be cosied up in the Little Knitting Box on such a cold day. The fog from yesterday had cleared, darkness had lifted, and the town exuded a crisp, winter finish, icy roofs dotted along Main Street, frost creeping from the corners of the window pane at the front of their store and others along the way.

The Little Knitting Box was the cutest store in Inglenook Falls in Kaisha's opinion, and so they were frequently told by locals and visitors alike. At the rear of the store was a shelf up high on which stood Cleo's grandma Eliza's old Singer sewing machine, a black 1930s piece with gold embossed writing that wasn't used any more yet still shone proudly next to its hardwood case. The cash register sat on an island in the centre of the store and in front of that, a display table with yarns in a rainbow of colours as well as a good selection of knitting patterns to leaf through, gloves in all shapes and sizes, and beanie hats with particularly festive patterns on that would be swapped out for other items depending on the season. Baskets dotted around the store held more stock, white card poking out from each with prices recorded on them; two ladders held yarn displays up against the walls; and more shelving kept alternative yarns. A small coat rail in the front corner held pre-made garments – a few sweaters, and cardigans for men and women. A collection of chunky, soft scarves hung along a rail next to the garments, inviting customers to either choose the yarn and make the items for themselves or, instead, buy them from here. Kaisha always had a knitting project going on while she was working in the store; the last four scarves for sale had been made by her, and right now she was working on a teal, angora sweater to replace a similar one they'd sold last week.

'This cider is just what I needed.' Dylan finished up his drink first. 'But now we need to get going with the decorations.'

Cleo and Kaisha had been staring out of the store window across at the markets, taking in the start of the season. The most wonderful time of the year. But now, they followed suit, finished their drinks, and pulled boxes in from out the back.

Dylan was already opening out the stepladder in the store, avoiding a customer who'd come to choose some new buttons for a cardigan she was knitting her grandson. 'We'll do anything that goes up high first, then I can leave you guys to it and go home to relieve the babysitter.'

'After you grab the tree from Mitch's place?' Cleo checked.

'Already sorted, stop worrying.' He kissed the tip of her nose.

Kaisha looked through how many sets of lights they had and ensured all of them worked, doing her best not to watch the romantic gestures and listen to the exchanges and feel the loneliness that had a way of being so much worse at this time of year. Cleo enlisted Dylan's help to put snowflake decorations on the ceiling as Kaisha reminded them not to let them hang too low or customers would get tangled. They looked good as they went up, fixed with thin pieces of wire on the ceiling at intervals, some in silver, others white.

It wasn't long before the Little Knitting Box glistened with a

mixture of shiny snowflakes and lighting. And when Cleo was satisfied she didn't need Dylan for anything else, at least not yet, he
went on his way while Cleo and Kaisha untangled lengths of fairy
lights and began to distribute those around the store.

Kaisha wound one set up the side of a wall ladder and down the
other side, replacing the yarns as she went. Cleo added a loopy line
of delicate white lights along the shelf with the Singer sewing
machine, and Kaisha had enough height to put the lights around
the doorframe and stepped back to admire her handiwork seconds
before she would have been knocked to the floor by a tree coming
in through the door.

'One tree, as requested,' came a voice, and it wasn't Dylan's.
Finn poked his head around the pine branches. 'Hey, roomie.'

Kaisha wasn't going to let him wind her up, not beneath Cleo's
watchful gaze, and she managed a smile in return. If Cleo thought
his moving into the apartment was too much of an imposition,
she'd be upset at having done it to Kaisha, and it would add to the
fear already building that something was going to go wrong
between now and the day she was due to say, 'I do'. Yesterday, a
newspaper article that told of brides' disasters with everything from
torn wedding dresses to ruined venues when the weather did its
worst hadn't gone any way to quell this bride-to-be's nerves.

'We'd like it to go in the window,' Kaisha instructed, shutting
the door to the store behind Finn as the cold whipped inside.

'Do you have a stand?' he asked as she turned her attentions to a
customer who needed talking through a knitting pattern.

'I think so...'

Cleo headed out back, calling over her shoulder, 'Coming right
up.' But she was back in a couple of minutes to say, 'Sorry, no luck. I
thought Dylan might have brought it down. It's at the very top of
the wardrobe in your bedroom, Kaisha.'

Kaisha wished the customer happy holidays and sent her on her way with more instructions on the pattern she hadn't quite got to grips with. 'Let me get it. I'll take the stepladder.'

'Why don't you let me fetch it?' said Finn. 'I'm taller than you and that way we won't need the steps, I hope.'

Cleo put her hand through the branches of the tree to hold it upright while Kaisha reluctantly told Finn to follow her upstairs. No way was she sending him into her bedroom on his own; she couldn't even remember whether she'd left anything out on the bed like a pile of clean underwear, which no doubt he'd have fun passing comment on.

Upstairs it felt odd to have him in her space. She was used to Cleo or Dylan asking to come up if they needed to – Cleo had taken a nap on the sofa more than once trying to recover from her busy life – but having a man in here was strange and something about Finn made Kaisha particularly nervous. She supposed she'd better get used to having him around.

She opened up the wardrobe doors fully so he'd be able to pull out the box containing the tree stand and pointed up to the top shelf.

Finn took off his coat. 'Too restrictive,' he grinned and Kaisha tried not to be discombobulated by the electric-blue eyes that twinkled with mischief and left her wondering what he was really thinking about. The way his lips twitched suggested it was nothing to do with Christmas trees and stands.

He reached up and the stretch made his T-shirt ride high enough that she could see his waist, the toned torso, and scar she'd caught a glimpse of once before at the Inglenook Inn. He pulled out the box but spluttered as a whole heap of dust came down with it, landing on his face. Kaisha couldn't help but laugh.

'Don't just stand there laughing at me, it's in my eyes,' he pleaded.

'Sorry.' She took the box and set it on the floor. 'Go wash them, the bathroom's this way.' She waited for him to follow while he pulled the oddest faces trying to get rid of the dirt in his eyes. She had to lead him to the basin after he bashed into the door and he didn't look amused, which was probably why she was.

He splashed water onto his face and she handed him a towel when he was done. Standing in her bathroom, he took up most of the doorway with his muscular frame and it was hard to believe that, as of tomorrow, he'd be actually living here.

'Come on,' she urged. 'Let's get downstairs, Cleo will still be holding the tree.'

Back in the store Cleo was leaning in smelling the pine. 'It's a good tree.'

'Chopped it down myself,' Finn told her.

'That was quick.'

'I started work this morning. Mitch needed the help, I need the money.' He set up the stand and heaved the tree into position, asking Kaisha to hold it steady while he tightened up the screws to fix the trunk in place.

She caught a waft of pine mixed with whatever shower gel or shampoo he used on his blond, dishevelled hair that had a few pine needles in it already. She almost reached out to pluck them out for him, but stopped herself before he cast a smug look her way. Touching him was probably exactly what he wanted, and besides, working on the farm, he'd likely have plenty more debris on him by the end of the day.

'Straight?' he asked, standing back and almost colliding with Cleo.

'Looks good to me,' said Cleo, while Kaisha readjusted her focus from him to the holiday decorations.

He reached up to pull off a stray twig from the top of the tree and his top rose again, revealing the scar. Kaisha had seen it twice already, but it was new to Cleo.

'How did you get that?' Cleo asked.

He looked at his torso, following Cleo's gaze and Kaisha's. It was a hard body not to look at a third time. 'Oh, that... bar fight.'

Cleo was obviously as lost for words as Kaisha was and swiftly moved on to something else. 'Did Kaisha show you your room?'

'She only showed me hers.' There was teasing in his voice but he added, 'I'll have to leave it until tomorrow, Mitch needs me to go right back.'

'Say hello from us and a big thank you for the gorgeous tree,' Cleo smiled. 'We'll see you tomorrow. I've got a key cut, all the sheets are washed and ready for you.'

'Appreciate it, thank you.' He looked to Kaisha and winked. 'Looking forward to moving in.'

With a smile he left, but after Cleo turned back to take out more decorations from the other boxes he looked through the window and waved to Kaisha. All she could do was wave back and wonder how on earth she was going to cope with having this man in her apartment for the next few weeks. Infuriating in one respect, but so attractive in another. She wondered now just how much trouble this man was going to bring their way.

Cleo climbed up the stepladder ready to wind a set of twinkle lights from the top of the tree. 'Are you sure you're okay with Finn moving in?'

'Mr Bar Brawl and a drunk? Sure.'

Cleo stopped what she was doing. 'I probably shouldn't have asked about the scar.'

'I expected him to say car accident or something like that, not that he was in a fight.'

'I would ask Dylan for details but he doesn't give much away about Finn, only that he's a good friend, and he's not had the easiest time. When he says that I try to think of Mitch and how everyone around here crossed the street when he came close, until we got to know the reasons why he hid away in the cabin in the woods.'

'You think we should give Finn a chance?'

'It couldn't hurt.'

Kaisha helped Cleo negotiate the branches as they wound the lights round and round until they reached the bottom. 'Having someone share the rent will be good.' She decided positivity was the way to go and Cleo was right: kindness at this time of the year was important. The man must have some good qualities if Dylan was willing to give him a chance to prove himself to be the close friend he claimed. 'I'll have more spending money over the holidays.'

'Always a good thing,' Cleo agreed with a smile as they made a couple of adjustments on the tree so the lights were evenly spaced.

'I'm well aware you still don't charge me much rent though,' said Kaisha.

'We've talked about this, no need to mention it again. You know I won't take any more.'

'I do know.' Kaisha had raised it once before, how Cleo could charge double and it would still be a fair rate.

'You're doing me a favour by staying there. Having the apartment occupied means the store is more secure, and if I had an official tenant paying full rent I wouldn't be able to go and have a break upstairs, or keep things like Christmas decorations in the cupboards. I'd have to find somewhere at home to put them, and let me tell you, there's definitely no room with two adults and four children, not to mention guests arriving soon, and wedding paraphernalia all over the place.'

'Bet you can't wait to see your dad.'

'I am excited,' she smiled. 'Talking of parents, how are yours?' Cleo shunted a couple of the boxes Dylan had placed at the side of the store containing tree decorations over towards the window and began to unwrap items inside.

'They arrived safely in Cape Verde, lucky things.' Kaisha opened the second box and took out a set of delicate blue baubles, some with snow patterns on them, others plain, some matt, a couple metallic.

'Golden sands, crystal-clear waters.' Cleo scrunched up her nose. 'Sounds hideous.'

'Doesn't it just. They needed to get away; it'll do them good. Dad is less stressed already.' Which was why they'd taken a long holiday, just the two of them. He was in his late fifties but had retired from his job as an insurance claims officer due to ill health in the form of high blood pressure, migraines, and a deep loathing of the company he worked for when they treated their employees with such little respect. Although Kaisha wouldn't mind betting her sister, Bree, had added to his stress levels too with her wayward nature and lack of taking responsibility. How could Kaisha possibly add to that by confiding in her parents about what had happened over the past year, how Bree had betrayed her and damaged her sense of trust? Her dad didn't need two daughters to worry about, one was quite enough, so Kaisha had put on a brave face and got on with things.

'Where shall I hang this one?' Kaisha took out a delicate, glass reindeer fixed in a leaping position, with thicker, white glass to represent dappled spots on its torso.

'High up,' Cleo advised, 'to avoid wandering hands from my kids and others.'

'Good idea.' Kaisha stood on the raised platform in the window where the tree was already drawing the attention of people passing by and hung it so it could be seen by whoever came through the door. 'It'll be your turn for warm climates, beaches, and beautiful oceans soon.'

'Dylan booked the honeymoon, I'm so excited. We head off just after New Year's on a holiday for the two of us, kid-free – we won't know what to do with ourselves.' Cleo positioned two small, rattan-weave reindeer in the space next to the tree and smiled in delight when she switched on the lights woven into the frame and they glittered away.

'You'll both have an amazing time. You deserve it.'

'I just hope the wedding goes without a hitch.'

'There's no reason why it wouldn't.'

'Dylan tells me to relax and go with the flow, but it's easier said than done. I wish I wasn't such a stressy person but it's in my genes.'

'You wouldn't be you if you didn't do a little worrying, but you'll soon be married to a wonderful man, and I for one can't wait. Imagine how gorgeous the venue will look with a roaring fireplace, delicate twinkly lights, white-covered chairs either side of the aisle.'

'Keep telling me those things and I'll be just fine.'

When the tree was fully decorated, Cleo tidied away the boxes and stacked them in the far corner of the store room out of the way.

'I can put them back up in the apartment if you like,' Kaisha offered.

'We'll leave them in here for now, otherwise Finn won't have much room in that tiny second bedroom.' She watched Kaisha. 'And you're really okay with this?'

'Stop asking me, I've told you it's not a problem.'

'I'm not sure I'm fine with it but I have to trust Dylan and his instincts. And Finn can't have enjoyed not even having a bed to sleep on at his grandad's.'

'No, I don't suppose he would have.'

'Remember the arrangement is only short-term so if you want to kill each other, try to bear that in mind.'

Kaisha laughed. 'I'll do my best.'

When Cleo's phone rang, she took the call out back while

Kaisha served their next few customers. Sometimes it worked that way. They could be quiet as anything, then all of a sudden a few people would come in at once and you'd be trying to help them all at the same time.

'What's going on?' she asked the second Cleo made a reappearance because any fool could see something was up.

'The wedding officiant is double-booked and can't do the wedding.' She was taking a deep breath already, their earlier conversation in mind.

Kaisha ushered Cleo out back again, away from any prying eyes. 'Sit down. No need to panic.' She pulled over the small wooden chair from the corner and, keeping one eye on the store, told her, 'We'll find another one.'

'The wedding is Christmas Eve. I struggled to find anyone who either wanted to be available then or who wasn't already booked.'

Kaisha thought for a second. 'I'll deal with it. I'll call every number I can find, we'll make sure this isn't a problem.' She sounded convincing even though she didn't feel confident at all. With it being the holidays, it was highly likely that any other officiants were already spoken for or else they had plans with family and friends.

Cleo checked the time. 'I need to go. Dylan has a conference call and I promised I'd be back in time so he doesn't have the background noise of Tabitha and Emily to contend with.'

'You two play tag team a lot and somehow it works.' That was what she longed for one day: a partnership built out of love and mutual respect. 'You go, be mom, and by the time it's closing at the store this evening I bet I've got an officiant sorted.'

'It's really not your problem, Kaisha.'

She picked up the glove Cleo dropped in her rush to get ready. 'It's what friends are for. Let me help, I want to.'

'I have a list of officiants I've already tried, I'll email it over to you. You search for anyone not on the list and I'll call all the names I already have in the vague hope there's been a cancellation.'

'Sounds like a good plan to me.'

'Between us, we'll have a solution.'

'See, sounding organised and positive already.' But by the time she ushered Cleo out the door, Kaisha wasn't feeling all that hopeful herself. It was crazy short notice; it wasn't going to be easy.

As promised, Cleo sent over the list via email and Kaisha began her own internet search, calling name after name. And after a dozen contacts, still no luck, and here was another customer in store looking as though she might need some help.

Kaisha was about to offer her services to the woman when Finn came through the door hauling a couple of black bags. 'If you frown like that,' he told her, 'the wind might change and that look will be permanently etched on your face.'

'Charming,' she said through gritted teeth. 'And I'll try to remember the advice, thank you.'

He held the bags out to her. 'Where do you want these? It's greenery from the farm. Mitch said to bring it on up, Cleo wanted it for the school or something.'

'I'll put it out back for her to collect later.' She took the bags, dismissing any need for help from him. 'You've just walked a load of dirt in, by the way.'

'I'll clean it up, don't worry.'

'Broom's in the back.'

He ducked past her to find it but she grabbed his arm. 'I'll get it or you'll make the floor even worse.'

Once she'd handed him the broom, he whistled his way around the store, sweeping up more than just the dirt he'd brought in with him, no doubt trying to stay in her good books, and when he handed Kaisha the broom back and announced he was done, the customer hovering by the ink worsted basket with a knitting pattern in her hand turned and said, 'Finn Thompson?'

'Guilty.' He gave her an inquiring look before a smile spread across his face. 'Well I never, Judge Ramsey.'

In a surprise move the woman put everything she was holding onto the counter and opened her arms to wrap Finn in a hug. 'How are you? Not getting in too much trouble these days?'

'Of course not, I learned my lesson.' He seemed suddenly aware of Kaisha. 'Judge Ramsey caught me doing a bad, bad, thing.'

He might be smiling but Kaisha wasn't – she had to share her apartment with this man soon. Bar brawls? Bad things? It was getting worse by the second.

'Finn and a friend stole my favourite garden gnome,' the woman told Kaisha, 'and then they sent me a ransom note.'

Kaisha started to laugh along with Judge Ramsey.

'It's no laughing matter,' said Finn. 'She gave us community service and we had to clean her car inside and out every week for two months.'

'Serves you right, I'd say.' Kaisha put the hanks of yarn the woman had chosen into a brown paper bag.

'I'm hoping he learned his lesson,' Judge Ramsey beamed.

'I have, don't you worry.' Finn used another smile to charm the woman although she was already looking at him as though he could do no wrong, no matter that she knew better. 'What brings you to Inglenook Falls? It's a bit out of your neighbourhood.'

'I moved into a lovely cottage not too far from the station; always wanted to retire to a town like this.'

'So no more courtroom battles for you then,' said Finn.

'No, I'm retired, just do the odd wedding these days. Much kinder to the soul, far easier to sleep at night.'

Kaisha's ears pricked up. 'Weddings? Are you serious? This is just meant to be.' When the woman looked from her to Finn she added, 'Oh no, not us two. But the owner of this store, she's getting married and the wedding officiant pulled out last minute.'

'When's the wedding?'

'Christmas Eve.'

'I shall be entertaining then I'm afraid.'

Kaisha's spirits sank. 'Fair enough.' She handed the woman her change and receipt. 'It was a long shot.'

'The owner of this store is marrying Dylan,' Finn put in hurriedly before she could leave.

'Dylan Bakersfield? Well I never, what a small world.'

'You know Dylan?' Kaisha asked.

'He was this young man's accomplice in gnome-gate.' She tipped back her head and laughed. 'I never did like the first woman he married, but I've met the owner here a few times and she's lovely, so kind and helpful.'

'So what do you say?' Finn pleaded, using his charm arsenal to full advantage.

She thought about it. 'I'll rejig my schedule.'

Finn hugged her so hard Kaisha was pretty sure the woman's feet actually left the floor.

'Put me down, young man,' she scolded, although she was smiling.

'Can you really do it?' Kaisha put her hands across her mouth, daring to hope, and even exchanged an excited smile with Finn – she couldn't help herself.

The woman took a business card out of her purse and handed it to Kaisha. 'Tell Dylan to get in touch as soon as he can and we'll take it from there. She turned to Finn. 'It's wonderful to see you. Give my regards to your family.'

'I will, and see you at the wedding… I'm best man.'

'Well, this has just made my day.' She waved her farewells and left Finn and Kaisha a little dumbstruck.

'That was weird,' said Kaisha, 'but in a good way. Talk about fate intervening. Cleo isn't going to believe this.'

'Yeah, it was nice to see her.'

She realised it was a nice thing to happen in more ways than one. Finn had a history with the woman and she clearly held an affection for him. It was hard to square this version of him with the one she had in her head, the impression he'd created when he showed up at the inn, then at the Garland Street markets.

'I can't believe you held her gnome to ransom,' she mused.

'There's a lot you don't know about me yet.' And off he went, leaving Kaisha to text Cleo the good news.

Dylan came into the store a while later to collect a couple of boxes of garments to take over to the Inglenook Falls markets. The sweaters had sold in unprecedented numbers compared to last year and already Kaisha and Cleo were worried they wouldn't have enough to keep the stall going until Christmas.

'You're looking pleased with yourself,' he said to Kaisha as she pointed out the boxes that could go.

'I am, because I found you a wedding officiant.'

'What are you talking about? We organised one of those a long time ago.'

'Cleo didn't mention it? The wedding officiant was double-booked.'

His face fell. 'She never said a word, she kept the kids out of my way while I had a meeting and then I rushed out the door.'

'She was probably hoping it would be sorted and I'm pleased to say it is.' She handed him the business card but he didn't recognise the name until Kaisha recounted the retired judge's conversation with Finn. That got Dylan laughing.

'We wanted fifty bucks, each,' he said, 'to return the gnome. She took hold of the tip of my ear when she reprimanded me – boy did that hurt – and she sentenced us to hard labour on her car.' He looked at the business card again. 'I'll make an appointment as soon as I can, and thanks, it was quick thinking to ask her.'

'It was my pleasure, she seemed lovely.'

'Not so lovely if you're on the wrong side of her like Finn and I were.'

Kaisha was only relieved that the judge hadn't known Finn via any other crime, one a lot more serious than the kidnapping of a garden gnome.

When Dylan left with the boxes, she brought through a chair from the area out back of the store and put it in the corner so she could carry on knitting. With stock dwindling, it was time to multi-task and more garments meant another worry off Cleo's mind. Cleo had given her a chance, a job, four years ago. It had been her constant, her security, ever since.

And it was the reason why she'd never walk away from the store, she wouldn't leave Cleo in the lurch. How could she?

Her own dreams would just have to wait.

4

FINN

It was going to be fun sharing an apartment with someone who very obviously didn't want him there, although that could be because his arrival at five thirty this morning took her by surprise when she came out of the bathroom. Working at the Christmas tree farm now, his mind wandered back to his encounter with Kaisha.

'What the hell?' She'd clasped her towel against her body when she emerged from a long, hot shower. Finn could tell she'd been in there a long while because it looked like a steam room when she came out.

'Sorry, I should've given you a time. But I did say I was moving in today.'

'It's still dark outside.'

'What can I say? I'm a morning person.' He actually wasn't but today he had to get this done before going to work. 'What are you doing up so early anyway? I figured I'd sneak in, put my bags in my room, and leave before you even knew I was here.'

'I have work to do.'

'People buy knitting needles and sweaters at this ungodly hour?'

'If you must know, I have a lot of knitting to carry on with. Stock doesn't make itself, you know.'

He leaned against the door jamb. 'I'm sure it doesn't. What are you making? Scarves, gloves, sweaters, sweater vests, balaclavas?' He saw the hint of a smile and it felt like an accomplishment that she'd simmered at least a little.

'Sweaters. They're a really good seller at the markets.' She tightened her towel around her body yet again. 'I'm going to get changed.'

And that was how they'd left it this morning. Not a great start. But now, five hours in to his working day at the farm, he was already exhausted and, no matter the atmosphere there, couldn't wait to get home to the apartment once he finished up here.

'Not used to physical labour?' Mitch asked.

'You could say that.' Already he'd cut down more trees than he'd thought could possibly exist in one field. He'd dragged trees to Mitch's truck and loaded them up, he'd gone out to the fields and hung around as families selected their favourite specimen so he could chop it down to order, he'd taken trees back to the little hut Mitch had made into a kiosk and netted them before sending happy customers on their way.

'By the end of the season you'll be used to it,' Mitch assured him as he heaved the last of the trees onto the truck before setting off to Bampton where he had a young worker, Jude, selling the trees so fast this was the second load today. 'And don't worry, it'll be dark in a few hours so closing time isn't too far away. You okay to hold the fort until I get back?'

'Sure thing.' Finn wasn't afraid to get dirty, he didn't mind hard work, but he couldn't deny he was really looking forward to his first night in a proper bed.

Holly emerged from the fields and held up her camera. 'I've got some wonderful photos, want to see them?'

He grinned. 'Sure. It'll give me an excuse to stop.'

'Mitch only works you hard because he doesn't know how to take it easy himself.' She showed him the shots she'd captured of a family of four selecting their tree, the delight evident on their faces, not an ounce of tension for anyone.

But Finn had never known family life to be like that. 'Nice,' he said instead of voicing his real opinion. 'I'd better go help them.' The family had appeared by the kiosk and he took payment. No need to wonder which was their tree – he'd seen them out in the fields posing for the picture, the tree adorned with an enormous, right-in-your-face red bow.

'I'll watch the kiosk for you,' Holly offered. 'I could try to get the tree myself but Mitch wouldn't trust me with a chainsaw or an axe.'

'I could teach you.'

'No,' she laughed. 'I don't want him to think I'm perfectly capable, which of course I am, because he'll have me chopping logs. At the moment I say the log burner needs filling up and he gets to it. Terrible, I know, but I repay him in other ways,' she winked.

It was one of the first times Finn felt jealous of the coupledom his boss and his other half shared. Having someone there on a cold winter's night wasn't something he'd ever experienced, at least not in the true sense, where the person had your back. Any previous relationships, if you could even call them that, had been physical rather than much else. He'd never had someone who got him and was a friend as much as a lover.

He picked up the axe and headed out to the fields, chopped down the tree, and hauled it back to the kiosk, where he put it through the netting machine. He was sure this family would have face ache by the time they got into bed tonight if they didn't stop smiling quite so much.

When a couple went on their way after Holly sold them one of the pre-cut trees near the kiosk she asked Finn, 'How are the new living arrangements?'

'I only dumped my things this morning.' He ran a hand across the stubble of his chin when it itched and sure enough a few pine needles fluttered onto his jacket. 'I'm not sure my new roommate fully appreciates my presence.'

'Kaisha?'

'Colourful Kaisha, I call her.'

'She's a lovely girl. Quiet, keeps to herself, but very kind.'

'She seems to be, yes.'

'She's close to Cleo, has been ever since they began working with one another. I'm sure she'll warm to you eventually.'

'How could she resist with my charm?'

'Well, that is true. By the way, the tree in the window of the Little Knitting Box looks amazing. I hear you took it up there for them.'

'They seem happy with it.'

'Does Kaisha have one for the apartment?'

'I didn't see one, but I'm not sure there's even room – the living area is what you might call compact and she's got some mannequin thing with clothing draped over it. Scared the crap out of me when I let myself in first thing. Thought it was an intruder.'

'I think Kaisha still needs a tree, no matter how small the apartment is. What's Christmas without one?'

After she left, Finn tidied up the kiosk and sold another three pre-cut trees. He had to hand it to Dylan and Cleo – they'd picked a great town to become a part of, and even though their house wasn't here, the fact that the store was and they knew so many people gave them a presence, a sense of belonging that surely made them feel grounded. Perhaps he should start his time in this town by getting Kaisha on his side. A housewarming gift was in order...okay, so technically you bought a housewarming for the person moving in, but why not a gift for both of them? And here was the perfect place to find one, just like Holly suggested.

By the time Mitch returned, Finn left happy, exhausted, with a five-and-a-half-foot pine beauty on his shoulder.

He'd make Kaisha like him and show her he wasn't all bad, although the fact that he cared what someone else thought was an entirely new experience for Finn. Coming to Inglenook Falls sure was pointing out a lot of ways in which his life hadn't quite panned out as well as it probably should have. He had nobody special at his side, he didn't belong anywhere, he didn't even have a permanent workplace.

It had never bothered him much, until now.

5

KAISHA

'Keep me updated, give Jacob a kiss from me,' said Kaisha, putting down the phone when she heard her new roommate come into the apartment. She hadn't been very nice to him this morning and he was Dylan's friend and would play a major part in the wedding, so with a deep breath she decided she should at least try to get on with him.

'Surprise!' Finn announced the second she turned around. From her position on the sofa, curled up in a ball as she spoke to Cleo, all she could see was a tree and Finn's arm holding the trunk in the middle of the branches. His head poked out from one side. 'It's a beauty, don't you think?'

'Please tell me that isn't for the apartment.'

'Of course. I'd hardly bring it in if it wasn't. Don't tell me you don't like to have a Christmas tree to wake up to every morning.'

'Oh, I love it all right.' She nodded over to the corner of the room behind the door.

He leaned to the other side so he could see what she was looking at. 'Ah. Houston, we have a problem.'

'I picked it up an hour ago from the Inglenook Falls markets.

Got it cheap because they don't like the trees hanging around too long once they're chopped.'

'It's a good one.' He stood, arm still in amongst the pine needles of the tree he'd brought.

'Yours is better. It's fuller, taller, and mine is a little bit on the stumpy side, you have to admit.' She could tell by the smirk that she was spot on with her description.

'Well, now we have two,' he announced.

'And where exactly are we going to put it?' She pulled her chunky, ocean-blue cardigan around her torso. She hadn't been home from the markets all that long and so the ancient heating system hadn't had time to kick in properly.

He looked around. The living room really was so small that there was nowhere to put it apart from next to the other tree. 'Bear with me.' He gestured for her to hold the trunk and off he went out of the room.

When he came back he had an idea. 'Why don't we put the smaller tree in your bedroom? This one won't fit – it's not because I don't think yours is good enough to be on show out here,' he said before she had a chance to object. 'I mean, you can have the larger tree in your room if you like, but you'll have to fight the branches every time you need to get to your underwear drawer. Not that I know where that is,' he stumbled. 'I haven't been snooping.'

She tried not to associate those two things – Finn and her underwear – because it made a hot flush creep all the way up her body.

Actually, this was fun, seeing him so awkward when usually he was so full of confidence in her presence and it was she who squirmed with embarrassment.

'It's the only solution,' he said. 'And I can't take this tree back, I can't exactly glue it back onto its stump.'

'I don't suppose you can. Okay, I guess it'll be a treat to have a tree in my bedroom, why not? And how much do I owe you for my share? That must've cost a lot more than the one I got.'

'Call it a housewarming present. I got it on discount anyway.'

'A housewarming present… but you're the one moving in.'

He pulled a face and shrugged before they set about manoeuvring the smaller tree, not yet decorated, into Kaisha's bedroom. She was mortified to realise a lace bra was hanging on the handle of her wardrobe to dry and another on the bedstead because he'd most likely caught sight of them earlier. She wasn't used to keeping her bedroom door shut, a habit she'd quickly have to change now.

'Who were you on the phone to when I arrived?' he asked after they'd shifted the tree into position. 'I heard you mention Jacob. That's Dylan's son, isn't it?'

'Yes, he's at the hospital. Sprained wrist, nothing too serious, but still a worry.'

'Poor little guy.'

'He's going to be fine.'

'That's good. But hospitals are no fun, believe me. Broke my leg once when I was seven, then my arm when I was eight, a few fingers when I was nine.'

'Your parents must've labelled you accident-prone.'

'Something like that. Do you have many decorations?'

She wasn't born yesterday, she knew a distraction technique when she saw one, but she'd play along and change the subject. 'Would you believe none?'

'What, not a single decoration?'

'I usually go home for Christmas. Cleo decorates the Little Knitting Box so I've never felt I needed anything more up here. I guess it's always been kind of temporary.'

'Why aren't you heading home this year?'

Now it was his turn to hit a nerve and her turn to give him a short answer. 'My parents are away somewhere tropical on a much-needed holiday.' She left it at that.

He looked ready to ask more but, deciding not to be nosy she assumed, declared, 'You know there's nothing quite so sad as a tree without decorations. What time do the markets shut?'

She checked her watch. 'We've still got a couple of hours.'

'Come on then. Grab your coat and let's do this. If we're going to have two Christmas trees, we need to do it properly.'

She was too shocked to argue. It was one thing having him stay in the spare room, quite another to go off somewhere together.

'Wow, that's got some bite to it.' Finn had tried a sample of the chipotle cheddar from the cheese stall at the start of the markets, insisting he was too hungry to focus on buying ornaments until he at least put something in his stomach. Kaisha tried not to think about the taut stomach that would've had a good workout at the farm, hauling trees, chopping wood, bringing a tree back to the apartment.

'I warned you,' Kaisha giggled. 'Now stop thinking about your stomach and let's choose some ornaments. We won't be able to get everything here, but I'm in Manhattan tomorrow at the Garland Street markets so I'm happy to finish the shopping.'

'I'll be in Manhattan tomorrow evening as well.'

Was he suggesting they meet up? Do something together, again? 'I'm happy to do the shop.' She admired a baby-blue, miniature gift box hanging from a white satin ribbon and the two turtle doves decoration next to it. She ended up buying both.

'Then let me give you some money,' he said, still talking about what else they could buy.

'Really, I'll handle it. Otherwise when you move out, who gets custody of everything?'

'Good point. Might have to take you to court for those turtle doves.'

'I don't appreciate the sarcasm, you know.'

'Sorry.'

She did appreciate the apology though and he trailed after her when she moved to the next chalet, with fairy lights all across its roof shining against the dark sky. But when she asked the stall-holder for a couple of sets of lights he had to tell her he'd sold out after an unexpected rush and wouldn't have more stock until the day after tomorrow. He was taking names and numbers of customers so he could let them know when he had more.

'I guess that's that,' said Kaisha. 'I'll have to pick some up in Manhattan. Everyone knows you can't decorate a tree until you have lights – they're always the first thing to go on.'

'Don't stress, we'll get some eventually.'

Typical. She'd suspected this whole tree-decorating business was a bit of a ruse to get in her good books and Finn had looked bored as they'd browsed stalls and ornaments, part of the reason why she'd accept sole responsibility for choosing everything in the city tomorrow.

'Sorted,' said Finn all of a sudden and before Kaisha could ask what he was talking about he stalked over to Holly and Mitch, who had arms linked together and were sipping on mulled cider as they wandered around the markets.

By the time Kaisha caught up with them Mitch had already handed over his keys to the kiosk so Finn could go grab a couple of sets for himself. Just like that.

'Why are you shaking your head?' Finn asked as he and Kaisha made their way back to the Little Knitting Box to dump everything in the apartment.

'I didn't take you for a man who liked Christmas much at all, but first the tree, now the insistence we decorate sooner rather than later.'

'I'm trying to be a good roommate.'

When Finn headed off to the Christmas tree farm to fetch the lights, Kaisha curled up on the sofa in the apartment. The place had warmed up and was the cosiest it had been in a long while, and for the first time this year she didn't feel as though Christmas was going to be one epic let-down. The pine scent enveloped her in enough joy to keep her positivity flowing and she felt even more settled when she thought of her parents on their vacation, away from everything for the holidays. They'd messaged this morning and sent more pictures of glorious beaches; they were both learning to snorkel and her mum was already talking about where they could holiday next. They hadn't been away in years until now.

Kaisha called Cleo to find out how Jacob was doing.

'He's tucked up in bed, enjoying the fuss,' said Cleo, relief evident. 'Thanks for calling, I'll give him a cuddle from you.'

'Be sure to.'

'How's the store?'

'Oh yes, your other child.' They'd often joked over the years that Cleo was as protective over the Little Knitting Box as she was the kids. 'It's all in hand, you take as long as you need.'

'Dylan works from home, I can come and go as usual hopefully, and for once Prue is pulling her weight.'

'That's good to hear.'

'How's it going making more stock for the store? I managed a bit of knitting at Jacob's bedside while Dylan cooked dinner and amused the girls. I've finished the teal sweater with the stars on and knitted another hat with the yarn I had left over.'

'Great. I've almost finished the second of the long red sweaters with the turtleneck.' She was getting used to knitting between

serving customers in the store downstairs or at the markets, wherever she was. Cleo was very similar in that regard. Kaisha's sister,
Bree, on the other hand had never taken to crafts. Growing up,
while Kaisha used their mum's sewing machine to experiment or
make repairs to her own clothes, Bree was too busy spending a
fortune at retail outlets, throwing out clothes when she'd had
enough of them. 'Do you think I should knit a couple in midnight
blue? They take a while but they sell well and there's plenty of
winter left. Cleo... you still there?'

'Of course, sorry, but yes to the sweaters, good idea.'

'Everything okay?'

'It's fine, all going smoothly.'

'Why do I get the feeling you're not quite believing those words
even though you're saying them yourself?'

'Just a bit of hassle with the menswear for the wedding.'

'Hey, you leave that alone; your dress and the kids' outfits are
enough to contend with.'

'I suppose you're right.'

But Kaisha couldn't resist asking. 'Out with it, what's gone
wrong with Dylan's outfit?'

'Nothing. But he'd arranged to go to the store for the suit fittings
tomorrow, the only day he doesn't have meetings, and Finn pulled
out. We'll have to reschedule, but it's a busy time of the year for us
and the menswear store. Honestly, juggling things in this family is
never easy – you'd think I'd be used to it. And Dylan seems sure
we'll get it sorted in time.'

Kaisha's hackles rose. It was irresponsible, that's what it was,
and she knew Mitch wouldn't have a problem with Finn making the
appointment, so what was so vital that Finn couldn't get there?
Surely the best man was supposed to help proceedings rather than
hinder them.

When she finished her call, she poured herself a large glass of red wine and, soon after, Finn came through the door.

'Hi honey, I'm home,' came his voice as he walked into the living room.

He looked impossibly handsome in his charcoal-coloured jacket, jeans, and work boots, his blond hair mussed by the wind outside and the light rain she'd heard spattering against the window panes since she'd cosied up inside. And when he was holding a couple of boxes of Christmas lights and beaming like a kid, it was very hard to be annoyed at him. In the interests of peace, Kaisha offered him a glass of wine.

'Not for me thanks, got to be up early again tomorrow.' He pulled another small bag from his jacket pocket and brandished an ornament from inside. 'What do you think?'

She looked quizzically at it. 'Not exactly traditional.' It was a Santa in sunglasses standing with a cocktail in one hand beneath a palm tree. Not her taste in holiday decorations at all.

She picked up one of the boxes after he set them on the table. 'I'll do the tree in my room then if you do the lights on the one in here.'

'Better to do the one in here together, don't you think? A joint effort.'

She didn't say anything while he went to hang up his coat on the hook just inside the entrance door in the hallway that led to the living room and bedrooms all on the same level.

'Why do I get the feeling I've done something?' he said as he came back into the room and she tried to bustle past him.

'No, not at all,' she insisted as she disappeared into her bedroom. She called out, 'We'll get it done quicker by doing a tree each.'

She took out the lights and pulled them into a long line on the bed in preparation for winding around the branches. When she caught sight of him in her peripheral vision she jumped. 'Why are you sneaking up on me?'

'I'm not, but I know what it's like when a woman says one thing and means another.'

'I don't follow.' She refocused on the lights, plugged them in, and checked they all worked.

'I've done something, that much is obvious.' His T-shirt had crept up enough to show a patch of bare skin on his stomach as he rested his hands at the top of the doorframe. 'Come on, out with it. What is it? You hate the lights? You think I have terrible taste in ornaments?'

She almost let out a laugh before insisting, 'It's nothing, really.'

But he didn't leave. He changed position to lean against the door jamb. 'I wanted to ask: what's with the haunting mannequin in the living room?'

'Haunting?'

'You've got to admit seeing that on a dark night would make anyone think we had an intruder.'

'It's made of plastic.'

'You know what I mean. What's it for?'

'I do the odd bit of dressmaking.'

'On the side?'

'Something like that.'

He harrumphed. 'I'm trying to be friendly, but look, I'm tired. I'm beat actually after a day at the farm. I might put the lights on the big tree and call it a night.'

'Whatever.'

He walked off but came back pretty quickly. 'One thing I really can't stand is when people won't say what they mean, so out with it.'

She bit down on her bottom lip again. 'I already told you how good friends Cleo and Dylan are to me.'

'Yeah, Dylan's a good guy, he's a good friend of mine too. Kind of why I'm best man.'

'And you're adding to their workload rather than helping them.'

'What are you on about?'

'You cancelled the appointment for getting suits fitted.'

'So?'

'So, it's three weeks until the wedding, you're kind of on a tight timeframe.'

'Have you ever thought perhaps some things are more important than a damn wedding?' And with that he smacked the edge of the doorframe and retreated into the living room.

It was then she noticed mud trailing from the wooden floor of her bedroom through to the hallway and when she followed the trail she realised the clumps of mud were coming from Finn's boots. 'Look at the mess you've made!'

He turned and noticed, swore under his breath. 'I'll clean it up.'

'Too right you will, you've only been here five minutes and already you're making more work for me.'

'What part of "I will clean it up" don't you understand?' He yelled this time and it took Kaisha by surprise so much that she retreated into her room and knew she wouldn't come out again until the morning.

'If I'd wanted a nagging wife I'd get married!' he yelled from the other side of the door and she heard what must've been his boots coming off, each one landing with a thud, and nothing else afterwards because she put music on loud enough to drown out any reminder that this apartment was no longer her own.

She was sharing, and with the most infuriating man possible.

Right now she'd already started counting down the days until he left.

6

FINN

He'd always had a bit of a temper, although he probably shouldn't have lost it with Kaisha. But nagging him after he'd made the effort to buy a tree, pick up the lights and another ornament – which she clearly hated and didn't even ask the meaning behind – despite the fact he'd done nothing but try to fit in with her hadn't gone down well. And having a go at him about not keeping the appointment time with Dylan? That was crazy. It was none of her business anyway.

He came out of his room early, greeted by the scent of pine that was like a warm welcome. Pity the atmosphere inside this apartment was as frosty as the window panes this morning even though Kaisha had already escaped somewhere. He tugged on his warmest thermal socks and picked up the heavy-duty gloves Mitch had given him yesterday. Thank goodness he had, because his regular gloves never would have withstood all that hauling of wood, time in the fields, the damp, the wet, the cold.

He looked at the tree in the living room, neglected without a single light or ornament to be seen, and it was a reminder that him being here had got off to the worst start possible even though he'd tried his best. Maybe he shouldn't have compared Kaisha to a nagging wife. He didn't know much about women but he did know that comments like that one usually made a situation worse rather than better.

At the farm it was busy as usual. A low mist hung in the air, making it hard to see in the fields, but it didn't deter people from coming to find their perfect tree. Finn had become a dab hand at using the bow saw in a short time, and although his shoulders ached and his calves burned from the exertion yesterday, it felt good to be out in the very fresh, wintry air again. It was a distraction from what was to come later, the reason he couldn't show up to the suit fitting as Dylan had arranged. And if they went by his measurements, the suit, shirt, and any other paraphernalia wouldn't be a problem, especially if he headed out to the store on his own when he could. He really didn't see the big deal – which had made him all the more irritated that Kaisha was making it out to be something worse than it was. She seemed to worry about Cleo and Dylan more than Cleo and Dylan worried about themselves. Finn hadn't told Dylan his reason for not being able to make the appointment. There was a saying that a problem shared was a problem halved, but in Finn's experience a problem shared just meant he thought about it, he experienced it, plus he had to talk about it when all he wanted to do was bury it as deep as he could.

As he reached the end of his shift, Finn had wondered whether Kaisha would pick up more ornaments in Manhattan or whether she was too annoyed and the tree in the living room wouldn't be there when he got home. But when he arrived back at the apartment, the tree had survived any culling. He showered and changed, ready to head to the station, and made the decision that if he was going to be here until the end of the year, he needed to make another attempt at keeping the peace. So, he'd pick up more ornaments himself. That way, Kaisha couldn't accuse him of being the baddie she already thought he was.

He fell asleep on the train journey from Inglenook Falls to Manhattan, exhausted from his day. But that wasn't necessarily a bad thing. He was somewhat mollified and ready to meet the family, a stressful event whenever it happened. The last time had been Thanksgiving and look how that turned out. Finn had left the last meet-up in a ball of fury and frustration, fuelled up on liquor, and disgraced himself at the Inglenook Inn. It had paved the way for Kaisha's disapproval and it was clear he had a lot of ground to make up if they were going to be roommates who didn't totally hate each other.

He weaved his way through the crowds in Manhattan and walked all the way to East 74th, where he stood on the opposite side of the street to his grandad's pre-war apartment. The tree he'd picked out stood proudly in the window up high, its coloured lights illuminating the window panes and shining down onto the street. There were other trees dotted in other windows so that the whole building looked like a wooden advent calendar with novelty coloured boxes to open. He looked up at the window he had looked out of countless times over the years. As a small boy he'd gazed down at the city below, watching cars, garbage trucks, the hive of activity he wanted to get in amongst. As a teenager he'd looked out way into the distance, more at the sky, knowing he could escape somewhere else and leave behind the memories he didn't always want to recall. And more recently he'd looked out wondering whether one day he could ever call New York home again, whether it was time to come back for good.

His grandad buzzed him in the main entrance and he took the stairs up to the third floor.

'They here yet?' was the first thing Finn asked when his grandad opened the door to the apartment. It was far too quiet in here for two people who couldn't stand each other to be contained within unless Grandad had taken to gagging them. Not a bad idea, maybe one to try. The thought gave Finn a little lift of amusement at least. He took off his coat and ran a hand through his hair to rid it of the damp that pervaded the city on days like this.

'Not yet. And I'll remind you all, it's to be a peaceful get-together this time.'

'So not our usual performance then,' Finn clarified.

'What do you think to the tree?'

'Good change of subject.' Finn went closer. 'It looks impressive from the street, even more so now.'

'Beryl helped.'

'Very tasteful, tell her I approve.' He stood by the log burner and looked past the tree to the skies looming above, dark and menacing as though a storm might be brewing.

Grandad shuffled over to stand beside him. 'Might get a thunderstorm tonight. Although I'd prefer snow.' Wearing a taupe cardigan that looked a size too big for him, he pushed his hands into the pocket of his cords, the same grey as the moccasin slippers on his feet. Little round spectacles he'd worn ever since Finn could remember only came off when the lenses needed a polish or when it was time to go to bed.

'Both are hazardous in my line of work. I spend my time outside remember, have a little sympathy.'

'How is the job going?'

'I'm enjoying it more than I thought. It's hard, but it's different.'

'Doing something with your hands at last. You were never cut out for office work.'

'I don't think chopping wood and felling trees will be forever, but I like change.' He held his palms in front of the hot air drifting up from the log burner and rubbed them together, still not fully warmed through after being outside.

'I know you do.' Grandad walked slowly away from the window and over to the wing-backed chair. 'That's why you never stay put in one place for very long.'

'Don't start,' he chastised, although tongue-in-cheek. His grandad had always respected his need for freedom, the desire to get away.

Finn flopped down in the chair opposite, longing to have a chat with his grandad all by himself and not have his parents appear at all. He'd been successful over the years when it came to minimising time with either of them. A quick hello, separately, and they all seemed to be able to survive that. But in Manhattan, all together? A recipe for disaster.

'How was it sleeping in a bed at last?'

'So good I can't even tell you.' Despite the frosty atmosphere between him and Kaisha last night. 'Thanks again for letting me crash here as long as I needed.'

'My door is always open to you, you know that.'

The buzzer rudely interrupted them and Finn prepared to face the inevitable, wondering which one of his parents was first.

It was his mother. Figured. She'd always hated to miss out on anything and liked to be one step ahead of his father however she could.

'Finn, hello.' She held out her arms and he hugged her. 'Good to see you. I do hope we can keep things civil tonight.' She had always been one for keeping up appearances, whether it was her perfectly applied make-up or the smart business suits she wore even though she hadn't worked in over a decade, or the care she took not to let slip any sign of emotion when it came to her son. She was, at best, nonchalant. That was the word Finn usually associated with her when it came to their relationship. It wasn't that she didn't care but it was as though she believed if she challenged him in any way he'd run for the hills and perhaps never come back. How could a woman be so afraid to talk to her own son?

'I will,' he said. 'If you will.'

She opened her mouth to reply but instead gave his grandad a hug and asked about his health, mainly about the cold he'd had on and off for the last month.

'I'm still living, stop fussing,' were his final words on the subject. They all knew what that tone meant.

The buzzer introduced a visible tension in his mother's shoulders because she knew it was her ex-husband arriving, and he appeared shortly afterwards, brandishing a gift bag for his dad.

'You didn't have to bring me anything. Your company is all I need, son.' John took out a box filled with cheeses, pickles, his favourite sea salt flatbreads. 'But this, I'm grateful for.'

'I knew you would be. Hide it from Beryl, I'm sure she won't approve.'

Andy Thompson had once been blond-haired like Finn until grey had wiped out any trace of the same shade. He wore his hair short, favoured jeans and well-fitted shoes most days, a hangover from his office days, and always the same crisp aftershave. He'd just turned sixty but had taken early retirement and between that and his sporting a partner who had to be a good twenty-five years younger, you'd never guess his age when he walked into a room. Not unless you were expert enough to spot the frown lines etched on his forehead, the dullness in his eyes when you caught him unsmiling and disengaged from the conversation.

Finn made coffees, extra strong for himself and Grandad. They'd need the boost if they were going to get through this ordeal.

The aroma filled the air, Finn distributed the mugs and the stilted conversation began. So far everyone was on their best behaviour and he hoped it lasted.

'Strong enough?' he asked his grandad.

'Perfect. Beryl would have words if she could see it.'

'How is Beryl?' Beverly wanted to know. 'Are you still happy with her?'

'She does a great job, Mom,' said Finn before his grandad could answer. 'You already know that. No need to fuss.'

'I only want to be sure, that's all.'

'She's good company,' Grandad confirmed. 'She stays late sometimes when we get carried away playing board games. Her son apparently joked we're like an old married couple.'

'You don't mean?' Beverly put a hand across her chest.

Grandad was chuckling behind his coffee cup as Andy's attention was piqued too. 'You two aren't... you know?'

'And what's it to you lot if we are?' Grandad's expression dead serious at first, it soon gave way to a smile. 'Of course we're not. She's young enough to be my daughter.'

'She's not a gold digger, in case that's what you're worried about,' Finn added. 'She comes from a reputable agency. I stayed here for a while, remember, so I've seen what good company she is for Grandad.' He wanted to put stop to any more suggestions of moving Grandad to a facility where he'd have round-the-clock care. Grandad didn't want it and his parents needed to let the idea go.

'Oh yes, you did stay here,' said his dad, wincing at the heat of the coffee. 'Can't have been comfortable. How's the new place?'

'Small.' And with one annoying roommate.

'How long have you rented it for?'

'Only short-term.'

'So you'll be moving on again soon?' His mum asked. She was clasping her coffee mug as though sipping from it might interfere with her pristine appearance.

'Don't know yet,' Finn shrugged. 'More coffee anyone?' He'd finished his in record time as though every gram of caffeine could knock a bit more strength for this into his psyche. So far being here wasn't all that bad but the Thompsons had a history of making family gatherings spiral out of control. Take two Christmases ago as the perfect example. They'd been all together for lunch, presents were opened, faces were strained more than they should be and as soon as his parents hit the liqueurs after they were full of festive food, a row broke out. It was over the wooden sleigh his dad had made for him when he was nine. Andy bemoaned the fact they'd got rid of it when it was so fancy, Beverly commented it had made good firewood, and that was it, the gloves were off. They'd bickered so much that Finn and Grandad hadn't been able to focus on their game of Jenga and Finn got so angry he smashed the entire structure from the table across the floor. And still they'd continued arguing because then the row moved on from the wooden sleigh to debating who had been responsible for spoiling Finn and Grandad's game.

'No more for Dad,' said Andy at Finn's offer of more coffee.

'I'm still quite capable of making my own decisions,' Grandad said in frustration.

'Aren't you supposed to be watching your caffeine intake?' Beverly asked.

'She's right, Dad,' Andy added. Wow, were they agreeing on something?

'I'll have another cup when I'm done with this one,' said Grandad, ignoring the weight of his son's stare.

'Anyone else?' Finn offered.

'Not for me, thanks,' said Andy, whose girlfriend usually had him on some health regime or another, whether it was cutting carbs, trying a new fitness fad, or turning vegetarian, and shortly after that pescatarian when she decided they hadn't made the right move. He even wore a watch that counted his steps although quite why, Finn had no idea – he played golf, but that was it in the way of exercise and it wasn't as though the eighteen-hole course changed much every time he visited.

'I think I'll wait too.' Off the hook for more coffee duty, Finn was suddenly more focused on getting out of here than on prolonging whatever it was they'd been summoned for. Grandad hadn't given them times and dates to choose from; he'd instructed them all to be here on this day, at this time, and there was no room for negotiation.

'The tree is wonderful,' said Beverly when the silence crashed around them again.

'I'm glad you like it,' said Grandad. 'And I've made sure all my favourite ornaments are on there. Not difficult, the tree is a nice big one thanks to Finn.'

His parents nodded their approval and Finn's focus drifted across the many decorations adorning the branches. The familiar ice-blue baubles were there, all six of them, each one with a slightly different snowflake pattern. From this angle he spotted the glittery plaques too – one for him, one for his sister Mackenzie – each one with hand and foot prints made when they were babies, a keepsake handed to their grandparents. His grandad kept every little thing that meant so much to him and Finn knew that no matter how much his family fell apart, to come here was to feel grounded, to retain a sense of self when everything was up in the air.

'It's a good tree,' Beverly repeated. What kind of family were they if they found it impossible even to make small talk?

'It's impressive,' Andy confirmed, looking to Finn. 'Did it come from the farm you're working at?'

'Sure did.'

'Are you planning to look for a real job in the New Year?'

'The one I have now is hardly a pretend job, Dad.'

'I didn't mean that. I—'

'How about you come and chop up a few dozen logs in the

freezing cold, or haul trees to waiting cars and trucks for families hoping to have a more magical Christmas than we ever managed? Then you'll see it's a real job.'

'I don't know why you couldn't stick with your engineering work,' his dad batted back.

'So you didn't mean *real* job, you meant something you'd be proud of, happy to tell your friends at the country club about.'

'I want you to have a secure future, that's all. And engineering was a good career, well paid, you'd be set for life going back into that. I don't understand why you lack any commitment to following a career path. It's life, son.'

Finn couldn't hold in his rebuke. 'Oh, I don't know, Dad, perhaps because it was never what I wanted to do in the first place!'

His dad actually seemed shocked when he really shouldn't be. Finn had always felt his dad's disapproval, his distance, but he'd never confronted him about it. What was the point? He'd gone into engineering thinking it was the right thing for him, but when something wasn't what you wanted deep down, carrying on regardless was a sure way to fail at it. Not that he'd really failed. He just didn't want to do it any more.

'You know he didn't want to be an engineer,' Beverly said. 'Don't deny it.'

And Andy couldn't. By the look on his face he remembered exactly the criticisms he'd thrown Finn's way when Finn had wanted to do something else entirely. 'I don't think it's unusual for a father to want the best for his son.'

'Even if the best isn't what he wants,' Beverly slung back, her voice viper-like. The calm seas of her mood had turned turbulent and she was angling for a slanging match. 'You never appreciated his talents, his wishes.'

'And you did?'

It was as though Finn and his grandad weren't even in the room.

Whatever they said now, it didn't really matter anyway. After the tragedy that struck the family, nothing had seemed important for a long time and Finn had glided on through school, taking each day as it came, escaping when he could. And when he'd begun to follow a path towards an engineering career, it had carried him along for a time, especially the parental approval and respect that came with it. He'd hoped that over time it would help him forget what he'd once yearned for. But it hadn't. It had eaten away at him like everything else and being happy never seemed within his grasp.

'Stop yelling, the both of you.' John was still sitting down but his voice bellowed despite his fragility compared to the rest of them.

Finn had to steer them away from this if they were going to survive the evening. They'd all promised to make it a peaceful occasion, and Grandad didn't deserve anything less. 'Grandad, are we going to get down to the reason you summoned us all here?' He wanted the focus to be on something else other than him, his choice of work, lack of career aspirations.

'We're family and it's almost Christmas, this is what normal families do,' said Grandad. 'They get together, they catch up, they're nice to one another. It doesn't have to be about anything more.'

It didn't, but they all knew that wasn't what *this* family ever did, at least not since before they'd fallen apart in ways that could never be fixed.

Grandad got up and went over to the bureau that had been in the same position in this apartment since Finn was in short trousers and came here after school for ice-cream and his grandma's famous blueberry pie with its golden crust and lattice top. 'My will,' he announced, and sat down with a clutch of papers on his lap.

'You've already given us a copy.' Beverly's face pinched at the coffee she was still sipping and she set it down. It seemed her relaxed, let's-try-to-be-civil attitude had walked out the door already.

'Dad, this is a bit morbid for Christmas drinks or whatever this is tonight.' But Andy set down his cup too, ready to listen.

'This will is slightly different, I've made a few... tweaks.'

'What kind of tweaks?' Finn asked.

Grandad peered through the lower half of his bifocals to see the documentation carefully. Not that he needed to if he'd already made the so-called tweaks. 'Originally I'd written that this apartment would be left to you, Andy, with a part share for Beverly, who has always been like a daughter to me. Andy, you could've bought Beverly out or come to some other arrangement. Perhaps you'd want to get rid of this place instead.' His voice wobbled on that sentence and Finn knew this last option wasn't what he wanted but he accepted that after he was gone he would have little control.

Finn wondered, was this will going to force his dad to keep the apartment for good? Or was he about to remove Beverly from the equation? Surely not. They'd always got on well; the divorce hadn't rocked that bond like it would when most marriages ended. Finn had sometimes wondered whether his mum stood by because of the money but any fool could see how much she loved his grandad.

'What's the change, John?' Beverly's voice, soft, urged him to continue but when Grandad began to cough she went to fetch him a glass of water.

Grandad set the water down on the side table when he'd recovered. 'I have a condition if you three want that arrangement to be upheld.'

'And what's that?' Finn asked.

'I want an end to this ridiculous family feud. My dying wish—'

'You're not dying, Dad.' Andy finally sat back in his chair ready to listen.

'I will be soon, I'm ninety-six. So... if you'll let me finish... my dying wish is that you three spend time together and try with each other. It might not work, but I want you to talk, be together without it resulting in one of you walking out.'

Beverly laughed but only for a second because John wasn't joking. This was serious. And right now Finn couldn't recall a get-together when one or all of them hadn't stormed away in a rage.

Beverly and Andy looked at one another, they looked at Finn, and then when John spoke again, they all turned to listen.

'The way all three of you are acting... well, it's not what Thompsons do. If your mother were still alive, Andy, and if dear Mackenzie were—'

'Okay, you can stop right there.' Andy snatched up his coffee mug and took it to the kitchen, leaving the others in silence.

Finn gave his dad a few minutes to calm down before joining him. As he hovered he looked down at the door jamb where the pencil mark and Mackenzie's name were etched when his younger sister's height had once been measured alongside his. 'Come back, Dad. Grandad asked us here. We need to listen.'

'I know we do.'

'You know, if this is what he wants, we don't have much choice.'

His dad nodded. He was steadfastly looking out of the kitchen window. By now any possibility of snow had been thwarted by the heavy rain lashing at the window panes. 'Mackenzie would hate this, all the arguing, the bitterness.'

Finn bristled. 'Yeah, well she's not here, is she?' And with that he went back to his mum and his grandad and they all waited for Andy to grace them with his presence.

'I want you all to make a real effort,' Grandad went on. 'This isn't some whimsical notion I'll forget about. This is family. Our family. And enough is enough.'

Nobody said a word.

The others were sitting down again but Finn hovered by the

tree, a place of safety in his eyes where he was a part of this but floating on the periphery.

'What are you suggesting, John?' Beverly was as anxious to know where they went from here as everyone else in the room.

'This new will I've had drawn up does not leave this apartment to any of you.' Grandad ignored the look of shock on all their faces. 'My solicitor has a copy of this one and only on my approval will he tear it up. If that happens, we'll revert back to the will I had before, a copy of which is in my possession waiting to be signed and dated again.'

'This is a little dramatic, John,' said Beverly.

Andy didn't say anything.

'Dramatic it might be,' Grandad continued, 'but it's also the only way.'

'Grandad, you've seen what they're like in the same room, it's a wonder they haven't ripped each other to shreds,' said Finn. 'Fact,' he added when his mum looked about to voice her protestations. 'How do you reasonably expect us all to spend time together? I think it's too late for that.'

'You will do it, or this apartment won't go to your father. Which means it won't then be sold for you all to get a cut of the money – there's no chance of it ever being handed down to you, Finn.'

'So who will it go to?' Finn asked. His dad had taken a sudden interest in his own feet, arms resting on his thighs, leaning forwards, looking down with his hands clasped. Finn had expected anger but perhaps it was simmering and he was busy thinking of the best way to resolve this so he didn't miss out on what was rightfully his.

'No idea,' Grandad replied. 'Your grandma was always fond of churches, I could leave it to one of them. Or cats. She loved those and was always pestering me to get a couple; I could find a good cats' home.'

'That's crazy,' said Beverly.

'No.' Grandad stood firm. 'What is crazy is all this.' He gestured to the three of them. 'This has gone on too long. And if you all want this apartment to be yours to do with what you will, that's my condition. And it's my final word.'

'We should listen to him,' said Andy, still not making eye contact with anyone.

Finn shook his head. 'That's just typical. You know, they say money brings out the worst in people. All you can see is an apartment with a hefty price tag slipping through your fingers. I'll bet you sell up the second it's yours. If you ever get your hands on it, that is.'

'Don't be rude to your father,' Grandad urged and picked up the water to head off another coughing fit. When he'd taken a few sips he added, 'Being rude isn't a good start. And Thanksgiving, as well as this gathering today, has shown us all that this family has problems. I might not be around much longer to help wade through these events, so it'll be up to all of you. I can't bear the thought of it always being this bad. But I accept that what I want might not matter at all, and I might be kidding myself that I can push you all together.' He put the papers down now. He didn't really need them but Finn suspected he was going to hand out copies so they'd all know he meant business. He might be in his nineties but he was still fully functional in mind and body, and the legalities over important documents weren't something he'd ever overlook.

'So why do it if you aren't sure it can work?' Finn asked. 'Why put us all through it?' Seeing his parents on the odd occasion worked just fine as it was, the shorter the visit the better, and never them both together like now. He'd seen them glare across at each other on more than one occasion tonight.

'It's what I want.' And that was that. 'You have three weeks, from now until Christmas, when you will all come here for breakfast bright and early.'

Finn harrumphed. A meal together? Sharing coffee was bad enough. A meal hadn't happened in years; he couldn't even remember the last time.

Grandad went on. 'Over the next three weeks I'll tell you where you are to go and what you must do.'

'This is a little unfair, John,' said Beverly, who'd never snapped at him but even Finn could tell the frustration was mounting this time. 'We're not pawns in a game. And we do have our own lives, three separate lives.'

Grandad whacked a hand down on the arm of his chair. 'Damn it, that's exactly my point!'

Beverly jumped and when John had a coughing fit yet again, Andy refilled the glass of water and passed it to him. Finn suspected he was panicking in case Grandad keeled over without amending the will back to what it was, meaning he missed out on a Manhattan apartment likely worth a fortune.

'What about my job on the Christmas tree farm?' Finn asked. If he hadn't worshipped his grandad, been eager to do anything he could to make him happy, he'd walk away right now. But it wasn't going to be an easy three weeks, that was for sure.

'You'll find a way to make it work,' said Grandad. 'You told me your hours are flexible and it's not for long. And after the three weeks? Well, at least I'll have tried.' He looked over at the photo on top of the mantel of Mackenzie with her grandma, their faces bathed in sunshine after an afternoon at the beach one spring, trousers rolled up to the knees to take advantage of the mild temperatures that day and the cool water that lapped around their ankles. Finn had stared at that picture enough mornings when he stayed here and now it was as though Mackenzie were here telling them all to get a grip and do this one small thing Grandad wanted.

'What happens if we don't do it?' Beverly asked. 'I'm not sure we can manage it.' It was one of the first times Finn had seen his mum look truly panicked, helpless even. 'You can't be serious about leaving it all to a church, or cats.'

'If I don't get my wish then the apartment will be sold to the real estate agent who's been sniffing around for a long time, dropping in leaflets, canvasing the building. They're desperate for it and I'd be sad for it to leave the family but it would give me a big injection of cash, which I'd distribute between the various charities I've got in mind. Including churches and cats,' he finished.

'It seems a bit far to go, taking something away from your family just because...' She brushed a piece of lint from the tweed skirt she wore over black tights and slender fitted leather boots. Finn wondered, did she ever pull on sweatpants and just chill out?

'Just because they can't get along? It's a desperate effort from me – try to remember that when you're all together over the coming weeks. Remember my sister, Eleanor?'

'She was a miserable old...' Andy began but soon shut his mouth.

'She was,' Grandad said, the hint of a smile appearing. 'I won't deny it, but look at the family feud that went on. As far as I know, her kids didn't speak to her for years before she died, and I'm sure they don't speak to each other now either. She was miserable, regretful. I saw her a week before she went and she begged me not to let the same thing happen to our family.'

'This may be a foolish question,' Finn ventured, 'but how will you really know we've done what you ask us to do?'

'Call it intuition. I'll know. And thank you for coming here this evening, there aren't any other changes to my will. Unless you're going to fight over my bureau or this wing-backed chair,' he chuckled.

'I love the bureau,' Beverly admitted.

'It's yours,' said Andy.

Finn couldn't imagine his dad's new girlfriend, Paige, letting that bureau within fifty feet of her spacious, spotless residence in Connecticut where nothing over five years old appeared to exist – apart from her and his dad, that was.

Grandad stood up slowly. 'Now get out of here, all of you, down to the Italian I took you to the day you got engaged,' he directed to Andy and Beverly. 'I've booked a table. You can start this plan by sharing a meal together but I don't want any part of it, I've had enough, I'm having an early night.' He looked at them, none of them moving. 'Off you go.'

Finn shrugged on his coat. The sooner this was done the better.

The moment they were outside, Andy checked his phone and tapped out a text, probably to Paige at a guess. She'd always had him on a tight leash – at least that's the impression Finn got.

'You can put that away at dinner,' said Finn.

'Finn, he's still your father, no need to be rude.' Beverly looped a chenille scarf around her neck and pulled on a heavy, blush-pink coat, totally the wrong colour for a Manhattan winter when traffic splashed its way around the city.

They walked sedately to the restaurant, not far from Grandad's apartment, all of them trying to digest what was being asked of them. Inside, seated at the table, his dad, presumptuous as always, ordered the wine without asking whether anyone else even wanted it or if they'd prefer something else.

'I might order a white,' Beverly announced, signalling the waiter and doing just that.

'You're only doing it to prove a point,' Andy muttered.

'What, to show that I'm perfectly capable of ordering my own drink?' she countered.

'Could you two try to remember why we're even here in the first place,' Finn hissed before the waiter interrupted, had his dad taste the Burgundy he'd ordered, and glasses were poured for both men. Finn could've used a beer rather than wine but he'd learnt a long time ago that staying quiet was often a good way to get through times like these.

Beverly thanked the waiter for her glass of wine. 'Tell us about your job, Finn.' His mum's silent understanding of why they were here precipitated the change of subject.

As Finn told them all about Mitch's Christmas tree farm, what his duties involved, the small town of Inglenook Falls, his dad's fingers twizzled the stem of his glass as though he'd rather be anywhere else than here. But then, didn't they all feel that way?

'Mitch is a good boss, leaves me to it when he has to, pays a good rate.'

'Enough to fund more travelling?' His dad held up his hands in defence when Finn shot him a look. 'I don't mean anything by it except the question itself. Must you always think the worst of me?'

'Right back at you.' But Finn simmered. 'The job is enough for what I need right now, and I have some savings too.'

'Even though you've travelled extensively?' his mum pondered, her glass mostly drained already. She did that when she was nervous and sometimes the liquor worked to relax her, other times it only served to wind her up more.

'I travelled but worked at the same time. I only needed board and food wherever I went, never stayed anywhere posh – house shares a lot of the time – but I moved on quickly enough before it became a problem, before anyone annoyed me enough to want to leave.'

'Dylan's always had your back,' his mum smiled. 'I'm glad he found you work, he's a good kid.'

Finn smiled. 'Hardly a kid now, he has four of his own.'

'Is that right? That's a lot of kids.'

Finn explained Dylan's first marriage, Cleo and the kids who'd come after. 'They're getting married Christmas Eve.'

'Romantic. And you're definitely going?'

'I'll be his best man. You look surprised.'

'You were both very close growing up but I didn't think you were in touch with him any more.'

'I'd not seen him in years but we've stayed in touch on and off.' Finn hadn't missed his father's cell phone on the table, his gaze lingering on it as though it could save him from having to try to make conversation.

Finn gestured to the waiter and ordered a beer. His dad could keep his fancy wine and drink it all himself for all he cared.

Andy tucked the phone in his jacket pocket and didn't comment on Finn's beer. All three of them only had eyes for their menus but the options swam in front of Finn's eyes. He didn't want to be here, he didn't want to do this. He would do anything for his grandad, but this? His family had long made him miserable and he suspected they were well past the point of no return.

'Anyone on the horizon for you?' his mum ventured when Finn had sunk a few good gulps of beer.

'Women you mean? Since when did you care about my love life?'

'I'm trying, okay.'

'Nobody special,' was his only answer before the waiter came over and took their orders.

Once again it was just the three of them and Finn tried to make a bit of an effort too. 'How's Byron? Didn't get a chance to ask the other day.' His parents had been too embittered with each other and throwing insults back and forth to even try normal conversation. Perhaps that little performance had prompted his grandad to make the changes to his will.

'He's fine.'

'How's his business?'

'I know you can't stand him, so why ask?'

'Because like you, I'm trying here.' Although she was right. Finn didn't like the man at all. Tanned, slicked hair, and teeth a shade too white, he was loud and overbearing. And every time Finn saw Byron, Byron would man slap him on the back as though they were pals. It was guaranteed to rile him.

He turned to his dad next. 'How's Paige?' Got another boob job? Tummy tuck? Whatever else she hadn't managed to alter yet and whatever had maximum hit on Andy's bank balance, he was sure.

'She's fine.' His dad wasn't giving anything away either and Finn gave up when their food arrived, glad of a distraction. In fact, he'd never eaten pasta so quickly; it would likely come up the other way when he walked to the station later if he didn't slow down.

Meal over, Finn was about to take out his wallet and pay his share when his dad suggested cognac to finish the evening.

'Since when did I drink the stuff?'

'A simple no would've done,' Andy huffed and took a cigar from the inside of his jacket pocket.

The waiter was quick to come over and tell him he couldn't smoke it here.

'I wasn't going to, I'm showing my son, if you don't mind.'

'Did you have to be so rude?' Beverly bristled after smiling at the poor waiter, who considered himself told and slunk off to an easier-to-manage table no doubt.

'He made assumptions,' said Andy. 'I don't appreciate it.'

'Were you really showing me?' Finn quizzed, more to avoid his parents launching into another row than because he was interested.

'Of course,' he shrugged. 'And I have two.'

'I feel the same way about cigars as I do about cognac.' With that, Finn excused himself to go to the bathroom, took his time, and when he returned his parents were up to their old tricks again. At least the bickering stopped the second Finn re-joined them and his dad told him he'd taken care of the bill.

'I could've paid my share,' said Finn. 'With the proceeds from my real job.'

'Don't start,' his mum sighed.

'We should probably call it a night.' Finn let the matter go.

'It's early yet, son. How about we find a bar? Plenty of them around.'

'I have to get back to Inglenook Falls.' And a bar was asking for trouble.

'I'm trying here. I'm doing what your grandad asked.'

Finn didn't really know how to argue with that. 'Another time, but I really do have to get back.'

'Wait a minute, both of you.' Beverly stopped Finn putting his jacket on and he sat back down. 'Your grandad is keen for us all to start treating each other a little better. We've all been guilty in the past of not respecting each other's wishes, of being rude, hot-tempered—'

'I can't listen to this, Mom.' Finn picked up his jacket again and shoved an arm into one sleeve. He felt like a yo-yo, going one minute, then back again, fighting one second, all making an effort the next. 'Think about it. You're talking as though we're three adults on the same level. But we're not. You two are the parents. I'm the child. Being civil is one thing but ignoring the lousy childhood you gave me is a step too far. I can't do it.' He turned and left them behind in the restaurant.

'Lousy childhood!' His dad's voice belied how much he'd had to drink and his breath stank of cognac when he followed Finn outside and came up close. 'You want to go ask other kids about their childhoods, kids brought up in poverty, kids abused, neglected. We never did any of those things.'

'You're right, you didn't.' What was the point in even trying? He was never going to get them to realise that this, the way they were with each other, was their fault. Life had thrown crap their way and they hadn't dealt with it, at least not in the way they should've done. How could he just forget that?

'We do take some of the blame,' his mum admitted.

'Some?' Incredulous, Finn had the overwhelming urge to run.

'You had a home,' his father snapped, 'you were safe, you never wanted for anything.'

'Well, I think we all know that's not true, don't we?'

'We need to arrange another time to try to move forwards.' And there it was again, his father's ability to block out the things that mattered, switch a situation around and treat it like one of his business meetings, as though he were at the helm of a big project rather than having retired from the game.

'I work seven days a week.' Finn buttoned up his jacket ready to begin the walk to the train station. He'd welcome the cold tonight. He wanted it to penetrate right through his clothes, wake him up to the unpleasantness of the evening.

'Do it for your grandad.' His dad's last attempt to impress upon Finn the importance of this was simple yet effective.

'We'll come to you in Inglenook Falls.' Beverly pulled on maroon leather gloves to cover manicured nails. 'Won't we, Andy?'

'Sure.'

'Fine,' Finn relented. 'Text me, you have my cell phone number.' He'd need plenty of warning to psych himself up for that visit.

A taxi trundled past, too fast for the street and so close to the sidewalk that it hit the puddle in the gutter and dirt splashed in their direction.

His mother swore. 'I'll have to get this damn coat dry-cleaned now.' There were charcoal-coloured splodges all the way up one side.

'It's a stupid colour to wear anyway.' Andy lit up a cigar.

'It is not,' she snapped.

'It's hardly winter attire,' Andy argued back. 'Look at the colour!'

And that was how Finn left them, arguing in the street like a couple of mangy cats, while he set off for the station.

He only felt himself relax when he got back on that train and heard the announcement of the destination, Inglenook Falls.

Who would ever have thought a small town could be so appealing to him after so much travelling to far-off places around the world?

7

KAISHA

Manhattan was mayhem today and the Garland Street markets, in their second year, had attracted way more footfall than ever before. Kaisha was manning the stall with two other helpers and they'd been rushed off their feet, but at least it got her away from Inglenook Falls and the tension in the apartment. She wasn't used to having a house guest and she certainly wasn't used to dealing with somebody else's moods.

Last night, Finn had come home late, banging around, the odd swear word thrown in. She'd heard his boots thud on the floor and had felt anger rising until she heard the closet door tucked just inside the front door open and then a scraping sound that implied he was using the dustpan and brush.

'Those are one-hundred-per-cent cashmere,' Kaisha advised a customer handling a pair of cream gloves, 'and there's a scarf to match if you're interested.'

The woman took them both as a Christmas gift for her other half. Kaisha served a couple who were laughing together as they chose matching sweaters to wear to a family event. Kaisha and Cory had once laughed in the same way donning Christmas sweaters and acting goofy, and at this time of the year it really was the little things you missed.

By the time Kaisha finished work and left Manhattan with Mitch, who'd offered to take her back to Inglenook Falls, she was so tired she fought to keep her eyes open.

'It's so much busier than last year,' Mitch remarked as his truck battled through the traffic and finally they left the city behind.

'Good for business.'

'Not sure I want to do it again next year, I've got enough going on with the farm and the local markets; this might be my last year in the city. I know Holly would like me home more.'

Kaisha smiled. Holly and Mitch were a couple who'd found their Happy Ever After for sure. 'How is Holly?'

He indicated to pass a car, his head moving as it needed to do to check his mirrors. 'She's good, plenty of commissions for magazine articles and photographs coming her way.'

'You make a great team.'

He put his wipers on when the rain started up again. 'Talking of teams, how's it going with Finn?'

'Fine.'

'You know, when Holly answers "fine" to any question it usually means she has more to say but really doesn't want to.'

'You never used to be this talkative,' Kaisha teased.

'Blame that one on Holly, she's always luring me out of my shell, as she describes it. But I can't complain; I was the hermit in the woods and I tell you what, it's far nicer being a man people greet in the street than one they cross over to avoid. So come on, what's going on with Finn? Is he at least behaving himself? He's a good worker, but is he a good roommate?'

'He seems to make the effort, occasionally. We both do.'

'But...' He glanced over at Kaisha. 'There's always a but...'

'I'm not sure I trust him all that much.'

'What makes you say that? I have no qualms about him managing the cash register at the farm.'

'I don't mean that sort of trust. I don't think he's going to steal from me or anything. I'm talking about loyalty, friendship, that kind of trust. I've spent a lot of time with Cleo and Dylan and they're very good friends, but the wedding is stressful enough and I don't want to see Cleo more wound up than she already is. Finn is best man and already he's turned up drunk at the Inglenook Inn for Thanksgiving, he's cancelled an important suit fitting with Dylan but wouldn't give a reason why, and he called me a nagging wife.'

Mitch's laughter rumbled around the truck that was empty in the back except for pine needles. He'd left the few remaining trees that hadn't sold inside his market chalet with their roots in plastic containers of water so he could put them out again in the morning. 'It sounds like you're getting under his skin a bit. I'm not saying you're doing anything wrong, you're looking out for your friends, but maybe give him space.'

'Hard to do when we live together.'

'True, but talking from experience, sometimes all us men need is physical and emotional distance to deal with whatever is going on in our heads and then we're ready to talk.'

Mitch dropped Kaisha home and she was relieved to find the apartment empty, although when she went into the living room and saw Finn had decorated the tree, her breath caught in her throat. Perhaps she was being unfair to him, assuming he was up to no good. Here was a tree decked with delicate white lights, a silver star at the top, a reindeer dangling by gold threads leaping from the branches. She even smiled when she saw the Santa in sunglasses standing beneath a palm tree with a cocktail in one hand.

Was she being too judgemental when it came to this stranger who'd descended into her life unexpectedly? Just because Cory had turned out to be a bad seed it didn't mean every other guy was.

Perhaps Finn was one of the good ones, like Mitch and Dylan. Maybe he deserved a chance.

Kaisha made a decision there and then. A peace-offering. She'd cook Finn dinner tonight and after a day on the farm he'd surely appreciate it. Maybe then they could start over and begin being a bit nicer to one another. If it was going to be this tense the whole time he was here, it would spoil the run-up not only to the wedding but to Christmas too, usually a time of joy that she looked forward to as soon as the leaves in the fall dropped and signalled the promise of cosy winter months, her most favourite season of all.

She opened the fridge to see what was lurking. She'd been planning on opening a tin of soup, having it with the chunk of crusty bread she still had left over from the bakery, which would be fine if it was toasted, but instead she took out the chicken she'd planned to make a huge hotpot with and freeze in portions. She took out carrots, parsnips, potatoes, herbs, white wine, an onion, and began to chop. She wasn't the best cook in the world but she'd made this recipe so many times before that she was confident it would be more than just edible; it would taste good. When she was a teen, she'd been hooked on cooking shows and had experimented in the kitchen most weekends, but she didn't have the knack. Somehow she misjudged quantities, didn't pay attention to detail, burned some things, undercooked others, and Bree had never held back on telling her how bad a cook she was. Kaisha had taken it all in her stride, dusted off the teasing, because it was kind of true.

By the time Finn came through the door, Kaisha had everything underway. The smell of garlic and thyme filled the tiny kitchen, the rice was almost ready, the peace-offering was in place.

'Hey.' He'd taken off his boots already and was checking the floor for debris, which made her feel terrible for having words with him about it before. She was just like he'd said, a nagger. And it didn't sit well. She'd never been that way before. She was always

carefree and easy-going, at least before her life got so complicated.
But these days she seemed to be taking her stresses out on anyone
who was around. And unlucky for Finn, he was right in the firing
line.

'Hey there,' she smiled at him as she picked up the oven gloves.
She opened the oven and waited for the blast of hot air to subside
before taking out the hotpot.

'I'll get out of your hair,' he said.

'But it's dinner time.'

'Which is why I'll leave you to it. I'm heading to the café, it's pot
roast tonight, on special according to the sign in the window.'

'Finn...' She set down the heavy oven dish. 'I've cooked for you
too. I thought it could be a way of making things easier between us.'
She was glad her face was still coloured from the oven heat and that
he couldn't tell how awkward she felt saying this to him. 'We have
to share this apartment until New Year's, I thought it would be more
pleasant if we got on, that's all.'

'You cooked for me?' The cute smile he seemed to have saved
for special occasions until now came out to play. 'Can I do anything
to help?'

She remembered the rice, which would be a soggy mess if she
left it much longer. She picked up the sieve to strain it. 'Grab some
cutlery; we can sit at the little table if you clear it first.' She'd seen it
earlier, stacked high with packaging from Christmas ornaments.
With the rice safely rescued, she said, 'And thank you for decorating
the tree today.'

'Mitch wanted me to start so early this morning and stay behind
tonight, so it meant a nice long break during the day. I sneaked back
here to do it.'

Finn got to work on the table while Kaisha spooned out rice,
adding a generous portion of chicken hotpot to each serving. The
potato top of the hotpot was golden and crispy and when they even-

tually dug in to the meal, Finn was all compliments. 'You can really cook.'

'Call it practice makes perfect. Really, I'm terrible in the kitchen – ask anyone, although I haven't cooked for anyone around here so you'd have to ask my family.'

'You can't be that bad.'

She covered her mouth, the food a little hot to have taken such a big portion, but she was so hungry. 'That chicken hotpot has taken a long time to perfect. I can make a good chilli, but don't even ask me to attempt a lasagne unless you want the kitchen to look like World War Three has arrived, and as for biscuits and cakes, I left those alone a long time ago after a series of disasters – cookies so hard my mom broke a tooth, cupcakes that sank and had no taste after I forgot to add the butter. I'd weighed it out, added everything else, and then when they were in the oven, there it was looking at me. I figured, couldn't make that much difference.'

'Sounds like you picked the right dish to serve tonight. This is amazing, and I really appreciate it.'

'The tree looks good too. Thanks again for doing it. I've done the one in my room but it's nowhere near as professional-looking as this one.'

'Glad you like it. You can take the ornament I bought for you and put it on your tree if you'd prefer.'

She pulled a face in confusion before realising he meant the tropical Santa. 'It's fine out here.'

'You hate it.'

'I do not.'

'I bought it for you, you know.'

'I appreciate it.'

'I'm not sure you do. It was supposed to remind you of your parents, having Christmas away somewhere tropical.'

'Oh...' She'd completely missed the point. She didn't know what to say so instead mumbled another thanks and asked, 'Seconds?' after he finished what was on his plate.

'I'll get it, I'm not a guest. Can I get you some more?'

'Still working on the first lot, thanks.'

'Be complimented,' he called back as he went into the kitchen. 'Seconds means I liked it enough to want more.' And when he returned to the room he said, 'Otherwise you'd never know whether I was pretending it was good.'

She waited for him to sit down at the table. 'Can I ask you something?'

'Go on.' He tucked in to the second portion with as much enthusiasm as he had the first.

'You said once that you got the scar on your torso from a bar fight.'

'And you're worried about the company you're keeping,' he said after finishing another mouthful. 'It wasn't as dramatic as it sounds. Wrong place at the wrong time. There was a fight going on, I tried to leave and got knocked into the path of trouble, if you know what I mean. I fell across a table that had glass already smashed on the surface, a shard of glass did the damage. There was a lot of blood. Sorry,' he said when he saw her face.

'Could be worse; I could still be eating.' So he hadn't been in the actual fight, he'd tried to walk away. It was oddly reassuring to know.

They finished their meal with plenty of chatter and as Finn finished the second portion and declared he was full, Kaisha suggested they open a bottle of wine. 'I picked it up at the liquor store weeks ago but never got around to opening it. I always figured knitting needed to be done with a clear head unless Cleo wanted some pretty odd garments going on sale at the markets or the store.'

'You've got a point there. Not knitting tonight?'

'Not tonight.' She found the corkscrew and glasses and Finn did the honours, opening the bottle of Spanish merlot and pouring each of them a measure.

'You really love knitting, don't you?' He smiled, looking at the turquoise sweater she was wearing. It was one of her favourites, which she wore a cream shirt beneath and which skimmed the top of her hips. 'Do you make your own sweaters?'

'I make most of them. Not always, but this is one of mine.'

'A woman of many talents.' He sat on the armchair while Kaisha settled at one end of the sofa.

'The markets are using so much stock, it's hard to keep up with ready-made garments. We're at it all year round, but doing all the knitting by hand takes time. I did float the idea of a knitting machine to Cleo but she wouldn't hear of it.'

'What else do you knit?'

'Scarves are hugely popular at Christmas and they're super easy to make. To be honest it's the actual knitting, the therapeutic clickety-clack of the needles, I'm hooked on rather than the garment I end up with, whether it's for me or someone else.'

'It's easy to put a lot of hours into a job that you love.'

She got the impression there was more meaning laced beneath his words than what showed on the surface. She took another drink of wine for confidence. 'What's your passion? What's the one thing you'd love to do if money was no object, time not a factor?'

'Now that might be letting you see a bit too much of me.'

'We're sharing an apartment, I've cooked you dinner and told you how awful I am in the kitchen unless it's a well-practised recipe, so I think it's your turn.'

He began to clear up the plates. 'I'm a bit of a nomad, don't settle anywhere and that includes in any job for too long.'

What was that supposed to mean? It was hardly answering the question, was it? She didn't get a chance to ask him anything more before he escaped to the kitchen. She followed after him to grab a cloth to mop up a dribble of wine left on the table.

She waited until they were standing side-by-side at the sink sharing the chore of washing the dishes, him with his hands in the suds, her with a cloth to dry and put away, to delve more. 'You came back to Manhattan, that must mean something.'

'I came back to see family and for Dylan's wedding, but it won't be long before I'm on my way again.'

As much as she missed having her apartment to herself, part of her didn't like hearing his plans for leaving. 'It seems a shame.'

'Why? I'm free to do what I like. No ties, no hassle.'

It wasn't how she ever wanted to be. Having a home, roots, kept her grounded. The past year without Cory had been tough but it would've been harder without her friends around. 'Dylan's here as well as your family, he's a good friend.'

'Always will be. You must have friends like that who you don't see for years and when you do it's as though you caught up yesterday.'

She smiled. 'Actually, yes, my friend Taylor from school. We were friends in second grade and haven't lost touch since even though she moved to Boston with her family. I hadn't seen her for seven years when we last caught up, and it didn't make a bit of difference.'

'Well, there you go,' he shrugged. He set the last of the cutlery into the drainer and shook off his hands.

'Sometimes it's easier, you know.'

'What is?'

'To put down roots.'

'Like you have, you mean?'

'I love Inglenook Falls. I was a city girl for a long time but this town is special.'

'And the Little Knitting Box?'

'Special too,' she smiled.

'But it's Cleo's business.'

'She pays me well, I get this place at a cheaper rate, I love what I do.'

'So it's a win-win then?'

'I guess it is.' She hung up the sodden cloth on the rail used to pull open the oven door. 'What's your next job to be after the Christmas tree farm?'

They took their wine back through to the living room. 'I'll turn my hand to pretty much anything – bar work, manual labour, whatever I can find.'

'And you're happy to do that forever?'

'I could ask you the same... are you happy to stay working at a little store in a small town forever or do you have bigger dreams?'

She topped up both glasses of wine to avoid the question. 'I'm happy, content, there's a lot to be said for it.'

'What's with that mannequin?' he frowned as he faced off with the plastic model. 'I feel like it's looking at me all the time.'

'It's not real.'

'In the shadows I keep imagining it is.'

'Get over it,' she laughed, remembering it wasn't the first time he'd mentioned it took him unawares when he thought it was a real person. 'And I can't move it anywhere. Your bedroom was my dressmaking room but now...'

'Yeah, leave it where it is. No way do I want to wake up to that in the morning.' He stood up and went over to the mannequin and lifted the hat off its head. 'Who's this for?'

'It's part of an outfit for the school Christmas pageant. I'm making the costumes.' She'd left the holly and berries drying on the rim of the black felt hat.

'How many do you have to make?' He balanced the hat back on the mannequin's head.

'Nine in total.'

'That's quite a commission.'

She patted the white all-in-one that was on the back of the sofa. 'The hat goes with this, a snowman costume. I've made black pom-poms to sew on for the coal buttons, I've knitted a red, black and green scarf, and the hat will finish it off as well as the carrot tied with elastic that the little boy can pop on his nose.'

'Sounds ingenious.'

'Hard work, more like, but they paid me well and this is the last costume of the lot.'

'It sounds as though you could start a whole other business the rate you're going.' When she said nothing he looked at her. 'That's what you want, isn't it? You want to go out on your own, make things. What else do you want to make?'

Her silence confirmed her answer and his persistence and interest made her want to tell him more. She hadn't told anyone else and it was hard to keep it all in.

'There's a dress hanging on my wardrobe—'

'The plum dress?'

She allowed herself a small smile, knowing he'd taken an interest. 'I made that dress and a turquoise one just like it, plus a black one in the same style that I gave to my friend Taylor when I last saw her.'

'I'm impressed.'

She stood up and turned around on the spot. 'I made these myself,' she said of her jeans, patting the rear pocket and then her upper thigh. 'And I embroidered the floral design too.' The wine was making her talk more or maybe it was the subject matter bringing out her enthusiasm.

He moved closer to admire the pattern and all of a sudden she realised his focus was on her butt. 'I made the lilac shirt I had on yesterday too,' she said, sitting back down again. 'I'd say sixty per cent of my wardrobe is homemade.'

'It really is your dream, isn't it?'

'Not a word, I haven't mentioned it to anyone here.'

'My lips are sealed. But may I ask why you don't want anyone to know?'

'My parents always hoped I'd get a job working in an art gallery or perhaps for a media organisation after my degree and that was what I intended, but at university I was friends with a few fashion students. I loved what they did; I'd make garments, get their expertise, and then I just couldn't stop. A hobby became that little bit more over time. Knitting was my passion for a long while until I discovered dressmaking.'

'Nothing wrong with finding your true passion.'

'My parents had no idea what I was thinking getting a job at a store but they are happy I'm settled.'

'They worry?' He'd topped up his wine and hers.

'Not so much about me. About my sister, she's caused them a lot of trouble over the years.'

'And you think sharing your desire to do something different might upset them?'

'Not at all. But I want to tell them when I'm ready. I've had a crappy year personally, but when the time's right, I'll be able to make plans.'

'Why has your year been so bad?'

She hadn't meant to blurt that out. 'You're very nosy, aren't you? There was I thinking you were quiet, you'd not want much conversation when you moved in.'

'Maybe you got to me with your dinner.'

'Don't let me make you mac 'n' cheese then or you might want to move on quicker than you planned. Cheese sauce is one of the hardest things to make.' When his mouth twitched into a smile she said, 'What's that look for?'

'You like having me here, I can tell.'

Oh no, had it sounded that way? Had she flirted without realising? 'I do not. You've taken my dressmaking room.'

Eyebrows raised and with a cute smile, he let it go. 'Cleo must know about your talent.'

'She does, but she doesn't know I'd like my own business. How could I desert her when she's so busy, when her own life has been up and down over the years too?' She filled him in on a bit of Cleo's background, the postnatal depression she'd always worried would get her, the loss of her mother, the anxiety when things got on top of her.

'No wonder you get so angry at me when it looks like I'll mess things up. You know, it's an admirable quality, caring so much about your friends.'

She shook her head. 'This is what I don't understand. You see the value in closeness, friendships, but why don't you want any of your own?'

'I'm Dylan's best man.'

'I know, but you're planning to move on, again. And that's if you don't mess up the wedding for them. There's still time,' she teased. But she soon turned serious. 'A best man has responsibilities. Like choosing the suits, getting measured up in time, being there for the groom.'

'I failed that one already, but I gave him my measurements, and it couldn't be helped.'

'Where were you?'

'With family. My grandad and my parents.'

'You make it sound like that's a bad thing.'

'Believe me, it is.' He scratched at his chin, his strong hands distracting Kaisha for a moment.

'Come on, your turn.' Time to put a stop to the melancholy this line of conversation was generating.

'My turn for what?'

'Well, I've told you plenty about me, but I was the one who asked the question in the first place. What are your dreams, what would you do if money were no object, if nothing stood in your way?' she reminded him.

'I don't have any.'

'Of course you do, everybody does.'

'Well I don't.' He turned his head, looking up as though he was trying to listen out for something. 'Can you hear that?'

'Stop stalling.'

'I'm not.' He put his wine glass down and left the room, a puzzled look on his face.

When he didn't come back she followed him out to the kitchen, where his body was half beneath the sink, half on the floor, and she tried to ignore the way the muscles on his stomach moved as his arms wrestled with something under there.

'What are you doing?'

He poked his head out. 'Your tap is dripping. What type of faucet is it?' She looked at him blankly, which seemed to amuse him. He pushed himself up again and staggered so close to her he put his hands on her upper arms and shunted her out of the way.

'I'll have to call a plumber in the morning.'

He shook his head, tested which faucet had the issue and then bent down again. 'We can't leave it dripping all night, so I'll switch off the water supply and go to the hardware store first thing. I'm sure Mitch will let me duck off for a while. Do you have one nearby?'

She mumbled the name of the nearest one but asked, 'Are you sure? I could just call a plumber.'

'Total waste of money.'

'I'll do my teeth then if that's okay with you.' She didn't wait for an answer because he'd held her stare long enough to make her feel on edge, and not in a bad way.

'Bathroom's free,' she said when she came back to the kitchen and filled a glass of water.

Finn headed off to use the bathroom and when he came back, crouched down to turn off the water supply. She tried not to gawp at his taut rear in well-fitted jeans. 'Wait a minute,' she said nearly causing him to bump his head. She bent down to his level. 'You're not one of those men who mends things and then has to get an expert to fix up a botch job are you?'

'Sorry to disappoint,' he smiled up at her, their faces closer than ever before, 'but I'm pretty handy around the house. I told you that you liked having me here.'

'Wouldn't go that far.'

Time to escape. She headed for the safety of her bedroom; it was enough distance to gather her thoughts. She hadn't found out much more about this man tonight, but something told her that her roommate was a lot more than brash and unreliable.

Kaisha had a feeling there was a whole lot more to discover about Finn Thompson.

And maybe if she gave it time, she'd find out.

8

FINN

When he saw his parents, Finn set down the axe by the kiosk at the Christmas tree farm and pulled off his gloves. Andy and Beverly stood at least a metre apart, as though getting any closer might be far too stressful for both of them.

'What are you doing here?' His breath, white on the air, disguised how hot he was from chopping firewood. He'd thought they'd text first, give him warning, but they hadn't.

His mum was first to speak. 'We want to honour your grandad's wishes and make an effort. And dinner didn't go all that well, did it?'

'So you think showing up when I'm working will help? I did tell you to message me first.'

'And risk you telling us not to bother?' Beverly was spot on; he would've told them to stay away. 'Can't you take a break?'

His dad looked hesitant to say anything, to risk stirring up the situation. Hands shoved in pockets, he looked around the farm, taking in the space, and for once he looked almost content. Maybe he was like this when he wasn't in the city meeting up, perhaps he was a different man these days. Stranger things had happened.

Finn had already taken a break to go to the hardware store, extended the break to fix the leaky faucet at the apartment. He explained all this to them. 'I won't be able to get away.'

Mitch was coming over and the last thing he wanted was for him to be generous enough to give him more free time but it's exactly what he did.

Stomping away from the farm, Finn told his parents, 'You have one hour, then I'm back here. I can't afford to lose pay or worse.'

His mum didn't have appropriate footwear on at all. It reminded him of the one and only year that as a family they'd tried to go out to another farm in Connecticut and select their own tree. It had ended in a full-scale row and after that, they never did it again.

Today, his parents had driven down and parked behind the little log cabin and so at their request Finn climbed into the back of the car and they headed up to the café on Main Street.

'This is a cute place.' The bell tinkled above the door to the café. What was it with Inglenook Falls? Finn got that it was a small town, but every store seemed to have one of those old-fashioned bells, and he hadn't seen a single CCTV camera since he got here.

They ordered muffins and coffees and settled down at the last remaining table, the café packed more than usual, most likely because of the season and the draw of the markets.

'How's the job going?' his dad asked, using a knife to cut his cranberry and cinnamon muffin into quarters.

'Fine.'

'You looked like you were working hard when we got there,' his mum told him. 'We saw you chopping the wood.'

He hadn't realised they'd been watching him before he went over to the kiosk. 'At least it's tiring me out. I sleep well.'

'Better than the floor at your grandad's,' agreed his dad. 'I heard you didn't find the sofa too comfortable.'

'My feet hung over the edge,' Finn confirmed. 'Kind of gave up on that.' And hadn't they already talked about him crashing out at Grandad's? It had been a sore subject for long enough.

'Dad enjoys your company, he's glad you're around for a while.'

'And I like spending time with him.' He could've come back just for the wedding when Dylan contacted him, but now he was here, he was pleased he'd come well in advance to give him more time with Grandad.

'I do wish he'd reconsider moving somewhere closer to one of us,' said Beverly.

'This again? Really?' Finn bristled. 'The apartment is his home, it's where he belongs.'

'I worry, that's all.'

He supposed he shouldn't criticise her for that. 'Between Beryl and all of us popping in, I doubt Grandad will have a chance to get lonely or have anything happen to him.'

'I suppose you're right,' she relented. 'He seems to get on with Beryl well.'

'She's very bossy, reminds me of Grandma.'

With his parents pleased at his summation, they finished their coffees and food. Finn filled them in on what he knew about the town, but when Enid, who worked in the café and had introduced herself to Finn yesterday, looked like she was taking way more interest than she should, he pulled on his coat. 'We should go, I need to get back.'

'Photo first,' Andy reminded them. 'Remember what your grandad said.'

'Right,' Finn conceded. He took out his cell phone, flipped the camera around but Enid was there in a flash.

'Let me!' She motioned for him to pass her the cell phone after she'd brushed off her hands on her apron. 'I'll get a nice family picture. You could even use it for a holiday card one year.' She waved her arm in front to direct them into position, closer to each other. 'Bit closer… bit closer still… and smile!'

Finn had no idea what the picture looked like and grimaced through a second attempt, a third, and a fourth before thanking Enid, plastering a smile on his face and sending the final and most respectable shot to Grandad before they could escape into the open air.

But Finn tried to get out of the café so fast he bumped slap-bang into Kaisha. 'Sorry, I didn't see you there.'

She put a hand to her orange hat in case it might have been knocked. 'Not to worry, I had my head down to escape the cold, wasn't really paying much attention to my surroundings. And thank you for fixing the faucet, I appreciate it.'

His mum cleared her throat and he knew he couldn't avoid the inevitable introductions. 'Kaisha, these are my parents, Andy and Beverly.'

She pulled off a glove and held out her hand. 'Delighted to meet you.'

'And are you a friend of Finn's?' his dad asked.

'I suppose you could say that. Finn is my roommate.' When she sensed Finn wasn't enjoying any part of this she added, 'Be sure to check out the markets, Inglenook Falls does Christmas very well.'

'She's a chirpy young thing,' said Andy, trying to read more into it than there really was, when Kaisha had the good sense to get inside the warmth of the café.

Finn grunted an agreement. His parents had never met a girl-friend of his, not since he'd brought someone back to the house the day before his fifteenth birthday and she'd witnessed one of their blazing rows and told the entire school about it. After that he'd rarely been in relationships that lasted longer than a carton of milk and never had the need to introduce his other half to his family. Brief flings were fun, but when emotions and talking became part of it, he walked the other way. Kaisha was the first woman in a long time to hold his interest conversationally and that was only because they weren't a couple.

The stilted conversation didn't last too much longer before Finn left his parents and made his way back to Mitch's farm, checking his cell phone when it pinged to find a reply from Grandad. For a man who was born well before mobile telephony even existed, he had no hesitation with technology and welcomed it to keep in touch with his family. He'd loved its convenience when Finn was on his travels around the world to this country and that. This time he'd sent back a thumbs-up emoji, to which Finn replied, 'This changes nothing.'

'A picture speaks a thousand words,' came his grandad's quick-witted reply, which made Finn smile before he pulled his gloves on and went back to work.

* * *

That evening, Dylan and Finn headed out to the Corbridge Hotel, a new, upmarket venue at the edge of town. They'd come here for a drink at Dylan's suggestion.

'Were you desperate to get out of home, away from the kids?' Finn asked as they sat down.

'Neither.' Dylan took a mouthful of no-alcohol beer given he was the driver. 'Okay, I admit, sometimes it's nice to get some head-space, but I also figured you and I haven't had a proper chance to catch up since you came back to New York, not counting that quick breakfast between my business meetings. Have you decided yet how long you'll be staying this time?'

'Not sure. It depends on Grandad.' Sitting at a table by the window in the main hall, guaranteed to be occupied unless you reserved it because of the opulent decor in the grand reception, the roaring fire, and the glass domed roof offering up a blanket of stars above on a clear night, Finn picked at the label on his own beer bottle. Full strength for him.

'How's he doing?'

'He's slowed down a lot, but he's not doing too badly and he has Beryl to keep him company. She keeps an eye out for him and it stops Mom and Dad from obsessing about moving him to a home closer to them. The idea is still there, they still make the odd suggestion, but he won't budge. He belongs in that apartment, nowhere else.'

'Sounds as though Beryl is a good solution.'

'She makes sure he doesn't miss medical appointments, they play cards, do sudoku, and chat politics like a TV talk show sometimes. Grandad's only complaint is that Beryl monitors his caffeine intake.'

'I remember you telling me he liked his coffee like tar,' Dylan smiled.

'Still does and sneaks one every time she's not looking.'

'Are you missing the city now you're out this way?'

'I'm not missing sleeping on the floor. I might only be mid-thirties, but my body felt every moment of lying on that hard surface.'

'Does this mean you're happy I arranged for you to share with Kaisha for a while?'

'The bed is comfortable, I have a room, it's close to the Christmas tree farm. What more could I ask for?'

'How's it going between you and Kaisha?'

'I'm behaving, if that's what you mean.'

'I didn't mean that. I was asking how you're getting on, that's all.'

'I'm surprised she doesn't fill you in on all the details.' Finn signalled for another beer.

'I don't see Kaisha much. I hear things through Cleo but, then again, I barely see my own fiancée as much as I'd like. We're both rushing here and there with the kids, it's a crazy life.'

One Finn had never wanted, or at least he didn't think he did. 'Kaisha's nice enough. Quirky, friendly, not too nosy.' He didn't reveal that Kaisha had cooked for him – it sounded too intimate a gesture, even though it had been a friendly way to start over after they'd clashed.

'I hear your parents were in Inglenook Falls today.'

'Word travels fast.' A muscle in his jaw twitched.

'Mitch,' he explained. 'He brought more trees to the markets this afternoon. I was on a run after a morning of back-to-back meetings, and he mentioned it. How did it go?'

'How it always goes.'

'Not well, I take it.'

'Tense seems like an apt description.'

'It did surprise me when Mitch mentioned they'd stopped by.'

Finn divulged the truth about his grandad's request. 'He's pretty insistent we sort things out once and for all.'

'And you don't think it'll work?'

'Of course it won't. It's been too long, we're all different, you can't gloss over everything that happened, much as we might want to.' His voice faded out momentarily. 'They didn't take parenting all that seriously when I was growing up, I got used to being independent and keeping my distance. Changing that now is crazy, but I'll do it for Grandad.'

'Do they still argue?' Finn's look gave him the answer. 'Must be hard to be around.'

'Always was.'

'Do you ever talk about…'

Finn suspected Dylan hadn't finished his sentence because they never spoke about the unspeakable. Finn's sister, Mackenzie, was a topic well and truly off limits. Dylan had once mentioned her to another friend, perhaps as a way of explaining why Finn could sometimes be such an asshole – he was forever getting into scuffles, or occasionally became verbally abusive after a few drinks if someone said the wrong thing – and he'd reacted pretty badly that time. He'd pinned Dylan up against the wall, anger blazing in his eyes, and told him never to mention her name ever again.

Finn swigged on his beer, surprised when Dylan carried on the line of questioning. 'Don't you think that's half the problem?'

His bottle paused before it got to his mouth this time. The hand resting on his thigh clenched into a fist. 'I'd rather not talk about it now either if that's all right by you.'

Dylan held up his hands. 'Sure thing.'

There were times he'd wanted to talk about Mackenzie, almost done it too, but admitting his feelings out loud to anyone else let a little window open into his soul. Stuffing it all back inside and holding his head up high always seemed much easier and far less painful.

'How is this reconciliation with your parents going to work?' Dylan ventured, helping himself to a handful of peanuts from the bowl in the centre of the table.

'No idea.' Finn threw a peanut up high and caught it in his open mouth.

'I tell the kids not to do that in case they choke.'

'Yes, Dad.' Finn grinned and took a handful of salty nuts to eat after he'd spoken. 'My parents constantly bicker but they're going to have to get over themselves and try, for Grandad's sake. Kind of like his dying wish, except he's very much still with us and probably enjoying watching us suffer.' He explained how he had to send photographic evidence each time, how his grandad made him check in, kept on their backs to ensure they were keeping up their end of the deal.

'On a different note, the suits are ready to collect,' said Dylan. 'You'd better hope you've given me the right measurements.'

'I'm sure I'll squeeze into whatever you've given me. How about

I go to the store myself and try it on, beg them to make last-minute alterations or switches if needs be?'

'I'd appreciate it.'

Finn wondered whether Kaisha's protective instincts over the happy couple were responsible for Dylan mentioning it again. She sure was persuasive and firm and the thought of her now made him smile, at least inwardly. He didn't want Dylan questioning him. 'On to more important issues. Are you absolutely sure you don't want a bachelor party?'

'I'm having one like we agreed, beers at the little log cabin.'

'Dull.'

'It's what I want, I don't need to get wasted.'

'Sure you do.'

'I don't, and I don't want to stress Cleo out. Managing our jobs and our brood sober is hard enough.'

Finn wondered whether Dylan ever got to have any fun. He didn't know Cleo much at all, but it sounded as though Dylan, Kaisha, everyone, treated her with kid gloves and trod ridiculously lightly. 'Fine, on one condition. Ditch the no-alcohol beer tonight so we can make a night of it. Might not get another chance.'

'I'm driving.'

'Leave the car here, I'm sure we can clear it with reception.'

'Cleo's expecting me.'

'Text her, she won't mind. Come on, we haven't been out in forever. This is me being your friend, your best man, giving you some fun before you really settle down. Although much more settled and you'll be in carpet slippers smoking a pipe.'

Dylan relented and after a quick word with the receptionist about the car, they ordered in a jug of house beer.

It felt good to have his friend back. The friend from days pre-women, pre-Prue – who had changed Dylan's life and stomped all over him, from everything Finn had heard on and off over the years.

Social media made the world way smaller and even though he hadn't been home very frequently, or spoken to Dylan, he hadn't missed out on much.

They sank a few beers each, borrowed a deck of cards, and played their way through several games of poker for what money they had left in their wallets – not much given the cashless society nowadays, although it was probably a good job. They ordered nachos smothered in chilli and melted cheese to soak up the liquor. And when Dylan's cell phone pinged again and he was otherwise occupied in the restroom, Finn replied to Cleo's message himself saying Dylan was having a lot of fun tonight and he was too old for a curfew, and he might just change his mind about getting married if she kept going on at him.

Another round of beers came and this evening couldn't have gone better until Cleo sent another message and this time Dylan picked it up. Judging by his face, he'd seen exactly what Finn had messaged the last time.

'I was messing around.' Finn pulled a face. 'Didn't mean any harm. She'll see the funny side, won't she?'

Dylan was still frowning. 'You don't know Cleo. You've met her, what, three times now?'

'She seems very nice. A little tense maybe.' Dylan's silence hinted he should probably stop shooting his mouth off now if he had a hope of salvaging this.

'She is nice, and she's nothing like Prue.'

'That's a good thing, right?'

'What I mean is that Prue was headstrong, didn't let things bother her, stomped all over other people's feelings if we really want to put an accurate description on it. But Cleo doesn't. She thinks – well, she overthinks a lot of the time. She worries, and I don't mean in a nagging wife kind of way, I mean deep down she worries even when she doesn't know she's doing it.'

'It was a joke,' said Finn. 'I didn't mean anything serious. I apologise.'

'You have to look at it from Cleo's point of view. She barely knows you.'

'Does she think I'm going to lead you astray, take you to a strip club, get you in trouble?'

'More than likely, yes.' Dylan took out his cell to call a cab.

Cab ordered and coats on, Finn suggested, 'How about I go into the store tomorrow and apologise?'

'I'm not sure, might be best to leave it before you do any more damage.'

He was about to tell Dylan to lighten up but his buddy had been there for him since before puberty hit, he knew more about him than anyone else, and Cleo's feelings mattered so much to Dylan that he had to stop being such an ass. 'I'll go to see her and I promise I'll make it better not worse. And I'll get to the menswear store tomorrow, sort my wedding outfit.'

'I appreciate it. And don't cancel any more appointments on me or be late to anything – she's crazy stressed that something will go wrong with the wedding. It's taken me long enough to persuade her that marriage isn't just a bit of paper, it's more than that.'

'Wait, you had to persuade her to marry you?' The beer was talking as he man slapped Dylan on the back. 'But you're such a catch.'

'Can't deny it,' Dylan grinned as he buttoned up his own coat against the icy wind that met them outside the foyer of the Corbridge Hotel. 'But, try to remember that I'm the one lucky to have her rather than the other way around.'

'Sounds like a match made in heaven. Now let's get you home to Cleo before she changes her mind.'

9

KAISHA

'Periwinkle blue is a beautiful colour on you,' Kaisha told a customer the next morning before the girl left the Little Knitting Box happy with her purchase.

'I hope you're not telling lies; she might get home and hate it,' said Finn as he came into the store having passed the customer on her way out.

Kaisha rolled her eyes and waited for him to shut the door as she waved goodbye to the girl, now on the other side of the window about to cross the street. 'Of course I'm not, it really suited her when she tried it on. What are you doing here anyway? Not working today?' She picked up the hanks of grey marl yarn from beside the cash register where she'd dumped them to help the customer and pushed them into the appropriate section of the hutch shelves on display.

'Late start for me. I was out with Dylan last night and there was beer involved.'

'I heard.'

He ran a hand across the stubble of his chin. 'Ah, Cleo told you. Was she angry?'

'No.' She tugged her chunky cardigan onto her shoulders properly again. The loose fit was comfortable but didn't take too kindly to too much moving around and saw fit to slide off whenever it could. 'Why do you think she'd be angry?'

'I sent a bit of a stupid text.'

'Stupid in what way?' She ran a duster past the cash register and repositioned the lavender sachets and cedar packets to keep mould and insects at bay.

The bell tinkling above the door interrupted them and the winter winds howled through as Cleo came in, her daughter Emily in her arms. 'It's wild out there today,' Cleo managed to smile, shifting Emily up her hip a little more. 'I think it's going to snow soon, but I'm keeping everything crossed it waits until Christmas Day or at the very least late Christmas Eve after the wedding.'

'I think the weather gods probably have their own ideas.' Kaisha smiled at Emily. 'Have you come to help us in the store today?' She tickled Emily's cheek as she asked the question. At two and a half, Emily was cute as anything but still swung between enjoying the attention of others and wanting only her mum.

Emily giggled and turned her face into Cleo's neck, using one hand to twirl the dark-blonde strands of her mum's hair that stuck out from beneath the woollen beanie.

'Dylan isn't feeling so great this morning.' Cleo's gaze drifted to Finn. 'I take it that was a warm-up to the bachelor party.'

'Not at all.' Finn held his hands up although Kaisha didn't miss the wince that accompanied the movement. 'The bachelor party will be far more sedate. Last night was my fault entirely; I haven't seen Dylan in so long I got carried away and persuaded him to give up the car keys and have a few beers.'

When Emily struggled, Cleo set her down and Kaisha took her hand so they could roam around the store. She seemed to love the kaleidoscope of colours dotted around, the warm feeling of the place her mum had owned and run since before she was even born.

'I'm sorry about the text,' Kaisha heard Finn say to Cleo. 'It was juvenile. And I apologise.'

'Apology accepted.' But Cleo didn't look too happy with him. Kaisha wondered whether she'd wanted to give Finn a piece of her mind and was either placated because he'd taken her by surprise being here now or had chosen not to add to any stress of the wedding preparations or the season.

'We've got it under control,' Kaisha assured her boss, who looked over to see what Emily was up to. Kaisha had found Emily a ball of yarn, which she was in the process of squishing her face into. Maybe they'd keep that ball out back and save it for the next time she came into the store.

'I didn't expect to see you in here,' said Cleo to Finn. 'Has Mitch given you the day off?'

'You think I'm taking advantage, don't you?'

'I never said that.'

'Didn't have to,' Finn shrugged.

Kaisha wondered whether she'd have to step in soon before someone said something they'd regret.

'I would never take advantage of Mitch, or anyone else for that matter,' said Finn. 'But Mitch heard my croaky voice in the early hours and probably figured he'd be wasting money paying me this morning. I'll go in later.'

'He's an understanding boss.'

'Once again, so sorry about the message.'

Kaisha had to give him credit. He was doing his best to appeal to Cleo's more understanding side, although it didn't seem to be working.

'You've already apologised.' Cleo checked the haberdashery display. Whenever she was here, even if she wasn't working, she found it hard to switch off and now she noted down on the pad of paper by the cash register a couple of items to restock.

'My grandma used to have one just like that.' Finn pointed up at the Singer sewing machine on the shelf at the back of the store behind the cash register.

'She did?' That had Cleo's attention.

'She spent hours using it.' Finn leaned against the counter, him one side, Cleo on the other. 'I swear she got excited if one of us ever had a hem come down, or got a hole in our jeans, or bought something that needed altering. She'd whisk the item away and get straight to it, no matter whether she was in the middle of preparing dinner or baking a pie.'

'Sounds exactly like my Grandma Eliza,' Cleo smiled. 'She always wore one of those housecoats so she was ready for anything – dressmaking, cooking, tidying. She was a woman who liked to be busy.'

'They don't make machines like that these days,' said Finn. 'My grandma's machine went a long time ago to someone in Grandad's apartment building, but I miss the sound, you know, the chug chug as the needle moved along the clothes, the sound as she hummed away when she worked.'

'My grandma used to do that too. Drove Grandpa Joe crazy.'

'Do you use the machine yourself?'

'No, it's here for decoration, a relic I'll never let out of my sight.' She briefly explained about the store she'd once had in the West Village, the store run by Grandma Eliza before she died. 'It didn't feel right not to have it here when I opened up the store in Inglenook Falls; it means a lot to me.'

'It's been looked after well.'

'I give it a dust most days, even a bit of polish sometimes. Sentimental I know, but...'

'Not at all. I get it, it helps you remember that person, feel close to them even when they're gone.'

'Exactly.' A moment passed between them. 'Finn… I'm sorry if I wasn't more welcoming when you came to town.'

'I didn't exactly give a good impression.'

'I hope you don't mind but Dylan told me a bit about your family.' She quickly added, 'I won't be spreading gossip, it's not my story to tell. But Dylan is always there for you, remember.'

'Even if I get him horribly drunk?'

'Don't push it,' she scolded, but there was a cautious smile lingering.

Kaisha watched the pair of them until Cleo took a phone call. It seemed Finn and Dylan's friendship ran deep and she was glad he and Cleo seemed to be at least talking rather than in battle against each other. She whispered in Emily's ear, 'I think this might be what you call a truce. Your mom is the best. And she's going to have a wonderful wedding.'

Kaisha was surprised when instead of scarpering upstairs out of the way, Finn came over to Emily, who was sitting with perfect posture, now unravelling the ball of yarn as though hoping to find the end.

'She's cute.' He took the ball of yarn and held on as Emily continued to pull at it.

'She is.' Kaisha touched a hand to the little girl's angelic curls and Emily gave her a toothy grin in return.

Cleo came out to join them when she'd finished her call and took some knitting patterns out of her bag.

'These are great,' said Kaisha. As well as pre-made garments, yarn, and haberdashery, the store had a library of patterns shelved for customers to select their own or for Kaisha and Cleo to make personal recommendations and match particular yarns to a customer's design requirements. 'I'll put them with the others.'

'There's a good range. One for a shawl, another for basic winter hats, one for a baby blanket, and another for a dog sweater.'

Finn was grinning. 'I hate to ask, but dog sweater?'

'It's been requested,' Cleo told him, sharing the amusement now she no longer seemed quite so wary of him. 'Come on, you,' she said to Emily, 'we need to get going, collect Amelia and Nathan from the airport.'

'It'll be lovely to see them again.' Kaisha attempted to wrestle the yarn from a none-too-compliant toddler. Amelia and Nathan were both from England but had met in New York this time last year and been together ever since. 'Why don't you go to the airport yourself, leave Emily here?' she suggested. 'The store's not been so busy with the markets on, Emily will be fine here with me.'

'I couldn't do that to you, I'll be a couple of hours at least.'

'I don't mind, honestly.'

'She'll freak out. For some reason she's taken to screaming the house down if I dare to leave home without her. Tabitha was never that way, it's taking some getting used to.'

'She won't freak out, she loves me, she's my number one fan. Apart from Ruby, that is.'

'It wouldn't be fair,' Cleo insisted. 'Come on, Emily, we'll be late at this rate.'

'Which means you'll rush and it won't be safe,' said Kaisha. 'And all that strapping and unstrapping of car seats will take forever. Go... leave her here, she'll be fine.'

'Are you totally sure?'

'Go, before I rescind the offer.'

'I'll be here for another hour,' said Finn, 'although I'm not sure whether that puts your mind at rest or not.' He pulled a face.

Cleo hesitated. 'I guess it would be easier.'

Kaisha ushered her out and, sure enough, the second Emily registered the tinkle above the door to the Little Knitting Box and saw her mum retreating across the street to her car, she was up on her feet toddling through the store and both hands smacked on the glass before she let out an almighty scream and the tears came.

Finn pulled a face. 'To be fair, she did warn you.'

Kaisha tried to console the little girl but the wailing continued. She waved another hank of yarn in front of her, this time a bright red. 'It's the same colour as Santa's coat,' she told Emily in a high-pitched voice.

'She's too young to know who Santa is.'

'Rubbish, kids know very early on.' But he was probably right and whether he was or not, the yarn wasn't working to distract Emily this time. At least she'd allowed Kaisha to pick her up and give her a cuddle.

'I find food often works,' Finn suggested. 'Does she have a favourite?'

'Easy, toast with raspberry jelly.' The sobs continued. 'What are you waiting for, go! The bread is in the cupboard, jelly in the refrigerator.'

Finn seemed to take forever. Time sure passed slowly when you had a crying child in your arms. By the time he came back Kaisha had settled on the floor out back with Emily on her lap still whimpering softly, every now and then letting out a howl. But as soon as she saw the glistening red topping on the toast she reached out for the first piece and Kaisha breathed a sigh of relief. 'Peace and quiet. Pass me a tissue?' She nodded over to where the box was sitting on the shelf and when Finn passed it to her, took out a tissue to wipe Emily's nose. Sitting on Kaisha's lap, she was happy enough now and seemed to have forgotten why she was even upset in the first place.

Kaisha leaned enough so that she could see out of the curtain to the store front.

'Customers?' Finn poked his head out. 'I don't think I'll be able to help them much, I'm afraid.'

Kaisha tried to set Emily down on the floor so she could get up but the kid screamed in protest.

'Give her to me,' said Finn.

'Seriously?'

'Just do it.'

'She'll cry again, I know she will.'

'If she cries, she cries,' he told her, holding out his arms. 'Big deal.'

Reluctantly, she handed Emily over and went straight out to a customer who wanted advice on crochet. And when a whimper turned into nothing more Kaisha lost herself in a sudden stream of customers, moving from crochet to chatting about the best colour for a cardigan for a newborn baby of which they had no idea of the sex – Kaisha advised you couldn't go wrong with lemon yellow or a snowy white – she found wooden toggles for someone who'd lost a button on an adult cardigan and had decided to replace all of them with something more trendy. And when she finally took the last payment on the cash register, she realised it was oddly quiet out back and she had a momentary panic she'd left Cleo's child with someone wildly unsuitable. But when she went into the back room all smiles, she stopped and leaned against the wall where the curtain hung to hide the part of the store in which they made coffees, took breaks, and kept surplus stock, watching Finn. He was sitting on the floor, his back leaning against cardboard boxes filled with yarn, and Emily was curled up against his chest fast asleep. His eyes were shut, too, and a gentle rise and fall of the material of his T-shirt showed he might not be far from sleep himself.

He looked attractive this way, with no sign of the annoying tendencies he had like invading her space, calling her a nagging wife, or causing trouble for Cleo and Dylan. This Finn was a softer

version of what they all saw and Kaisha watched him and Emily –
the delicate flutter of the little girl's eyelids and her mouth slightly
open, the way Finn's arms stayed strong around her even though he
was so relaxed. As though he'd never let his guard down when he
had someone to protect.

The bell to the shop door tinkled again but Emily didn't rouse.
And before Kaisha could head out front, Finn murmured, 'Don't
you know it's rude to watch people sleep? You might freak them
out.' He opened one eye to peer at her then shut it again. 'Go see to
your customers, we're doing fine here.'

It was only Enid from the café, who had come in for a new zip to
replace the one on her purse that had been broken for weeks. And
when Kaisha went back to Finn and Emily, his eyes were open
again.

'She's heavier than she looks,' he said.

'Here, let me get something to support her.' He was taking all
Emily's weight on his left arm with nothing beneath it and Kaisha
took a clear plastic bag filled with hanks of yarn from a box on a
shelf up high and wedged it into the space. 'Better?'

'Much.' His eyes locked on hers and there was a moment of
awkward silence before the tinkling of the bell and Cleo's calls from
the store announced her return.

Kaisha leapt up and out in the store, put a finger to her lips.
'Emily's fallen asleep,' she said softly to Cleo. 'She's out back with
Finn.'

When Cleo went to check on her daughter Kaisha gave Amelia
a hug. 'Great to see you. Where's your other half?'

'We dropped Nathan at the guesthouse to unpack and have a
snooze. I couldn't wait to come and say hello.'

'Well, I'm glad you did. How was the flight?'

'It went by very slowly. I was far too excited about coming back
to New York.' Amelia's green eyes sparkled, her dark-brown locks

hung loose across her shoulders, and she didn't look the slightest bit worse for wear after flying all the way from England. The glow she had about her also heavily suggested she was happy with Nathan and Kaisha guessed they were just as besotted with one another as they had been last Christmas when they got together.

'How are the markets this year?' Amelia wanted to know. They'd worked together at the Garland Street markets in Manhattan last year.

'Very busy, as always.'

'Is Cleo working as hard as I suspect she is?'

Kaisha smiled. 'You know her very well. She's crazy busy, but thriving on it of course. And the wedding organisation seems to be going smoothly. You guys making it here without any hassles is another worry to cross off her list.'

'I'm glad. And the wedding is going to be magical, everything is planned, nothing will go wrong.' She crossed her middle and index fingers on both hands.

'You sound just like Darcy, which is good. The more people reminding Cleo of that, the better.'

'I don't think Dylan will let anything stop him marrying her. He's been trying to get her down that aisle for a long time.'

'He sure has.'

'Tell me, how has Ruby been?' Amelia spoke softly so their voices from the front of the store didn't carry to Cleo out back.

Ruby, Dylan's daughter from his previous marriage to Prue, had been giving Cleo a hard time last year, pushing the boundaries, wondering where she fitted in to this relationship of her dad's that was soon to become permanent. Even though they were all living together and had been for some time, Ruby had begun to feel insecure and the situation had been stressful for Cleo. 'She's been super helpful, really on board,' Kaisha assured Amelia.

'That's a relief.'

'Anyway, I want to know about you,' Kaisha smiled. 'Things with Nathan going well?'

Coyly, Amelia told her they'd recently talked about living together. 'It's a huge step but it feels right.'

'Then I'm pleased for you.' Yet there was still a tiny pang of jealousy deep down. Kaisha remembered the excitement of moving in with Cory, the promise of a new future, the disappointment when it all fell apart.

'My nephew, Kyle, is still seeing Nathan's daughter, Scarlett, too.'

'That's good to hear as well.' Kaisha forced a smile because she was pleased things had worked out, she wasn't the sort of person to be resentful of other people's happiness. Or at least she wouldn't admit to it if she was.

When Cleo reappeared with a still-sleeping Emily in her arms, Kaisha held the door open for her and Amelia. 'We'll catch up again soon,' she assured Amelia.

'Look forward to it. And I can't wait to see your outfit for the wedding.'

'I'll be back in an hour,' Cleo whispered so as to not wake Emily.

Kaisha shut the door to the blistering cold and rubbed the tops of her arms as she turned to go tidy up the wall ladder of wool that had been fished through so many times it needed attention. The fawn was crossed over the strands of maroon, the turquoise was tangled with the angel blue, the sage green had fallen behind onto the floor, and someone had just heaped the powder pink on top of the desert rose.

She began to pull the different colours out and start over so that customers could distinguish between yarn colours and textures.

'What's this outfit like?' Finn's voice came from behind her and she realised he hadn't escaped upstairs as she'd thought.

'For the wedding? It's just a dress.'

'I assume it's pretty special given that friend of Cleo's mentioned it.'

He didn't miss much, did he? But she deliberately hadn't told anyone about her outfit in case they asked where it came from. 'She's being kind because I'm making the dress. It's been a project of mine for a while.'

'I haven't seen anything on the freaky mannequin.'

She grinned. 'It's not freaky. And I put the dress away for safe-keeping.' As soon as she knew she was going to have a roommate, she'd hung it in her wardrobe away from prying eyes. Over the last couple of years, Kaisha had made so many dresses for various friends and relatives that she'd almost lost count. She'd made a beautiful dress for her sister too but Bree had barely even thanked her for the gorgeous, mulberry skater dress before selling it on eBay and boasting about the profit.

'Do me a favour?' she said before he disappeared up to the apartment. 'Don't mention the dress to Cleo.' She'd always been discreet, not wanting Cleo to pick up on what she was doing, perhaps wonder whether she was going to leave her in the lurch.

He nodded in agreement before he went to grab his things and head to Mitch's farm.

Maybe she'd talk to Cleo eventually, tell her where her real passions lay even though she'd be forever grateful for finding the store and falling into friendship groups she never wanted to be without.

But, as usual, putting something off was far easier than tackling it head-on.

* * *

After a stint at the Inglenook Falls markets, Kaisha returned to the Little Knitting Box where Cleo was recommending a pattern for a shawl to one customer and ringing up a sale of the super-expensive vicuña wool they stocked in limited quantities to another.

'What's she making with the vicuña?' Kaisha wondered when the customer went on her way and all was quiet again. She hung her coat and scarf out back and joined Cleo in the store.

'She's making a stole.' Cleo had found out the few remaining hanks of vicuña and slotted them onto an upper shelf to replace what they'd sold.

'I bet it'll be gorgeous in the caramel colour. I still wear those vicuña socks you gave me as a gift years ago, you know. And I still love them just as much.'

'Let me know when they need replacing, I'll make you another pair.'

'Don't you dare. I'll buy my own yarn and do it myself. Talking of home projects, do we have any more packs of hemline machine needles?'

'We should have some with the haberdashery.' Cleo went over to the display. 'I was sure we did. Has someone requested them?'

'Me,' Kaisha smiled. 'My last one broke after the pageant costumes.'

'Well, you did work extra hard and the costumes were wonderful. Please say you're still coming to watch Tabitha in the pageant – we'd all love it if you did.'

'I wouldn't miss it for the world.'

'I think I might have another delivery box upstairs in the very, *very* top of your wardrobe.'

'Ah, the shelf I can't reach and therefore don't mind if you commandeer.'

'That's the one,' Cleo smiled. 'I'll take the stepladder from out back, go get the box down, and we'll replenish as much as we can so hopefully I don't need to put it back up there. When Finn's gone we'll have a lot more space.'

When Cleo disappeared to do just that, Kaisha stood at the front window with the Christmas tree, the frosted glass, the gorgeous decorations with the promise of the exciting festive season to come their way. It was dark outside now, any car that passed had its headlamps on, and Kaisha was reminded that not only would Christmas soon be here but the wedding would also be upon them. Then, they'd welcome in another New Year. But by then, Finn would be gone. And after seeing another side to him, she realised she'd got used to his company and she wasn't quite so desperate for him to leave. The loneliness she knew she'd feel with her own space once again sent a shiver down her spine.

'Here we go.' Back in the store, Cleo blew her hair away from her face and set the box down by the cash register before rifling through. She passed Kaisha a few different sorts of buttons – they had a bit of space, having not replenished at all over the last few days – and found four packets of hemline machine needles.

Kaisha popped three packets onto the hooks in the haberdashery display and kept the other. She went to get her purse but Cleo swished the suggestion of payment away.

'Kaisha, you go above and beyond for me.' She laid a hand on her arm. 'You're the best assistant I could ever have hoped for; you're a godsend.'

And there it was. The very reason she hadn't said anything about her dressmaking, the hobby that was already becoming a bit of a side business – the side business that, deep down, she longed could be more. She didn't ever want to lose this bond with Cleo. Her relationship with her sister had already been fractured beyond repair and losing another person from her life simply could not happen. Even if it meant her own dreams went on hold.

10

FINN

Finn knew he was going to need all his patience today. Honestly, he'd rather be having another beer with Dylan at the Corbridge Hotel – not that Cleo would let that happen again anytime soon – or sitting in the apartment putting his feet up after another tiring morning at the Christmas tree farm. Hell, he'd even rather be arguing with Kaisha than being right here, right now. But this was what his grandad had wanted, so here he was in New York by Central Park meeting up with his parents.

'Why he thought this was a good idea I'll never know,' Beverly huffed. She showed Finn the text as he reached them. No hello, no hug, just a frown of annoyance, which was nothing unusual.

Finn took the phone and looked at the message on the screen. 'You are kidding, right?'

Andy began to laugh. 'You've got to hand it to Dad, he's having fun with this.'

Finn managed a smile too. It was only his mum who couldn't see the funny side of hiring bikes and riding around Central Park. Grandad wanted photos, of course, to prove their bonding experience had really taken place and all three of them silently knew they'd be honouring his request.

'Right then, we'd better go hire us some bikes.' Finn handed the phone back.

'Could be worse,' said his dad. 'It could be pouring with rain.'

Half an hour later and they were geared up with cycles and maps of the area. There were over eight hundred acres of park to cover on two wheels if they liked, although Finn knew it would likely be in the first acre when he felt the strain and probably well before the second that someone lost their temper.

They hadn't been on the bikes long when Finn reminded them, 'We need to take a photograph.' Better to do it now while they were all still being relatively civil.

'Give me strength,' said his mum.

'Just get in the picture, Beverly.' Andy's impatience was beginning to show.

Finn, the tallest, took the selfie of all three of them astride their bicycles, together in a row, smiles – or was it grimaces? – on their faces, with the wintry park setting all around them. 'Remind me to take another in a while. Grandad will see we're trying.'

'Is that what we're doing?' When his mum asked the question Finn thought he might see the stress of the situation in her eyes, the worry lines carved by all the years that had passed when they hadn't been much of a family, but before long she complained, 'If I'd known we were doing this before I left my apartment, I might have worn more appropriate shoes. These cost a fortune.'

His dad seemed to find that amusing and gleefully started pedalling away. 'I'll lead and we'll head to—'

'Just join the West Drive, Andy, and we'll see where it takes us.' Finn's mum wasn't going to be bossed about but his dad had already taken the lead and it was up to her and Finn to keep up.

It was freezing today too. Even with his hands encased in a

decent pair of gloves, Finn had banked on shoving his hands in his pockets most of the time today. He'd never thought his grandad would be making them do this kind of pursuit together. It was putting danger with danger and coming up with catastrophe.

Finn was so tired he wondered whether he'd fall asleep at the handlebars after his busy morning. His thoughts drifted to little Emily and how she'd snuggled against him out back at the Little Knitting Box. He'd had to shut his eyes when Kaisha found them that way so she wouldn't see how he'd welled up. Because Emily had reminded him of the way his little sister used to rest her head against his shoulder as she watched television. She'd often fall asleep that way and he'd never once minded. Maybe he would have, had his buddies been around, but when it was just him and his sister there was a sense of calm Finn hadn't found since Mackenzie left their lives forever.

The chain on his mum's bike came off soon after they set off again. They'd wheeled the bike back to get it sorted. His dad had swerved into a little kid given that the last time he got on a bike was at least three decades ago but, lucky for them, the parent with him had accepted their apology and let it go at that.

Their cycle ride became a bit less fraught as they got into the rhythm. They all lapsed into a quiet melancholy as they pedalled surprisingly serenely along West Drive, taking in the scenery that in the winter didn't fail to disappoint. As much as Finn had treasured time away, coming back here always made him realise how much it was his home. And perhaps one day he'd be able to stop running from it, from the mess that brought so much pain.

They stopped at Strawberry Fields and there was a moment when Beverly and Andy almost agreed on something as they talked about their younger days, the Beatlemania that rocked the world.

'Your walls were covered in posters,' said Andy to his ex-wife. 'I don't think I ever knew what colour they were underneath all that paper.'

'The walls were white, why do you think I got so bored with them?' They were both looking at the *Imagine* mosaic on the ground in the centre of Strawberry Fields. The area surrounding them was lined with elm trees whose leaves had shed in the fall. Plants, rocks, and shrubs filled the space, a designated quiet area that kept their voices at a low whisper. 'And what I had in posters, you made up for in vinyl.'

'I sure did.' His dad looked at him. 'I seem to remember you finding my Beatles collection and my old record player round about your fourteenth birthday.'

'I don't remember.' Finn cleared his throat and read some of the information on a plaque nearby. Because he did remember. He remembered it well. He'd been making his own birthday cake that year. It wasn't an easy thing to do given the memories it conjured up but he'd stayed strong, decided he needed to do it. His mum had given him her apron to put on because they didn't have any others, and his dad's face when he came through the door wasn't one a son needed to see on his birthday. It spoke of frustration, sadness, disappointment, and he'd poured a large whiskey before heading to his study. Finn had only got more of his attention after schlepping into the basement to hide. He'd found the record player, the records, and put on the Beatles albums in quick succession. He'd thought he was in big trouble when his dad came down, glass of whiskey in hand, but instead of yelling at him, sending him to his room, Andy had taken out another vinyl record, put it on and they'd jumped about dancing to 'Birthday' by The Beatles. And when his mum came down to see what the noise was all about, she'd joined in.

'Finn, we're going.' His dad beckoned now and tugged him from his reverie, away from a happier memory with smiles they all needed to feel.

They got back on their bikes and made their way to the Shakespeare Garden and Belvedere Castle, locking up their bikes to do more exploring on foot. And from there it was on to The Loeb Boathouse, a stunning oasis surrounded by nature and well away from the city streets. They'd taken plenty of pictures and now it was time for some sustenance before they returned the bikes, sent the rest of the evidence of their day of bonding to Grandad, and Finn could finally escape back to Inglenook Falls.

The venue was at least casual as well as being chic and classy, and they ordered cake and coffees from the table they'd been given by the window with a view that momentarily distracted from the tension of the situation.

'I haven't been here in a long while.' Andy stirred sugar into his coffee and glanced briefly at Beverly.

She turned to Finn. 'We had our wedding here.'

'Really? Why did I never know that?'

'You probably did,' she sighed, 'but we wouldn't have talked about our wedding for a very long time.'

'I guess not. You were too busy talking about the divorce for as long as I can remember.'

'Lots of marriages end, Finn.' His dad set the spoon down but didn't touch his coffee. 'We know it had a huge impact on you.'

'You could've managed it better, the both of you.' It was like talking to a couple of kids. 'But let's not spoil today.'

'It's not been too bad,' his mum ventured. The weather had cooperated and the rain held off, the snow that appeared on and off on the weather report hadn't come and the brutal winds that had battered the window panes in the apartment in the middle of the night had given up trying so hard, letting the trees sway gently today.

'We could go as far as to say it's been pleasant,' his dad said and Finn managed a nod in agreement or at least acceptance.

'We probably do need to talk, Finn.' His mum said the words but there was enough hesitation there to know she wasn't even sure she meant it.

'I'd rather not,' he said.

His dad set down his coffee cup. 'You always were stubborn.'

'Wonder where I get that from. Once you have an idea about something, Dad, then that's it. You're not interested in anyone else's opinions, it's your way or the highway.'

'He's right about that,' Beverly chipped in.

Well, the truce hadn't lasted long. Finn sensed trouble brewing, finished his coffee cake and hoped to goodness they were going soon. But his dad seemed intent to prove his point yet again.

'I think you're being a bit unfair to both of us.' He was looking at Finn.

'In what way?'

'We tried with you when you were growing up, we tried to get you to do more things with us as a family, but as you got to your teen years you weren't interested. You were more enamoured with the family next door than you were with your own.'

Not this again. 'Dylan was like the brother I never had, his parents were like...'

'The parents you never had?' His mum's voice, laced with hurt, asked the question.

'To be honest with you, they were.'

'Son, you always think other people's parents are better than your own. I'll bet Dylan had his issues with his mom and dad – he probably didn't tell you, that's all.'

'How are the wedding plans going?' his mum asked.

'You always do that,' Andy accused. 'You change the subject. It's why we never solve anything.'

'Oh, so it's *my* fault. Never mind that I'm sitting here, I'm trying, all for your dad and his hare-brained idea that we can all be fixed with some kind of invisible glue. I've got oil on my new trousers, my feet are like ice blocks in inappropriate shoes, and now you're hurling accusations my way.'

'Maybe if you didn't have such a temper you'd see things rationally,' Andy bit back. 'You'd see I'm not saying it's your fault, it's all of our fault – not one of us communicates properly and when we do, this happens!' His voice went up at the end.

'This is why I couldn't stay married to you! You're impossible!' Beverly slammed down her cup but Finn had beaten her to it, put down his own, weaved through the first few tables and as his dad called after him, he didn't look back.

He fired off the photographs to his grandad to prove they'd tried yet again. Maybe he'd tag on one of his parents fighting to show they'd also failed again, but he couldn't bear to be here a second longer. He peddled his bike back to the hire rank and made his way to Penn station, not easing off his pace until he'd run to the platform and leapt onto the next train waiting to depart.

* * *

With a full day at the Christmas tree farm tomorrow, it was good to know at least he could chill out tonight at the apartment. But Finn found himself heading towards the Inglenook Falls markets instead, perusing the stalls like the other families, tourists, locals, all having a good time and welcoming in the holidays. He picked up a mulled cider at one, had chocolate tasters at the next, ignoring any pings on his cell phone until he finally accepted he'd have to turn it off to get some headspace.

The stars out here looked different to any he managed to see in New York City. The buildings in Manhattan hid so much of the sky but out here it was for everyone to admire. A blanket spread out across the little town.

'It's Finn, isn't it?' An attractive, smiling girl with chestnut hair recognised him and smiled as she came away from the cheese stall. 'Darcy,' she reminded him.

He patted a hand to his forehead. 'Of course it is, sorry, I had a momentary blank then.' He wondered if he should mention the state he'd turned up in at the Inglenook Inn for Thanksgiving but if Darcy was thinking about it she didn't let on and he was happy to overlook the memory. With it being a weekend, Finn wasn't surprised when Darcy's partner Myles joined her and introduced himself again. Dylan was next along with all four of his kids and meeting Ruby and Jacob was surreal. The last time Finn had seen them, Ruby was sporting cute pigtails and wore a sparkly fairy dress and Jacob had that uncoordinated way of a kid who was still trying to grow into his own body. But now Jacob had more confidence and Ruby was turning into a proper little lady.

'You have a beautiful family,' he told Dylan, who had hold of Tabitha's hand while Emily snuggled up against him in his other arm.

'Thank you.' Dylan was clearly taken aback by such a candid remark, rare to hear from Finn.

'Not that I'm going soft or anything,' Finn added with a grin as Dylan persuaded Emily to walk too and hold his other hand. She wasn't exactly light, Finn could vouch for that after she'd fallen asleep on him. And that day had evoked memories of Mackenzie. It had reminded Finn of how precious those we love are, and for once he hadn't batted the emotion away.

Dylan cocked his head towards the knitting stall. 'Come on, I'm grabbing Cleo and we're getting hot dogs. You're welcome to join us.'

'I'll hang around but I'll pass on the food, I've had enough to eat with my parents today.'

'How did that go?'

They weaved through the crowds to find the knitting stall, Kaisha laughing animatedly with a customer, red Santa Claus earrings swinging from her lobes. You couldn't deny the girl was fun – no wonder Ruby went straight to her. Even he had to admire the colourful clothes she wore, the bright-turquoise, glittery Doc Martens that caught a shaft of light unexpectedly.

'We went bike riding in Central Park.' Finn began to laugh out loud at the look on Dylan's face. 'I'm for real, it was Grandad's idea.'

'I'm surprised all three of you didn't end up in the emergency room.'

'Believe me, there were times I wanted to push each of them off, and the outing finished when I left them arguing in the restaurant.'

'That doesn't sound too good.'

'Grandad is convinced we need to persevere and I suppose in a way it's amusing that he seems to be having fun with it. I'm going along with the plan to please him, nobody else.'

Cleo came to join them and the family of six went on their way and Finn caught Kaisha's eye as she served her customer. She was smiling in conversation but when she saw him looking over she seemed to become flustered, as though his attention wasn't an annoyance as it might once have been. Perhaps she was beginning to like him. Although like him or not, she was off limits.

With a sigh he left the markets and headed home to get some sleep. His grandad had given him and his parents only two days to rest up before their next rendezvous. And who knew what he had planned next?

11

KAISHA

Kaisha opened the door to the Little Knitting Box expecting a delivery. Usually that was the only reason anyone rang the bell outside the store, which sounded up in the apartment. Personal visitors tended to let her know they'd arrived by calling her, but not this time.

'What are you doing here, Bree?' She hadn't expected to come face to face with her sister and her reception was as frosty as the path in front of the store, as cold as the fields beyond.

'I've come to talk.'

Kaisha turned her back to march through the store towards the stairs back to her apartment. 'Then you'd better come in.' She'd give her five minutes and that was only because she didn't want to stand around getting cold and she knew Cleo would be here any moment to open up.

By the time Kaisha opened the door to the apartment, Bree had caught her up and lingered on the top stair, unsure whether she was invited to go over the threshold. And when Finn emerged from the bathroom with only a towel around his bottom half and her sister's eyebrows shot up, Kaisha pulled the door behind her to block the view.

'Aren't you going to let me in?'

'We can talk here.' Kaisha had thought because Finn was working later today he would sleep through the whole visit but now she knew he was up and about, she didn't want to do this in front of him. 'We're not even speaking, Bree, and you just show up here. Typical.'

'What do you mean, typical?' Bree crossed her arms in front of a completely inappropriate-for-winter white shirt with black leather jacket over the top. Even her scarf wasn't enough for a New York December, a sheer, wine-coloured, loosely knotted piece of material that would do nothing to protect her from the cold.

'What I mean is that as per usual you expect you can say jump and everyone else will ask how high.'

'Like I said, I came to talk. I'm not asking you to do anything more.'

'You mean you want to talk and I should listen.'

'If I'm honest? Yes!'

When Bree raised her voice it was as though a shutter had come down in front of Kaisha. She stepped back and moved to shut the door but couldn't. She looked down, the hairs on the back of her neck prickling with anger. 'Is your foot seriously blocking me?'

'I know we've had our differences, but have you ever wondered whether you should hear me out?'

'After what you did?'

Bree flicked her dark ponytail back behind her when it crept over her shoulder as she bent down to brush her boot. The dust from the door or the door jamb had left its mark – just like Bree did everywhere she went. 'You know, you're pretty two-faced.'

'Me? You've got a nerve!'

'You come across as can't-do-anything-wrong, strait-laced

Kaisha, yet you're lying to our parents. You never told them what I did.'

This time a shiver ran right through Kaisha's body. 'Lying by omission isn't quite such a bad thing. And why do they need to know everything? It would only upset them.'

'Please, this has gone on for so long. I want to make amends. You can't tell me you're happy with the way things are.'

Tears sprang to Kaisha's eyes. 'You show up after all this time and expect me to let you in and make nice?' She kept her voice down because now she could hear Finn clattering about in the kitchen, probably making breakfast.

'Who's the man?' Bree tried to see past her shoulder.

'Go away, Bree.' And with that she timed it right and without giving Bree a chance to use her foot as a block, she slammed the door in her sister's face.

'Who was that?' Finn was hovering in the kitchen doorway with a bowl of oatmeal cradled in his palm.

'My sister, Bree.'

'You didn't want to invite her in?'

'It's nothing to do with you.'

'Take it easy, it was just a suggestion.'

'Yeah, well I don't need any suggestions, thank you.' She went through to the living room under the pretence of putting on the Christmas tree lights as she always did but what she was really doing was checking her sister had actually left. She hoped to catch a glimpse of her walking away and, fingers crossed, she wouldn't come back. What she didn't expect was to see her sister climbing into an expensive-looking, shiny car and driving off. Kaisha supposed she should be grateful her sister was the driver and she hadn't brought anyone else with her, especially the man who'd come between them.

Finn took the hint as she clattered around the kitchen herself and took his oatmeal to his room. Twenty minutes later and he was out the door without a goodbye. He usually called out to say he was off, whether out of politeness or friendliness she had no idea, and she found she missed it today. Her hackles rose all the more at the thought of Bree's inquisitive look at who was in the apartment with her, the fact she'd ruined her morning before it had even really started.

After a shower it was time to put a smile on her face and focus on work. She joined Cleo, who had opened the store and had likely seen Bree leaving given the timing. As Kaisha ran a duster over the old Singer sewing machine that sat proudly on the shelf at the back of the store, Cleo asked, 'Do you want to talk about it?'

'Not really, but thank you.' She stood on a stool and dusted the hutch along the very top. Cleo always kept a clean store, she was fastidious about it, and once that was done, Kaisha polished the glass in the front window, dodging the prickles of the pine needles from the tree, one eye on the surface and the smears she'd created, the other on the street to make sure that midnight-blue car didn't come back.

One of the teachers from the elementary school came in a few moments later, stressed out and prattling on about how one of the children had taken their costume home with them last night and it was ruined. 'I told them all to leave them at school,' she flapped. 'I should've checked. Their puppies used it like a chew toy. I'm so sorry.'

Kaisha put a hand on her arm. 'It'll take me no time at all to run another one up. I still have material, but it won't be the same colours.'

'Anything, please, and I'll pay double, whatever it takes.'

With the pageant happening tonight, Cleo was already on the phone calling another helper to take over the Inglenook Falls market stall for lunch to give the existing stallholder a break so she could man the shop and Kaisha could do the costume. That was what Kaisha admired about Cleo: her ability to just read a situation, know what was the right thing to do. If only Bree had done that they may never have fallen out, they could still be close as sisters, the best of friends even. But she'd committed such a betrayal that there was no going back.

When the teacher went on her way, Kaisha dashed upstairs and set up the sewing machine. She didn't have any of the brown and taupe material left but plenty of the blue so she put together the costume, the headdress that went with it. It was straightforward at least and it calmed her to sit there with her machine at the table in the living room, the silence filled by the repetitive tick, tick, tick of the firing piston as it plunged at material with a needle over and over again, only slowing when Kaisha let it, only speeding up when she allowed.

'Hey.' A voice came from behind her.

She put a hand against her chest. 'You scared me. I didn't hear you come in.' Finn had an arm leaning above the door jamb, boots still on. Her eyes must've flicked there because he quickly took them off.

'Why aren't you in the store?' he asked.

'Why aren't you at the farm?' she smiled, relieved he wasn't bearing a grudge at the horrible snarky tone she'd used on him that morning.

'I came back for some lunch, then Mitch asked me to man the stall at the market. Suits me; I've been lugging logs all morning and my arms are aching.'

She did her best not to focus on those arms that were blessed with defined muscles. 'I'm sorry I was snappy earlier.' She removed the cloth clamp from the next section of material ready to stitch it.

'Not a problem.'

And as he went to get his lunch she carried on, calming as she worked, losing herself in a simple task yet one that made her smile, especially when she was able to call the school to tell them she'd bring the costume along with her to the pageant this evening.

'I've got the place to myself tonight?' Finn asked when she went through to the kitchen where he'd just put a piece of bread on top of filling to make his sandwich.

She thought back to how he'd been with Emily: the first time she'd seen his personality shift a little, the way he'd been with the kids near the knitting stall at the markets too. She'd noticed him fist-bump with Jacob, being careful to avoid the wrist he'd sprained by going for the other arm, he'd winked at Ruby and won her over straight away. 'You should come.'

'Where?' he said between mouthfuls as he ate over a chopping board rather than get a plate.

'The Christmas pageant up at the school.'

'Not my kind of thing.'

'Course it is. Call it best man duty.'

'Not best man duty,' he groaned, but then asked, 'How long does it go on for?'

She shook her head and laughed, but didn't answer his question. All she said before heading back down to the store to relieve Cleo was, 'We're leaving here at 5 p.m. sharp, don't keep us waiting.'

* * *

'I'm expecting some serious performing to go on here tonight,' said Finn as he and Kaisha filed along the row of chairs to join their friends after Kaisha delivered the new costume to a very relieved actor-in-the-making. Dylan and Cleo, Jacob and Ruby were all waiting at the end of the row. Emily, a little young to sit still for long, was at home with Cleo's Grandpa Joe.

Kaisha turned and smiled at Finn. 'I bet you enjoy it. You must remember these as a kid.'

'I was never a star in these things,' he told her after they said hello to Cleo and Dylan, removed their coats, and took their seats. 'I was never Joseph, a shepherd, or a wise man; usually I got a part that was obviously made up so the less-talented of us didn't feel left out.'

'You don't need to be a main part to have fun with it.'

'Too right. One year I was a snowflake, another year I was a camel. I don't know if the latter is traditional or whether they decided I'd make a good animal and added it in.' When he smiled at her, nerves danced around in her tummy. 'Don't tell me... you were Mary or an angel, or some huge part, the star of the show.'

'No...' She shook her head, mouth twitching into a smile. 'I was the back end of the donkey.'

When he laughed at the same time as the lights went down a lady in the row in front turned to shush them. Kaisha thought she was going to have a fit of the giggles after being reprimanded and had to bite down hard on her bottom lip.

Tabitha was an angel in a long, white, flowing costume with sheer sleeves, a delicate, silver belt to gather it in at the waist, a fluffy halo on top of a headband. When she'd seen her costume on the mannequin in Kaisha's apartment one afternoon she'd been so excited and begged to keep it at home but Cleo had told Kaisha under no circumstances would that happen because she'd wear it outside to play, she'd traipse down Main Street with it on and by tonight it would've been ruined. Kaisha had been paid generously by the school; a collection had gone round parents who could think of nothing worse than having to sew their kids' costumes at an already busy time of the year, and after tonight the kids were free to take their outfits home.

They watched the pageant – the stable with its straw-covered roof, black curtains at either side bulging every now and then as the kids hid behind them, shepherds with their crooks, Mary and Joseph, who had to be two of the most confident little kids Kaisha had ever come across. The woman who'd told them to be quiet had unusually bouffant hair and Finn had made a joke that maybe he should ask her to pat it down, and when Kaisha's hand brushed against Finn's as she leaned to the side to see the stage better, she got a jittery sensation that reminded her this man who she'd once thought brusque was anything but when he let his guard down.

'She did brilliantly,' Kaisha whispered to Cleo after Tabitha came on and said the words she'd learnt by heart with clarity and confidence and even a little smile in their direction.

The kids gathered on the small stage, took a bow, and with audience participation sung a few carols to end the proceedings.

'Was it bearable?' Dylan asked Finn as they gathered their things to leave.

'I enjoyed it.'

'Did I hear you humming along to the carols?' Kaisha quizzed.

'Don't know what you're talking about.' But the grin was itching to come out, she could tell.

They left Cleo and Dylan waiting for Tabitha and outside the school, the crisp air made for them as they wrapped up in their winter layers.

'Look at those stars,' said Finn, head tilted back to look at the darkness above them punctuated with glittery spots. 'You don't see them in quite the same way in Manhattan – too many buildings, too much going on up high. But here…'

'I know exactly what you mean. Inglenook Falls is a special place. I love the city, always have done, but out here is something else.' Kaisha breathed in the cold air, warmed through in her coat and the mahogany scarf that she'd wound round so it came up to her chin.

'Does your sister live in the city?'

Her body instantly tensed up at the thought of Bree. 'No, I think she's staying somewhere in Connecticut.'

'You don't know exactly where?'

'Given you don't get on with your parents terribly well, you might see that families are complicated.'

Eyebrows raised, he said nothing as they made their way from the school to Main Street.

'I'm sorry, I seem to have a habit of biting your head off. Let's just say things with Bree and me are complicated.'

'I kind of got that from her visit this morning.'

'You think I should have let her in, that I should have listened to what she had to say.'

'Like you said, families can be complicated. Mine sure is. Actually, a better description for mine would be total nightmare.'

They walked on, past the top of the track that led down to Mitch's Christmas tree farm. Main Street was quiet, everyone at home tucked up in their beds or having cosy dinners. The lights wound around the bandstand shone prettily from a distance, the café lights dimmed as they walked past, and they could see Darcy and Myles's Inglenook Lodge set back from the street.

'Can I ask what happened between you and your sister?' Finn ventured.

'Long story,' she sighed, and changed the subject. 'What do you think you'll do after the wedding?'

'I don't know. Find work on the West Coast maybe. But I wouldn't go until the weather warmed up. I might hang around in Manhattan a while longer, be here for Grandad.'

'And your parents?'

'They'll soon be back to their own lives. We're meeting up because my grandad wants us to, he wants us to make amends, but I think he's a bit too hopeful. I think once the Christmas Eve breakfast Grandad has planned at his apartment is out of the way, Mom and Dad will quickly back off.'

They reached the Little Knitting Box and Kaisha opened up the door to the store, ready to go through to the apartment. But Finn hung back.

'I might walk for a while,' he said.

'But it's so cold.' She'd been hoping they could keep talking inside, perhaps over hot chocolate, a glass of wine even. Who would've thought she'd be feeling like this given the first impressions he'd made at Thanksgiving?

'I need the air after the pageant.'

'Do you have your key?'

A wry grin told her he was thinking the same as her, that they sounded a bit like a couple, looking out for each other. 'I do. And I just want to say, thanks for talking me into going tonight.'

'I'm glad you came. Goodnight, Finn.'

'Goodnight, Kaisha,' he breathed into the night air.

She shut the door behind her but stayed in the shadows of the store watching him go, looking as he walked along the street past the markets that had closed for the evening, back towards Main Street. And when he was out of sight, she went upstairs to the apartment they shared and sat at the chair beside the window looking out at Inglenook Falls.

Life was complex, people came and went, some left their mark, some you couldn't wait to let go of, others you wanted to hold on to as long as you could.

Her sister Bree was someone she couldn't bear to confront, sort through what happened with. Maybe it was the fear of making it a whole lot worse, a trepidation that things would be said that could never be taken back.

With a last look at the tree Finn had hauled in here for the both of them, the thought of that characteristic smile that quirked his mouth at the most unexpected times warming her right through, she turned off all the lights and went to bed. Finn was a man she was learning so much more about as time went on, although she had no idea why he seemed so sad a lot of the time.

She only hoped he'd stick around long enough to find his own happiness because she had a feeling Inglenook Falls and the friends he was making could help him to do that.

12

FINN

He didn't want or need more fresh air. The cold was biting tonight and the short walk from the school to the Little Knitting Box was enough. What he did need, however, was a moment. A moment to ask what the hell he was doing. Women had come and gone from his life over time and he'd never got emotional about them, he'd moved on as soon as he was ready. But with Kaisha it felt different even though they weren't involved.

He pushed his hands in his pockets and hunched his shoulders to keep the material of his coat shielding his neck as he sat up on the bandstand, the wood cold beneath his butt, the lights shimmering their way up the stair rail as well as the posts. An enormous Christmas tree, which he knew Mitch had provided, stood proudly looking out over Inglenook Falls. Working at the farm was one of the best jobs he'd had in a long while. He liked Mitch too – not nosy like some bosses could be, but friendly enough.

Sniffing the air, Finn couldn't detect a pine scent from the huge tree now, but then he spent every single day at the farm so maybe it had become a new kind of normal. Either that or it was so cold tonight that his nostrils were frozen and all sense of smell wiped out.

When his phone pinged, it was his dad confirming the time to meet the day after tomorrow. It seemed he was making the effort and Finn had already seen a bit of a change in him. For years he'd thought all his dad cared about was money, working hard, buying material goods to fill some kind of void, but lately, just seeing him with his own dad told him there could possibly be more to it. Perhaps he was just as guilty as his parents. They never would've won a parenting of the year award, but had he made it hard for them to be any different?

He had no idea. All he knew was that he had a full day working at the Christmas tree farm tomorrow, then he'd be working early morning the day after until mid-afternoon, but if he pointed out to his grandad that all this cavorting with his parents was exhausting, he'd get no sympathy. You had to admire the old man. He was as stubborn and persistent as his own son. He'd tell Finn to toughen up and get on with it, say that it should be a pleasure to see your family, not a chore.

If only it were that simple.

Phone back in his pocket, Finn went back to the apartment and even though the light beneath Kaisha's door had gone off he hovered outside her bedroom for a moment, tempted to knock.

But he lost his nerve and Dylan's warning to leave Kaisha alone rang in his ears loud and clear, so instead he went to his own room, shut the door, and was asleep the second his head hit the pillow.

* * *

Two days later and Finn was with his parents. Again. And when he met up with them he wondered who, if anyone, would mention that today was Mackenzie's birthday.

When silence greeted him he had his answer.

This time Grandad wanted them to trawl the city and take in the stunning holiday window displays, something Finn remembered having loved doing as a kid, especially with his sister. He wasn't quite so enthralled by it all now. There were too many crowds to battle, their joviality and togetherness yet another way of making him feel lonelier than ever.

Finn and his parents did their duty. They went to Bloomingdale's, Barneys at Madison Avenue, they saw the windows at Bergdorf Goodman, the lavish displays at Saks Fifth Avenue, and the magical wonder of Macy's.

When they were little, Finn and Mackenzie had always wanted to go to Macy's first but their parents had insisted they go there last, and tonight he understood why. Because as impressive as the glitzy, expensive windows of all the other stores were, being a kid at heart was magical and as kids they'd trawled this store more times than Finn could remember. He gulped at the emotion he felt, the absence of Mackenzie, the need he felt sometimes to talk about her even if it was difficult. His gaze focused on the miniature train in the window circling the base of the Christmas tree and he thought of how he and Mackenzie had fought trying to construct the track one year at Grandad's apartment. He'd wanted to have something more interesting than a simple circle, she insisted it be the usual round track and refused to budge. When he took over and made the track the way he wanted it, she'd stood by their height marks etched on the kitchen door jamb and sulked. Those height marks stopped after the last one of Mackenzie's, aged eleven, was recorded on the morning of her birthday. Finn had never wanted to do one since, not without her. If she were here now, he'd build that damn track any way she liked. He'd do anything to have her back.

He cleared his throat and sniffed to extinguish the sentimentality before anyone else saw and instead took out his phone to send some more photographic evidence to Grandad. He and his parents had already taken selfies; he'd even done one in the cab on the journey between the stores on 58th and Macy's, his mum being unable to walk any further. Why she always felt the need to dress to impress he had no idea. It had just slowed them down tonight when she tottered behind them, but they'd kept going. Perhaps that was the lesson Grandad was trying to teach them all with his endeavours, that even when they got on each other's nerves, even if they were all unique in their own way, they had to keep on moving forward; they were family.

Except they weren't. Not a complete one, not any more. And the more Finn thought about how nobody had acknowledged Mackenzie's birthday or mentioned how much she'd once loved to do what they were doing right now, the more his temper rose and he was forced to smother it, dampen the fire in his belly.

'I'm heading to the station,' he announced.

'Not yet.' His dad was still trying to hail a cab. 'We're going to the apartment for drinks,' he told them as the third taxi in a row sailed on past with the lucky passengers who'd got there first.

'Are you serious?' Beverly clearly had no idea about the drinks part of this evening either. 'I'm tired, all I want is to go home.'

'I've been hauling trees,' said Finn. 'I'll do it another time.'

'Come on, both of you. For Grandad.'

He had them there. And as a taxi deposited a family of four at the street where they were waiting and Andy raced to get it before someone else did, Finn reluctantly followed on.

His dad in the front and Finn and his mum in the back, this quick journey across town wasn't going to be pleasant. 'He failed to mention the post-activity drinks,' Finn grumbled.

'I didn't know either,' his mum hissed back.

His dad turned in his seat to look at them both. 'It was my suggestion.'

'Andy, what were you—'

'We keep sending him photographs; maybe this one time we show up and see him, prove to him that we're trying.'

Finn muttered under his breath. 'Unbelievable.'

'What was that?'

Finn could let it go but he wasn't in the mood. Tiredness from a morning at the Christmas tree farm as well as a blister on his hand from manipulating the saw and the axe had left him in a bad mood. 'You only want to go there and play nice so you get your hands on his apartment when he dies.' He didn't really mean it but it seemed spiteful words were a weapon he'd got used to brandishing over time.

'Finn!' His mum never backed his dad, at least not any more. Finn didn't see why she'd bother now.

'Since when did you care how he was spoken to?'

'I don't think this is the time or the place,' Andy sighed from the front seat. And they spent the rest of the cab journey in deafening silence.

Finn was first up the stairs at his grandad's and Beryl let them in. She was talking away at a rate of knots as usual, putting on her coat, telling them all how she was returning tomorrow to reclaim the title after Grandad had beaten her three games in a row at Boggle.

'See you soon, Beryl.' Finn held the door open for her. 'Coffees?' he offered everyone, but when Grandad's coughing fit was too severe to ignore, Finn helped him into his chair. 'You all right there, Grandad? You've had that cough a while. Maybe we should book you another appointment to see the doctor.'

He dismissed the concern. 'No need. And coffee sounds like the right idea to me.'

'Are you sure, Dad?' Andy came over. 'You don't sound well.'

'I'm not running marathons or doing a hundred push-ups a day, but I think I'm good to sit in a chair and have my family's company.' When Andy backed off, he wanted to hear about their day. 'I've had the photographs but I want to hear what it was like to see all those window displays. Always was one of my favourite parts about Christmas.'

Beverly recounted every street they'd been to while Finn made the coffees, super strong for Grandad, the way he liked it, less of a hit for his mum, who had to be told to take her cup she was so busy pulling pine needles from the feet of her pantyhose.

'Artificial trees are much easier, John; you don't get the needles everywhere,' she said as she took her coffee.

'Let's not pretend I'm getting any younger. This may well be my last Christmas and if I want a real tree I'm going to have a real damn tree!' His voice rose the best it could but another coughing fit took over. Before Finn could get to him, Andy was at his side, rubbing his dad's back. It was then Finn noticed Grandad's hand gripping hold of Andy's as though he were the child, Andy the parent.

'I'll get some water,' Beverly announced, her own coffee abandoned on the table nearest the Christmas tree. 'I didn't mean to upset you, John.' She put a hand on his shoulder and he covered it with his own, dismissed her concern, apologised for being cantankerous. 'Take the coffee away,' she instructed Finn.

Grandad began to get worked up again. 'You'll do no such thing.'

Beverly didn't argue, she simply got the water anyway. Andy took the armchair closest to the door and, at Grandad's instruction, Finn went to cut the coffee cake from the tin in the kitchen.

'Beryl bought it this morning,' Grandad called after Finn. 'She assures me it's fresh and one of the best.' He didn't take long to spring back whenever he looked unwell, but Finn realised he'd pretended to be in top form a lot lately. He'd make that doctor's appointment himself soon if the cough didn't go.

Finn soon returned with a tray with four plates, four portions of cake, and four times as much stress as he'd had when he got here, because now, all of a sudden, they were talking again about Grandad's health and being alone in the apartment. He slammed the tray down on the coffee table. 'Not this again. Grandad doesn't want to move, when are you going to get it through your heads?'

'If you listen before you bite our heads off,' said his dad, 'I'm not suggesting he do that. But we might need a second carer if he wants to stay here. Unless Beryl can do more hours? I'm worried about my dad being on his own at any time if he's like this.'

'She's a day carer, you know that.' Finn had recently asked her to extend her hours but she already did six days a week, she was happy with the overtime, and she had a family of her own.

'I'm not incapacitated.' Grandad was getting worked up again and Finn shot both his parents a warning look to rein in anything that was likely to upset him.

'I know that, Dad. Think about it though, for me?'

'I will. But do you finally see that I'll never leave here?'

Andy smiled. 'Since when were you ever going to back down?'

'This apartment is where your mom spent her last days, it's where I'll be spending mine. I want to hold on to my memories, not run away from them.'

Andy nodded, indicating an acceptance between them both that they wouldn't speak of this again. And then he went into the kitchen, where he tipped the rest of his coffee away. From his position in the living room, Finn could see his dad's shoulders hunched as he leaned against the sink and knew he was probably reading the subtext of Grandad's comment. Because Andy had run away from painful memories. He always had done. In fact, hadn't they all been guilty of doing so? Maybe Grandad's remark was aimed at all three of them.

'What do you think to the new ornaments?' Grandad asked

after he'd finished his cake in silence and Finn and his mum had demolished theirs.

Finn, glad of the lighter mood, looked at the tree. 'There are quite a few decorations there, am I supposed to know which ones you mean?'

'You'll know when you see them.'

Finn humoured him and went over to the tree. He looked between baubles, amongst glittery decorations, pine cones, and lights that graced the branches and eventually he had his answer, because there, at various intervals, were three identical bumblebee ornaments. In traditional yellow with black stripes, they had over-sized wings, smiling faces. Finn cleared his throat before he could talk. 'Where did you get them?'

'Beryl gave them to me as a Christmas gift.'

He'd told Beryl about Mackenzie and her love of bumblebees?

Beverly's eyes misted over but she didn't mention the ornaments. She only asked, 'Did you give her a gift?'

'I didn't give her the family jewels, not that there are any of those apart from your mom's emerald ring,' he directed to Andy, who was finally coming back through to join them after hovering in the kitchen as an avoidance tactic. 'I always thought Mackenzie would have that one day.'

The sound of Mackenzie's name being said out loud reverberated around the room, sending as much of a jolt through each of them as if they'd gone outside and stood in the street in shorts and T-shirt, the icy wind coming for them in no time.

'This is your problem all along, none of you talk about Mackenzie,' said Grandad. 'You all run from your problems instead of tackling them. Mackenzie wouldn't have done. She would've knocked sense into you all. She'd have had those beehives she always talked about too, she'd have made her own honey just like she said. She took after her grandma: vivacious, fun and full of life. Not to mention determined.'

'Yeah, well she's not full of life now, is she?' Finn rammed his hands into his pockets. Enough of the happy-families pretence. It was all a farce.

'Finn...' His mum's voice followed him out of the door of the apartment but he slammed it behind him, took the stairs too fast and was out on the street in seconds. He marched away from his family, away from the reminders, away from all of it.

And he headed straight for the nearest bar.

* * *

Finn woke up with a start as the train pulled into the station at Inglenook Falls and he only just managed to leap off in time before it departed again and he found himself goodness knows where. Unless this was the end of the line? He had no idea. He'd had way too many beers to be able to work out anything that complicated – it was surprising he'd managed to get on the right train at all.

He staggered from the station in the dark, along Main Street, and past the sign welcoming newcomers to the town. The stores were all quiet at this hour, though the Italian restaurant still had people sitting in the window enjoying a meal, the low hum of Mediterranean music drifting across the street when a couple emerged, laughing as though everything in their lives was perfect, as though it couldn't all change in an instant, their happiness gone in a fleeting few moments.

When he reached the Little Knitting Box, he rooted around in his pocket for his key. He finally found it buried deep beneath his wallet and his train ticket as well as the gloves he hadn't bothered with tonight, and his clumsiness saw the key drop to the ground. He nearly lost his footing when he bent down to pick it up but righted himself and aimed for the lock.

'Hey.' A female voice behind him made him drop the key yet again.

He picked it up and saw a face that looked vaguely familiar. 'I know you,' he slurred, pointing at the girl. Pretty, with dark hair that hung poker straight, she had a leather jacket on and was standing next to a fancy car. He'd only owned two cars before, both rust buckets, never anything so clean and slick.

'I came here a few days ago.'

'Bree!' he called out. 'I knew it! Told you.' He tried to tap the side of his nose to show his impressive knowledge but his finger clipped the tip of it. 'You're Kaisha's sister. Come in, I have a key.'

'I don't think—'

'Come on, you're family.' This girl was Kaisha's sister. Just because his family was a bunch of nightmares waiting to happen didn't mean Kaisha and Bree couldn't work out whatever was going on.

She followed him inside, where he did his best not to stagger into the cash register and went through the store room. The dim light from the moon that shone through a side window gave them enough visibility to see the stairs up to the top and the entrance to the apartment.

'Hi honey, I'm home!' he called out into the darkness when he eventually made it to the top of the stairs and negotiated the key in the locked door without dropping it like he had the one for the store. He flicked on the light and it wasn't long before Kaisha emerged from her bedroom. 'Oops, were you sleeping?'

'Are you drunk?' Her smile at his jokey greeting completely disappeared when her focus shifted to who he'd brought in behind him when Bree shut the door. 'What's she doing here?'

Bree stepped forwards. 'I just want to talk to you, Kaisha.'

'You've got a habit of showing up when it suits.'

'Only way to get your attention,' said Bree.

'Well, it's almost midnight and even if I did want to talk, which I don't, now wouldn't be the time.' Kaisha crossed her arms against the cutest snowman T-shirt that stopped at her mid-thigh, bare, long, slender legs leading up beneath. Legs that he took his eyes away from the second she caught him looking. 'Please leave.' She went back into her bedroom and shut the door with a bang.

Finn gave Bree a look as if to say he'd sort this, don't worry. He knocked gently on Kaisha's door.

'Go away,' came her voice.

'She's definitely not a morning person, but she's usually fine in the evenings,' he told Bree, who was still hovering near the doorway. 'Kaisha, come on,' he said against the solid door. 'It's your sister, come out.'

'Goodnight!' she snapped from the other side and then all he heard was music coming from the docking station he'd seen beside her bed.

'Women… I don't understand them.'

'She's got good reason to turn me away.'

'Yeah?'

'I get the impression she'd be even angrier if I told you any of the details. I'll come back another time.'

'You could try using the phone.'

'She won't take my calls.'

'Well, you're my guest tonight, how about a drink before you go?'

'I think you've probably had enough.'

'See!' He held out his arms as though this was a revelation. 'You two are very alike. You sound just like your sister.'

'Thanks for trying. I'll let myself out.'

He thought about knocking on Kaisha's door again but his head was spinning. Coffee, he needed coffee. Or maybe water. Or food?

Whatever it was, it had to wait until he'd shown Bree out and locked up the store again.

Back in the apartment, he had four slices of toast in quick succession, each slathered in butter, but he still felt wasted. He'd had so much beer tonight. He'd stayed in the one venue, the bartender serving him over and over, and lost count of how many he'd had. He'd played darts with a man who didn't seem to have any patch of skin that wasn't tattooed, pool with a girl who was interested in more than just the game, but it was at that point he realised he'd have to leave to make the last train.

He filled another glass of water and glugged it down and was just mopping up what he'd spilt – somehow it had escaped from the sides of the glass and onto his shirt – when he turned to see Kaisha standing in the kitchen doorway. She didn't look happy.

'Sorry, was I being noisy?'

'I don't think that's the problem, do you?'

'The smell of toast? Did it make you hungry?' He looked at the lonely piece of bread left in the bag. 'I could make you the last slice.'

'Bree, I'm talking about Bree. Why did you let her in?'

'She wanted to see you.'

'So?'

'She's your family.'

'You can't stand yours, I thought you'd maybe get why I don't want anything to do with my sister.' She turned to storm off, back to bed he presumed.

'I have a complicated relationship with my parents, but they're still family,' he called out to her retreating back.

'You admitted you're only spending time with them to appease your grandad.' She was back.

His head was pounding far too much for this debate and definitely too much for use of words like appease. Mind you, she was right. He was only doing the family thing because Grandad had asked, but deep down he'd wondered whether it might perhaps end up making a difference. 'If Mackenzie was here, she'd tell you to sort yourself out.'

'Who's Mackenzie? A girlfriend who put up with you?'

He harrumphed. 'Doesn't matter.' He leaned against the door jamb of the kitchen. It was that or fall asleep on his feet.

Kaisha took a step back and he hadn't realised how close he'd got to her until he caught a waft of perfume that had to be lingering on her pyjamas or in her hair.

'You need to take a bit of control over your life.' What was he thinking carrying this on? Suddenly he felt exhausted.

'Says the man who's filled to the brim with beer and who doesn't get on with his family, who drifts from job to job, never finding a home anywhere.'

'Hey, I get by, don't you worry about me.' All of a sudden she didn't seem so friendly. He'd only been watching out for her, trying to make sure she didn't push people away like he did, like his dad and his mum both did. What was wrong with them all?

'I'm not worried. But Bree, well, she's my business.' With a long sigh she added, 'I suggest you go to bed and sleep it off.'

He reached out and took hold of her arm before she got a chance to walk away. 'Don't go, not yet.'

'It's late, don't you have to work in the morning?'

He blew out from between his lips as her seriousness gave way to something else. 'I do. Mitch is a good man. I like it at the farm.'

'I'm glad you do.'

'You know, Cleo is a good boss too.'

'She is.' She was smiling as though he was ranting nonsense.

'And she wouldn't mind if you told her you wanted to go it alone.'

Her body stiffened again, back on the defensive. 'That's not a conversation I want to have tonight, do you understand? Don't you dare say a word.'

He held up both hands. 'Take it easy. I'm only talking to you right now, is that so bad?'

'My dressmaking is a hobby,' she insisted, even though he knew by now that she wanted it to be more. 'I have a job, a busy one.'

'But it's not really what you want to do,' he argued, although his head protested louder as it started to thump.

'I'm going to bed now.'

He didn't reach out this time but his voice followed her. 'Life's too short, that's what Mackenzie would tell you. Don't mess it up for good with your sister.'

'What's going on with Bree and me is absolutely none of your business,' she trilled as she departed.

He called back, 'She seems to really want to talk.'

'I'm sure she does. But she can go to hell.' He heard her door slam, followed by the distinctive words, 'Just stay out of it.'

'Well, that told me,' he said to himself and schlepped towards his own room, his bed, and collapsed face down on top of the comforter, where he stayed until morning.

Neither of them had even commented that he still had his boots on inside the house, dirt trailing in his wake.

13

KAISHA

'Soup delivery,' Kaisha announced, handing Mitch the tray of three big cartons at the door to the little log cabin down in the woods of Inglenook Falls. 'One veggie barley, two white bean and chicken chilli.'

'You're a lifesaver. Holly is laid up in bed, hasn't moved for two days. I really appreciate the delivery. I'm hoping today is the only day I have to stay away from the tree farm.'

Holly had had to cancel the photoshoot at the Inglenook Lodge yesterday with Darcy because she, along with Mitch, had come down with a heavy cold. Darcy was picking up soup for the sick in the café this morning when Kaisha went in for a leisurely coffee on her morning off, and when Darcy paid for the soup and was about to make the rush delivery, Kaisha offered to do it for her.

'I won't invite you in – I'd hate for you to catch this wretched cold,' Mitch explained, 'but do me a favour?'

'Of course. Anything.'

'Take one of these cartons down to the kiosk and give it to Finn. He looked terrible this morning, tried to pretend he was fine, but he's struggling and I need someone reliable to keep the business going while I'm on my deathbed.'

Great, just what she wanted: another run-in with Finn. But she took a carton. 'Of course I will, and you go recover from your man flu,' she winked.

'Cheek.'

She grinned and waved goodbye. She supposed she'd have to face Finn sometime and she'd been rude to him last night, again, when he was doing his best to help. But if there was one thing worse than knowing you had problems in your family, it was being told by an outsider to get on and fix them.

She followed the path from the log cabin through the trees and took the path down to where an old barn had been turned into the kiosk. The public came from further down but this was the way Mitch, Finn, and any other friends accessed the Christmas tree farm.

The soup container was still warm in her hands when she reached the barn and wandered around the outside to find Finn leaning a tree against the wooden exterior alongside several others. He stepped aside to prepare the netting machine with a new piece of material when he saw Kaisha and smiled but a customer lingering nearby grabbed his attention, asking how much water the tree would need in the first twenty-four hours, how much thereafter.

Finn answered the questions as he netted the tree, passing it through the machine with practised ease. It was only after payment and waving the customer goodbye that his face changed. 'Are you still talking to me?'

She handed him the soup. 'Of course.'

'I'm suffering.'

'I can tell.' Oddly enough, despite their words last night, it was funny to see him in such a bad way.

'I'm no drunk, just so you know.'

'You don't need to justify your behaviour to me.'

'No, but I'd like to. I enjoy a few beers, I'll admit, but the amount I had last night and on several occasions since coming back aren't really me. I guess I've literally been trying to drown my sorrows.'

'And has it worked?'

'What do you think?' He took off the lid and the scent of spicy chicken filled the air. 'Right now, Kaisha, you're an angel sent from the top of the biggest Christmas tree to make all my wishes come true.'

'Now you're freaking me out. Just drink it.'

'I will. And let me tell you, I know already that it'll taste far nicer than a beer.' He sipped tentatively at first, taking on the hottest part of the mixture, then drank more enthusiastically as it became easier to consume. Kaisha pointed a family of three in the right direction for the field of six-foot, or at least approximately that height, trees.

'How did you know where to send them?'

'This place has been running for a while, I've been down a few times. Holly had all the girls down here one day to do a winter photo shoot. We were all wearing sweaters from the Little Knitting Box, it was snowing and... well, the photos were very impressive and I think Cleo got a lot of orders out of it.'

'Good for her and her business then.' He downed the rest of the soup. 'No food the morning after a big session on the beer does something to a man. I grabbed a coffee at the café but Enid wanted to chat and I really didn't, so I scarpered pretty quick.'

'She does like a good conversation, you probably made the best choice. Anyway, I'll leave you to it.' She turned to go but his voice stopped her.

'I really am sorry if I overstepped the mark last night.'

'No, I'm sorry I snapped. You were only trying to help. But

seeing Bree there, inside the apartment, so late at night. It was a confrontation I hadn't expected.'

He sat down on the floor of the barn where it was raised from the ground enough that it was comfortable. 'Keep me company for a bit?'

'It's freezing.' Although she did have on her long orange coat, her longest cream scarf, and matching gloves that had kept her from feeling the frost first thing this morning when she set off for a walk.

'It's not so bad.'

'You've had soup to warm you up.'

'Good point.'

She stayed standing as another young couple came and browsed the pre-cut trees. 'Who's Mackenzie?'

His face tensed but then fell as though his hangover had finally sapped him of all energy. 'I mentioned her last night, didn't I?'

'Girlfriend?' Wife, friend?

'Sister.'

'So you know a bit about sibling relationships then.' She scraped the toe of her boot across one of the remaining patches of frost that still hadn't been scared away by the sunshine blazing overhead. The weather was set to change yet again tomorrow with a forecast of blustery showers, a threat of snow. She'd bet the tree farm wasn't so idyllic under those conditions. 'How old is your sister?'

He broke off to net a tree for the couple, take payment, and send them on their way with a 'Happy holidays!' sentiment she was pretty sure he didn't feel right now. 'She was eleven when she died.' He sat down again and shuffled up for Kaisha to sit alongside.

There was more frost here beneath their feet but she hadn't noticed before. 'I'm sorry, Finn.'

He shrugged. 'Long time ago.'

'Doesn't matter.'

'Isn't time supposed to heal?'

'I think we both know that's not necessarily true.'

'Is that why you haven't forgiven your sister for whatever she did?'

She looked out at thick wooded land, the pine scent carrying for miles and miles. 'It's not that simple. Even if I tell her I forgive her, I talk to her and have her in my life, I can't forget what she did. Which kind of makes the fact that I say I forgive her a bit of a lie. I can't see how I'll ever not be angry.' She covered her eyes with her gloved hands. 'I'm not explaining this very well.'

'You're doing just fine. What did she actually do? Might help if I know some details, might stop me giving the wrong advice.'

'It all seems so trivial when your own sister died,' she said guiltily.

'True.' But he smiled at her and her explanation soon came tumbling out.

'Bree is my younger sister. Only by twenty-one months, so she's always been one small step behind and I think it frustrated her. If I tried out new hairstyles it wasn't long before she did the same, when I went out with my friends she grew impatient with her stricter curfews, when I got a boyfriend she wasn't far behind with one of her own.

'My last boyfriend, Cory, was my most serious boyfriend. We were together for a few years, we moved into an apartment, we talked about the future on and off, although I always got the sense I was more settled than he was. Bree was single at the time, she went out to nightclubs with a vigour I could never manage, she took off travelling around America and Canada. She always loved her freedom, liked to blow off steam, but our parents grew frustrated with her because she wasn't putting any thought into her future whatsoever. But they tried not to drive her insane with their prodding; they left her to do it her own way. She carried on seeing the world, went to Africa on safari, saw hippopotamuses, elephants, buffalo, rhino. She saw polar bears in Alaska, she bought fancy shoes in Italy, braved the jungle in Peru.

'She got by on just enough money after using her savings, she worked jobs here and there, bit like you.'

'Nothing wrong with that.'

'There wasn't. She worked behind a bar, was a waitress for a time, a kitchen hand, she worked in a clothing store. You name it, she turned her hand to it. I think that was what kept her at least a bit grounded. But then she came home and got it together with a guy who was every parent's worst nightmare. He was wild, into drugs and partying, and I know Bree got dragged into it. Even when she ended things with him, which she did a dozen times or more, somehow he wormed his way back into her life. I think the travelling became an escape for her, a way to get well away from him.'

Finn had boiled the kettle as they talked, made two cups of coffee, and now they sat side-by-side on the raised floor of the barn as she carried on.

'Cory, my boyfriend, had always got on with Bree – I loved the fact that she was like a little sister to him. Or so I thought.'

'I think I know where this is going.'

'He was longing to do something different. I got the feeling I held him back by not particularly wanting to leave New York to live anywhere else. A move to Connecticut was all I managed, but I'm happy here.'

'And he wasn't?'

'He was happy for a while but he always had the itch to do more, go somewhere else. When I turned twenty-one, my parents gave me a bank account they'd been paying into my whole life. They hadn't wanted me to use it for college; they'd wanted me to have it once college was done, once I was older and would appreciate it more. I used some to go travelling in Europe but I didn't spend all that much so had quite a chunk of it still. Cory and I shared the expenses for the apartment we moved into as well, so the money stayed in my account earning interest.'

'What did you have planned for it?' When she looked at him he guessed. 'Dressmaking.'

'I thought that one day, when the time was right, I'd set up on my own. I'd start a dressmaking business and the cash injection provided by my savings could've rented me premises or at least a small shared space somewhere for quite a few months until the income began to build.'

Finn paused to direct a group to the fields beyond and gave them some yellow ribbon to tag their tree, told them to take note of the field number that should be on the nearest fence and then he'd know where to go and cut it down. Kaisha watched him, hardly believing she was telling him all this today. She hadn't even told her parents, which was the toughest thing of all. She'd had to make nice with Bree at the last family occasion, pretend everything was fine, because she worried about her dad's health and feared his blood pressure would skyrocket if he knew of the problems between his two daughters.

She carried on when Finn was free again. 'Bree stopped travelling because she ran out of money. She quickly grew frustrated living at home again, felt like a caged animal, she said, and Cory and I laughed along with her, sympathising over her having to live at home with parents after being footloose and fancy-free. Bree told us she hadn't worked much in the last few months but she'd done a lot of tours, had plenty of adventures and she'd used up everything. My parents were fine about it, the money was there for each of us to do what we wanted. And travel had been her passion.'

The group was already back and Finn picked up the axe. 'I have to go chop this tree.' He hesitated. 'Would you be able to watch the kiosk and I'll be back as soon as I can? I thought Mitch's helper Jude would be here by now but he must've been held up.'

'Happy to.' As well as the talking, Kaisha knew that while she was out here in the middle of nature there was no risk of Bree's car cruising on past.

He wasn't long and managed to haul a tree back for the customers. When he was done, he came back to her side. 'This has to be the longest day in history.'

'Still suffering?'

'You bet, but not too much to listen.' She squinted as the sun pierced through the treetops as it progressed around the sky on its tentative crawl. 'Swap places,' Finn told her. 'You'll be out of the sun then.'

'What about you?'

'I'll be fine. Now, where were we in the sister story?'

She launched straight back into it. 'Bree would talk to Cory and me about travelling – we'd while away many an evening in the pub with her stories – and I was interested, but Cory was enthralled. She wanted to go off again, she talked about Asia, maybe Australia, and somehow Cory and I found ourselves drawn in and talking between ourselves about doing the same. Cory told me he loved me but that my sister's experiences had reminded him that we were both still so young, too young to settle down. Over the coming weeks, as my sister slowly drove herself mad living with my parents while working a waitressing job to raise funds to get away again, I began to think I wanted to travel too. I thought perhaps Cory was right; we needed to have fun and then come back and settle down. I agreed to make some loose plans, to talk to Cleo about time off.

'I never talked to Cleo because the next day my sister came to me in tears: she couldn't hack living at Mom and Dad's, she was off travelling regardless of the lack of money. I think she was intending on putting the flight on a credit card, I've no idea. All she said was that she'd get work as soon as she arrived at her destination and I knew she'd done it before, I had no reason to doubt her. What I did doubt was whether she'd be as safe as before. I knew she'd been seeing that loser boyfriend again, most likely out of boredom, and at being home again, and I had visions of her partying hard the second she landed in another country. Call it sisterly instinct, but I didn't want her getting into more trouble. I figured, if I could go with her and at least be there while she settled and found work, it would be enough to steer her in the right direction.'

Finn found a bag of doughnuts in the cupboard inside the barn. His hungover stomach was obviously demanding sustenance for this enormous spiel. 'I'll replace them later,' he said, eyes closing in pleasure before he sank his teeth into the first glorious bite.

Kaisha removed her gloves, took one, and bit into the glazed dough. It was heavenly and all she needed to finish the rest of her story. 'I wanted to travel by then, I'd started to get excited, Cory was over the moon. But I still had to tell Cleo. I left it to Cory and Bree to go and book everything – plane tickets, accommodation. We were going to start in Sydney, Australia. The airfares alone were crazy money. Bree admitted she couldn't use her credit card and she was overdrawn so I gave her cash – I didn't want the bank swallowing up the money if I transferred it to her. Cory was supposed to meet her at the travel agent; it was the best one, she told him, they were au fait with overseas travel for people on a budget, people like them. But Cory's face when he came back to the apartment that night after not a word from him all day, well, I'll never forget it.'

'She ran off with the money?' He brushed away the sugar from the doughnut that had stuck to his lip.

'She did, all of it, thousands.'

'Drugs?'

'Thankfully not. She did at least fly to Australia, and she sent me a message saying she was sorry, she'd had a row with dad, he wouldn't loan her any more money, and she would pay back every cent with interest as soon as she found a job.'

'Don't tell me, she didn't.'

'She did. The first payment came a week later, another the week after – very small, but something. I cried every night, had to lie to my parents and say Cleo needed me desperately, that she was sick and I owed it to her to stay, and that was why I hadn't gone with Bree. I knew the lie would come out eventually unless I went away and I thought once I had enough money I'd go and see my sister, ask her how she could do this to me. The payments kept on coming, she paid me back every last cent. It took her months. I was still angry at what she'd done, but she'd proven she knew she was in the wrong, she'd put right her mistake.'

'So what happened? How did she mess up again?'

'You know earlier when you said you knew where this was going?'

'That's when I thought she'd run off with your boyfriend.' His laughter didn't hang around. 'Oh... I was right.'

'Cory eventually gave in to the urge to travel even though I'd well and truly changed my mind. We argued, he stormed out, and then he calmly told me he was leaving. I was devastated, but not as much as when a month later he called me and told me that he'd headed to Australia and was living with my sister.'

'As in...'

'As in living together as a couple, yes. Apparently they hadn't intended it to happen. There'd never been anything between them before, if you can believe that. He'd gone to Sydney, where Bree was still hanging around. She'd got a well-paying job with free accommodation and they'd arranged via Facebook to meet for a drink. One thing led to another... and the rest, as they say, is history.'

He handed her another doughnut. 'You need it.'

She grinned. 'One was quite enough.' She stood up when the

farm started to get busier with three cars arriving. 'Can you manage on your own? I need to get to the store.'

'I think so, I'll lock up the kiosk if I need to head out to the fields.' Most of the customers were milling around the pre-cut trees. 'Kaisha…' He stopped her from walking off quite so quickly.

She turned, suddenly cold now they'd been sitting for so long, and eager to walk.

'Thanks for telling me. And think about it.'

'Think about what?' She pulled her gloves back on, her fingers still sticky from the doughnut.

'My sister died. I'd give anything to have her back. No matter what she'd done, I like to think I'd take a chance at rebuilding what we once had. Life really is too short and I'd hate to see you have regrets.'

'I'll bear that in mind.'

He nodded in acceptance and before he could walk over to a customer she asked, 'What happened with your family, Finn? Was it your sister's death that broke it?'

He smiled at her, the face she saw now on so many mornings and last thing at night. 'That's a story for another day.' And with that, off he went into the fields filled with pine trees ready to grace another family's home with their Christmas spirit.

14

KAISHA

Finn wasn't a bad roommate. He was guilty of leaving dirt on the floors, he wasn't always quiet when he fixed a drink or snack in the kitchen at night, he sometimes bit her head off when she least expected, and he called her out when he thought she was in the wrong. But the talk they'd had overlooking the vast expense of land and pine trees had given her some sound advice and she'd taken it on board. She'd come away from the Christmas tree farm and thought about nothing else as the snow began to fall beyond the windows of the Little Knitting Box. Finn talking about his younger sister had got to her and she knew, if something happened to Bree, she'd never forgive herself for not at least hearing her out.

And now, here she was, on the bandstand in Inglenook Falls, darkness descending after her shift at the markets had finished. She hadn't wanted to do this in her apartment – something about the fresh air yesterday had made her talk freely, and she only hoped it worked as well now. She'd brought a woollen blanket from her apartment and laid it down before sitting, and she wasn't gazing up at the town's Christmas tree for long before Bree showed up.

Kaisha shuffled up so her sister could share the warm surface to sit on. It was a silent peace-offering that ignited a smile at least.

'Thanks for calling.' Bree tentatively handed her a cup of something hot. 'It's mulled cider. I picked two up from the markets, I remember you always liked it.'

'I still do.' She took the drink and cupped it between her hands, enjoying the way the warmth spread from her palms all through her body.

'I'd almost given up trying to talk to you. The other day when I came and your boyfriend let me in, that was the last time, I told myself.'

'He's not my boyfriend.'

'Seriously? He's gorgeous.'

Kaisha opened her mouth to snap something about her stealing her boyfriends but changed her mind. She filled her sister in on how she and Finn had come to be living together. Talking about something other than the reason they were really here made it easier.

Snowflakes drifted from the wood of the bandstand where they'd gathered earlier and settled, hiding from the wind and lasting longer than the others that had landed on the grass and long since disappeared. 'It was Finn who persuaded me to get in touch with you,' said Kaisha.

'He seemed drunk when I met him. Is he always like that?' The frown suggested worry, and Kaisha liked to think that's what it was. As much as Bree had competed with her over the years, she'd worried about her older sister at times too.

Growing up, Kaisha had been the more placid but also the more gullible. She'd believed local Eddie Rowlinson when he told her the crab apple he'd picked up was the same they used in their apple pies every year and it was only Bree's common sense and suspicion that something was off that stopped her taking an enormous bite of it, including the maggot poking its ugly form out of the flesh while Eddie looked on amused that his practical joke had almost worked. One day on their walk home from school, Bree tugged Kaisha out of the way of a speeding car she didn't see zipping round the corner. Several parents had seen it and praised her for her quick-thinking actions.

Kaisha liked to think that that girl, who'd once come to her rescue, was in there somewhere. But could she ever really let go of what had happened, what Bree had done?

'I don't know why Finn was drunk that night, but no, he's not always like that,' she clarified.

'Good to know.'

'He had a sister.'

'Had?'

'She died. She was only young.'

'And so he's convinced you to talk to me,' Bree surmised.

'His point was that life is short. And he's right, I wouldn't ever forgive myself if we didn't at least try to make peace with what happened.'

They watched as an elderly couple huddled together before hurrying across the street opposite the bandstand, arms laden with bags after a shopping spree at the markets.

Kaisha sipped at the mulled cider, the warmth of cinnamon and cloves and a hint of cardamom sliding down her throat. 'Finn made me realise it was time I listened to what you had to say.'

'All I ever wanted was a chance to talk, to explain.' Bree fiddled with the fingertips of her gloves. Kaisha had forgotten the quirk. Bree often tugged at the skin on her hands when she was stressed or anxious, sometimes causing the nail bed to bleed, and she pulled at the wool on her gloves now.

Kaisha put a hand over Bree's to stop her, the way she'd done when they were little. 'You'll ruin the gloves and make your fingers sore.'

They shared a tentative smile before Bree left her gloves alone and picked up her own hot drink from where she'd set it down beside her. 'I really am sorry for everything that happened, for what I did.'

'You're sorry for taking off without Cory and me? Or sorry you cleaned me out of money?'

She didn't answer right away. 'Both.' She sipped her hot cider. 'And I paid all the money back.'

'Not really the point though, is it? For all I knew, that money had gone forever. You put a fear into me I hadn't experienced before and then to top it off my boyfriend dumped me and got it together with you.'

The accusations sat on the frosty air, not in the least bit scared away as the wind picked up and cold whipped around them, their cheeks, their faces, warning them that winter would get worse from here on in.

'It wasn't planned, I swear to you, Kaisha.'

'It better not have been or I don't think I could even be sitting here now.'

'I promise it wasn't. I... I was with another guy when I left New York.'

'Oh no, don't tell me, Druggie Dougie?' He'd been a face in Bree's life but one she thought her sister had got rid of for good after she took off to Australia. It seemed she was wrong.

'I'm afraid so. And I guess that's the best name for him. He and I... well, the day I was supposed to meet Cory and go make the booking for our adventure together, Dougie turned up. We got high – his shout he said...'

'I thought you were done, you were never touching drugs ever again.'

'I don't know why I did it. I guess I was feeling down.' Her voice faltered. 'I felt bad about myself, trapped, I knew I was leaving and I thought it's one time and then I won't do it again.'

'That's what they all say.'

'I was a fool. But it really was the one time.'

'What happened then?'

'I was off my head – that was when it happened. I went and booked the trip for myself and for him.'

Kaisha almost dropped her cup. 'You bought *two* tickets?'

'When I sobered up and realised what I'd done, I went crazy at Dougie. Do you know what he said? "Whatever, babe, see you on the plane,".' She mimicked his laborious tone, the way he always talked as though each word was an effort to drag out. 'I hated him for getting those drugs, I hated myself even more for taking them, and how could I face you and Cory after what I'd done?'

'So you went anyway.'

'I had to.'

'No you didn't.'

'I couldn't bear to see you, the look of anger, pain, pity, shame. I thought if I use the ticket I could go, get a job, pay you back all of the money and I'd prove myself. Then I'd come back here and explain what had happened and hopefully, with the money back in your account, your anger might subside and we could start over.'

'What happened to the grand plan? And how did you and Cory...'

'How did we get together? It was completely out of the blue. He sent me a Facebook message, told me he was in Australia. I assumed you were with him but when we met up, that was when he told me you guys had broken up.'

Kaisha looked up at the sky above, the moon peeking out in a sliver of silver tonight. The mulled cider was all gone and she was feeling the cold seeping in wherever it could – around her scarf, up through any gap in her coat.

'I always wondered why I couldn't be more like you,' Bree admitted. 'You always seemed to get everything right. You knew exactly what you wanted, breezed through college, then landed a dream job. You even scored lucky in love. You didn't have waste-of-space boyfriends, you had sensible ones like Cory.'

'Cory wasn't perfect, as he proved. He's caused me enough grief to last a lifetime. We're very different, Bree, but don't assume it's always easy for me. I worry more than you. I hated the way you stressed Mom and Dad out too.'

'No more than other kids.'

'You're joking, right?' She took a moment to think of how to word what she wanted to say, work out how to get through to Bree. 'Dad has been sick more than once, you know that.'

'High blood pressure, I know,' Bree confirmed. 'Stress at work.'

'Stress full stop,' Kaisha snapped. 'I had to be the daughter who picked up the pieces. And you were a lot worse than other kids, you mark my words.'

'I tried not to be. That's why I tried to get away. I tried to leave Dougie and the trouble behind, I didn't want to burden them with it.'

'But you did. And who do you think Dad talked to about his concerns? Who did Mom talk to when they had no idea where you were or who you were with or whether that would be the day they got a call to say their youngest daughter was never coming home?'

'You make me sound like a criminal.' Butter wouldn't melt now for Bree in her tailored leather jacket, soft, dove-grey gloves, cherry-red lipstick she'd adopted as her shade as soon as she was old enough to wear it.

'Drugs are hardly sold at the candy store in full view of the law, Bree.'

'You're so patronising.'

Kaisha stood and picked up her empty cup. 'I knew this was a mistake.'

But Bree was quick enough to reach a hand out to her sister's arm. 'Please, don't go, not yet. I'm sorry, I messed up badly. I didn't come here to argue.' When Kaisha reluctantly sat down again she said, 'I was naive to think that Mom and Dad would stop worrying if I just left, or maybe I didn't want to see the truth. I made a mess of things and every time I thought I'd fixed it, I just managed to make it worse.'

'Quit feeling sorry for yourself and take some responsibility.'

'I do, believe me. I just want you to realise that not everyone has themselves sorted like you do. I'm not saying you have it easy and I'm not making excuses for being all over the place, but I promise you, I'm not any more.'

'I hope that's true, Bree.' She took a deep breath and let it out slowly to calm herself down. She didn't want to fight any more, she was tired of it. 'The reason why I shielded Dad in particular and didn't tell them what you did is because his health should be our priority and I didn't want his stress levels going up and something worse happening. Remember Mrs Zuckerman?'

'Our old neighbour?'

'She had a heart attack and Mom swore it was because she was always fretting about kids playing on her lawn, forever yelling at people. She was stressed. Dad was stressed. Mrs Zuckerman died, Bree. Do you see where I'm going with this?'

'You're doing it again, you're patronising me.'

'I don't mean to, I just get frustrated when I think you're not taking me seriously.'

'I do, all the time. But sometimes you take yourself too seriously. You worry too much about other people. And I'm guilty of cashing in on that. I let you come in and save the day for me, I relied on you to get me back to where I wanted to be and I shouldn't have done.'

It was the closest her sister had ever come to a meaningful apology.

'You never told Mom and Dad that Cory and I got together over in Australia,' said Bree. 'But they've known for a long while that something isn't right between you and me. And that makes it stressful for them anyway.'

When the wind howled again, Kaisha stood up. 'Come on, let's walk or we'll freeze.' She bundled up the blanket and tucked it beneath her arm before they strolled along Main Street, pretty lights of the stores illuminating the sidewalk, stars twinkling up above. 'Mom and Dad do realise there's an issue with us, but I'm careful not to give them details. I wanted them to think it would all blow over.'

'But I was with Cory for a month, you should've told them.'

'Wait, are you not together now?'

'God, no! Did you seriously think we were?'

'I assumed...'

'He really got the travel bug and left Sydney with feet so itchy I thought he'd got a bad case of athlete's foot.'

Kaisha got no satisfaction that he'd done the same thing to her sister as he had to her, although she was pleased to hear Cory was no longer in Bree's life. Over time she'd nearly driven herself crazy asking herself what if it got serious and they were married? What if they had a family together? What if she had to smile and play along forever more?

'I'm sorry about everything,' said Bree, 'but most of all about Cory.'

'I never told Mom or Dad. I carried on as normal, they think the split was amicable because I suppose I knew I'd fall apart if I admitted everything. And when Dad had another scare with his blood pressure and wound up in hospital, I vowed to never tell them the whole truth.'

Bree stopped dead in the street. 'You never told me. Nobody did. What happened?'

'He wasn't in for long. I just think everything got on top of him and he passed out. It was a hot day too, he'd been painting the dining room, he overdid it. But it was a timely reminder that he has to take care of himself. Anyway, I could hardly tell him his youngest daughter had shacked up with my ex, could I?'

'You should've told me he wasn't well, Kaisha.'

'I know.' Her voice came out soft on the wind. 'I'm sorry I didn't.'

'Were you trying to punish me?'

'Partly, I guess, and that was wrong. But if you'd come home then, I'm not sure I could've kept quiet about everything. At least the extra time gave me some space to get over Cory and accept that you and he were...'

'Me and him are nothing now, we never really were. We were never in a proper relationship. I think it was just something that happened and, for a while, became a habit. I don't think I was particularly sorry when he left, or surprised.' They reached the end of Main Street and crossed over to walk back along the other side. 'My biggest fear was not being able to pay that money back. All your savings and I'd taken them away.'

'I'm glad you paid me back too. But I can't believe Dougie got a free ticket out of it.'

They both used the same expletive to describe him at exactly the same time as they passed the top of the track that led down to Mitch's Christmas tree farm and it was a moment that bonded them together as they shared a smile.

'Is Dougie out of your life completely?' Kaisha wanted to know.

'I wouldn't spit on him if he was on fire.'

'And you're not...'

'Drugs? No, no chance. Nothing since that day. I suppose I've got Dougie to thank for making me realise I'll never touch drugs again.'

'Glad to hear it.' They reached the corner where they'd turn to be alongside the Little Knitting Box.

Bree stopped before they got to the store, her car parked alongside them. 'Where does this leave us, Kaisha?'

'I honestly don't know.' She'd spent so long being angry, resenting Bree in some way, her mindset wasn't going to change just like that.

'Can you ever forgive me for what I did?' The sheen in Bree's eyes was enough to let Kaisha know this was for real, these tears were genuine. Out of nowhere, maybe because she hadn't been looking for a while, her sister had actually grown up.

'I haven't lost out financially, but I wish you'd come to me when you did something so crazy with Dougie. I would've been angry about the money and had you pay it back, but the running away to the other side of the world was one of the worst things. And then Cory.'

'I wish I could take back what I did.'

Their parents obviously didn't even know Bree was home because they hadn't mentioned anything about it – her mum had even talked about Bree being in the sunshine at this time of the year. 'When are you going to tell Mom and Dad you're back?'

'I'm going to tell them everything when they're home, not while they're on their holiday.'

'I agree.'

'I'll sit them down and do it calmly, but I'm hoping by then I'll have work and my own place to live. I know that would go a long way towards showing them I'm fine, that they don't need to worry, and I'm a bit more responsible than I once was.'

'We probably don't need to ever tell them about Cory.'

Bree hesitated. 'I feel like that wouldn't be fair to you. I feel like you're covering up for me.'

'I think the rest of it will be enough for them to handle, and to be honest, I've moved on from him, I don't need to dredge it all up again. Sometimes, perhaps we need to keep things to ourselves. We're big girls now, grown up.'

Bree braved a smile. 'What are your plans for Christmas?'

'Cleo's wedding is Christmas Eve.'

'That'll be really special, she's like an older sister to you.'

'She is. But I still have a younger sister, I haven't forgotten.' The awkward moment between them was broken when a few delicate flakes of snow fell around them, dusting the front of the Little Knitting Box just beyond.

'Remember the snowman competitions we had growing up?' Bree grinned.

'Now there's something you were way better at than me. I always got fed up halfway through. The soaking wet gloves were never fun.'

Bree dug into her bag and took out a red, blue, and mustard woollen hat. 'Remember this?'

Kaisha's eyes glistened with tears and she gasped, 'How do you still have it?' She'd crocheted the hat when she was twelve years old and they'd agreed whoever made the best snowman – as judged anonymously by their parents – got to put it on the snowman's head. Kaisha had thought the hat lost the last Christmas they did the silly competition. But here it was.

'Of course I still have it. It's a trophy of sorts.' Bree gulped as Kaisha handed it back. 'Just because we haven't spoken in a while, certainly not properly or honestly, doesn't mean I haven't thought about you every single day. And even though I did what I did, doesn't mean for every second of that twenty-four-hour flight to Australia I wasn't wishing you were sitting right there beside me.'

Kaisha, in a moment of spontaneity, pulled Bree into a hug. It felt good after so many tentative hugs over time for the sake of appearances. 'Thank you for coming to see me.'

'Thank you for listening.' She took out her keys, ready to leave. 'Can we talk again?'

'That's probably a good idea.' She wanted Bree in her life; seeing her today confirmed it. Up until now she'd put up a barrier to stop her younger sister ever hurting her so much again. But she could see now that Bree had been hurting too, in a different way. And while trying to put right her mistakes, she'd fallen into a relationship with Cory, who had to share part of the blame for that.

'I'll see you then.' With a wave, Bree stepped towards her car.

'Drinks,' Kaisha called out, berating herself for yelling something so random. 'We're having bachelorette drinks at the store after closing in a couple of days. Would you come? Meet my friends?'

This time Bree's smile was genuine, not afraid to shine. 'I'd really like that.'

And when she drove away, Kaisha let herself into the Little Knitting Box, went on up to the apartment, and for the first time in a long while, she realised she'd actually been happy to see her sister.

15

FINN

'I haven't worn a pair of these in years,' Andy told his son as he bent over to do up his ice-skates beside the Wollman Rink.

'Another one of your grandad's bright ideas, Finn,' Beverly tutted, once again trying in vain to wrap her scarf in such a way that it didn't dangle down.

Finn didn't mind the idea himself. He wasn't a bad skater; he'd done it a lot as a kid. Perhaps Grandad had wanted to give him the upper hand on this one. 'Come on, it's freezing, can we just get on with this already?' He'd been laced up and raring to go in his own skates for twenty minutes and his parents were still trying to sort themselves out.

They finally took to the ice with the many tourists who'd decided today was the day they gave ice-skating a go for the very first time this season. Or at least that's the way it felt, with crowds finding their feet and hesitant at first. And Finn had already lapped his parents before his mum had even let go of the side.

'You make it look so easy,' she grumbled. His dad was concentrating too hard to talk. He'd never been one to multitask. Changing the oil on the car meant Finn couldn't ask him a question about his maths homework, fixing the kitchen cupboards one morning meant Finn had to literally wave a permission slip for school in front of his face to get him to acknowledge it, and after Mackenzie died he just got worse. He gradually retreated into himself more and more and nobody else got much of a look-in.

'Stop looking down,' was Finn's advice as he skated beside his mum and saw her making the same mistake again.

'I don't think now is the time to appreciate the view.'

'I didn't mean that, but if you look at your feet you're putting your weight forwards.'

She immediately stood bolt upright to take his advice but almost lost her balance completely before he caught her. 'Don't lean backwards either,' he instructed as they at least glided on a bit further.

'Can't we just get a photo of all of us with our skates on, tell your grandad we did it?' She ignored Andy going past them and then doubling back, not that you were supposed to go in the opposite direction.

'He's not stupid.' Andy had staggered to a halt beside them. 'He wants video footage.'

'You are joking, please tell me you are,' said Beverly, at last getting the hang of moving forwards with Finn alongside.

'Of course he's joking,' said Finn, 'he's winding you up. But we won't lie to him.'

'A couple more laps round,' Andy suggested, joining them.

'I'm not sure I can, my legs ache already,' said Beverly.

'At least you don't have to worry about your ankle,' Andy complained.

'Your dodgy ankle?' asked Finn. 'Your sporting injury?' He heard his mum snigger beside him as they shared the joke.

'It's playing up again,' said his dad.

This time, Beverly's laughter peeled around the rink. Probably more a release from the tension than anything else. But they should've been concentrating more because Beverly wobbled and almost fell, she used her arms to regain balance, knocked into Finn, who fell into Andy, and they all ended up in a heap on the floor.

Finn and his mum were still laughing hard, especially when his dad mentioned his ankle again. And they'd all been laughing so much that none of them realised they were being watched until Kaisha called hello to them from the edge of the rink. She was looking over at the tangle of bodies on the floor.

Beverly accepted she needed assistance and Andy held out a hand to help her to her feet. Finn's parents progressed round the rink themselves, leaving Finn to talk to Kaisha alone.

'What made you all laugh so much?' she asked, the tip of her nose a cute shade of pink with the cold. 'It must be progress; you all looked happy. And look, I got a photograph for you.' She showed him the image on her phone.

He caught his breath and straightened his coat. 'I guess laughter compared to a full-on row must be a development of sorts.' The photo wasn't half bad; they looked oddly happy. 'We were laughing at an old joke. Dad was complaining ice-skating makes his ankle hurt and I asked if it was his sporting injury.'

'And was it?'

'Hardly. I was in the school ski team and Dad came on a trip with us. We skied well the entire week but on the way home, at the gas station, he tripped up the kerb and sprained his ankle. He was on crutches for a while. He told some of the other dads he'd done it skiing, he was too embarrassed to admit the truth. Dads were very competitive at my school and I guess he had a reputation to maintain. Anyway, Mom and I knew the truth and at a dinner party he told the guests but one look from my Mom and we couldn't keep a straight face. We had to leave the room to recover.'

She was smiling. 'It sounds like a lovely memory.'

'It's nothing, ridiculous really and not even funny.'

'The best private jokes often aren't, but I think what makes them so powerful is the memories that come with them.'

The joke had reminded him of an occasion when things hadn't been strained, the odd time the family held it together and managed some semblance of normality.

'You guys really do look like any other happy family,' she assured him, checking out the photograph again. 'Let me send this to your phone.' They'd already had the foresight to swap numbers given they were sharing an apartment.

When she put her phone back in her pocket and tugged on her gloves he asked, 'What brings you this way?' Dylan might have warned him away from this woman but he was finding it hard to honour his promise to keep the thoughts in his head platonic.

'I met up for dinner with a friend from college, then we came skating for fun. We were just leaving when I saw you guys. You're not bad, you know. I watched you, you've got some skill.'

'Yeah?'

Her cheeks coloured and he suspected it wasn't entirely from the cold. She looked away briefly. 'Is it working? The family bonding?'

'You know, I think it might be a little bit.' He waved at his parents when they passed by again, not at each other's throats, chatting even, and every now and then Beverly would reach for Andy's arm to steady herself.

'I'm getting the hang of it,' his mum called over.

'Remember how you told me life was too short?' Kaisha drew his attention back her way.

'Sounds like something wise that I might say. Does this mean you're going to talk to your sister?'

'I already have.'

'You're a fast worker.' Standing at the edge of the rink, him on the ice, her on the safety of solid, non-slippery ground, their hands were almost touching on the barrier and he looked down into her eyes. But they didn't get a chance to say much more because her friend waved over at her.

'I've got to go.'

'Not before you tell me how it went with Bree.'

The smile told him what he needed to know. 'It's a start,' she said, eyes alight with the glow from the twinkly lights strung nearby from tree to tree. 'And sometimes that's all it takes.'

He watched his parents at the far side of the rink again now. A start. That's what this was. Not so long ago they'd have killed one another being in such close proximity for so long. But every meet-up, every dinner, outing, and engineered activity courtesy of his grandad had been a little start to offer them the chance of momentum.

Maybe this time they'd take it.

Kaisha went on her way, his parents left the rink all smiles for once, and they handed back their ice-skates.

As they walked through Central Park, Finn tried to maintain the progress they'd made tonight, quite unexpectedly. 'Mackenzie would've loved doing this, being here today.'

The canopy of trees above was so bare they could see a smattering of stars up above. By spring, blue skies would barely be visible, with pink blossoms expanding overhead, but tonight, the heavens above them were clear to see.

'She might've been a mom by now,' Beverly said to neither of them in particular, more to herself. And although Finn was taken aback that she'd spoken of his sister, he tried not to let it show. 'She was forever nursing those dolls of hers. She liked to tuck them into their cribs, rock them to sleep.'

'Remember the cars?' His dad spoke now and Finn again didn't let his surprise show that finally he was talking about the daughter he'd lost. Mackenzie's name was rarely mentioned and yet here they were launching into a conversation about her as though they did it all the time.

'I'd forgotten,' said Beverly. 'How could I forget those? She had so many.'

'I was envious of her car collection,' Finn admitted. 'I was a bit too old to be sitting playing with them but I used to pretend I was doing it to entertain Mackenzie.' She'd been serious about collecting all sorts of makes and models and she'd also inherited the wooden garage his dad had made and given to him when he was little but had barely used, favouring his go-kart or bike, or, later on, being in the kitchen.

'She sure loved those cars,' his dad reminisced. 'Remember how she'd come to the garage if ours was in for repairs? She never wanted to sit in the comfortable waiting room, always wanted to know what was happening on the shop floor.'

'Bet you hated that,' said Finn.

His dad fell silent but after a while said, 'I only ever wanted the best for my children.'

'Is that why you made me feel like such a failure about my unmanly interest in baking?' His words left him before he had a chance to filter. He should be focusing on the fact they were actually talking about Mackenzie, they'd had an okay time at the rink, rather than being antagonistic.

'You lost interest anyway,' said his dad as though he hadn't played any part in Finn's change of heart.

'Did you ever think to question why?'

'Look how far you've come, son,' his dad tried again. 'You got a good job, you travelled the world. You wouldn't have had half these opportunities if you'd make cakes for a living.'

'Well, we'll never know, will we? I convinced myself that baking wasn't enough, it would be a poor career choice, nothing more than a hobby. You made me think I was an imposter dreaming of a job that would never be mine; I was never allowed to make my own way into a world I was still getting to know.' He wasn't ready to admit his own reasons for not fighting back and pursuing his passion regardless – he couldn't help himself, he wanted the blame to fall squarely on his dad's shoulders right now. He was so angry still and he wished he wasn't.

'I don't have to listen to this.' Andy broke away from the trio in Central Park and marched away from confrontation. Same as always, unless it was confrontation with his wife, in which case he was often happy to go into battle.

But this time Finn refused to let him do it and followed after him. 'You do have to listen, Dad.' His own advice to Kaisha was firmly in his mind. If he let his dad walk, if Grandad's plan didn't do anything to bring the family together, he'd be a hypocrite. He had to at least try.

'Not here,' said Beverly, jostled by the crowds. 'There's a café up this street, let's go there and try to have a sensible conversation for once in our goddamn lives.'

When she led the way, they followed quickly on and none of them said a word until they were settled inside and the coffee was ordered.

'I won't deny the career I chose in the end, and on your approval, had its perks and I was happy for a while,' Finn admitted. 'Hell, I even thought it was right for me, but with no passion there I ended up quitting and went off travelling. I was being stifled, I felt trapped, but now I do whatever job I can find and I feel free.'

'I think your father wanted you to see that you could have work and hobbies,' his mum tried. She really was going all out to support her ex-husband today.

'That's not true,' Andy admitted, but couldn't meet Finn's eyes.

'What do you mean it's not true?' Finn asked before managing a murmur of thanks to the waitress who delivered the cinnamon rolls they'd ordered. Finn didn't have much appetite but he forced down some of his food when his grumbling stomach argued otherwise.

'That wasn't it, you've got it wrong.' His dad still couldn't look at him.

Finn swigged more of his coffee, but suddenly he didn't want to do this. He couldn't handle it. 'I'm going to call it a night. I've got work tomorrow and I'm worn out. Don't worry, I'll send the photograph to Grandad.'

'That wasn't it,' his dad repeated as Finn picked up his gloves from the edge of the table. 'Please sit down, Finn.'

Something about the way he looked, the hopelessness he conveyed, made him sit down again. Whatever Grandad's plan had been at the beginning, his dad wanted to talk for once, and usually discussing his emotions was something Andy Thompson didn't do.

'Remember when you made Mackenzie's eleventh birthday cake?' his dad asked him.

Rather than looking upset at the mention of her daughter, Beverly beamed. 'The bumblebee cake, I'd never seen anything like it. Intricate, complex, you have such a talent.'

Finn smiled, noting her use of the present tense, not that he'd shown his talents off in a long while. And making Mackenzie a part of this conversation somehow made it easier to hear his dad out. 'She had a fascination with bees.'

'That she did,' his mum smiled.

His mind went back to summer days with his sister. 'Remember when I got stung?'

'I've never seen you cry so much,' said his mum.

'Maybe don't broadcast that bit. Do you remember Mackenzie crying too?'

'I don't, but she doted on her older brother, I'm not surprised she was distressed that you were hurt.'

'She wasn't crying for me, she was balling her eyes out thinking the bee would die because it stung me. She stopped crying when I pointed out that I'd been stung by a big round fuzzy bumblebee rather than a honeybee, and it would probably go on to sting some other poor kid before the day was out. I thought she'd want a birthday cake made into the shape of a car, or a pretty pink number for her birthday like she told me her friend had the week before, but she begged me to make a bee cake. Her favourite flavour was chocolate—'

'Always chocolate.' His mum shook her head. 'I don't think any of her celebration cakes were ever anything else.'

'I made chocolate sponge and she helped me in the kitchen, watched me put it all together.'

'She wasn't the only one in awe,' his mum admitted. 'The way you melted the white chocolate and shaped it on bubble wrap and then fashioned those fat, round bumblebees out of fondant to dot around the beehive cake board left me speechless. I don't think I could've ordered a better cake from any of the bakeries in Connecticut.' Her warm memory faded on her face into something cooler as conversation lapsed and Andy still didn't say a word.

'Thanks, Mom.' She may not have fought his corner but at least she acknowledged his love of baking. He'd told a girl he met last year that if he could be anything in the world it would be a master baker. She'd run a hand across his tattoo before kissing him and telling him something unrepeatable about melting chocolate and what they could do with it, and he'd wondered what he'd ever have to say to get anyone to take him seriously.

His dad still wasn't talking and Finn felt his frustration rise until Andy took out his wallet to pay. Except he wasn't paying. He handed a photograph to his son. 'Here...'

Finn looked at the picture, curled up at the edges, faded colours that would've once been vivid. And he looked at his teenage self, next to his sister who'd turned eleven that day, the finished cake in front of them, her with a smear of white chocolate across her cheek, both of them laughing so hard he could see the tears in their eyes even now. Or perhaps he couldn't, maybe he just remembered the bittersweet moment in glorious technicolour.

'It's a nice picture.' He passed it back.

'Mackenzie died a couple of hours later,' Andy said, although nobody really needed reminding of the facts. Mackenzie had died of a brain aneurysm. Nobody could've predicted it, she was taken from them cruelly and suddenly on a day that should've been nothing but happy. 'When the ambulance came we just left everything as it was and went to the hospital.'

'I'll never forget it.' Beverly, head hung, toyed with a tissue as though she expected tears to come along shortly.

Finn would never forget that day either. He went to the hospital with his sister very much in his life and came home without her, realising never again would they laugh together, bicker, or rally against parents as kids often did. He'd gone from being one of two to an only child, and the loneliness hit him with full force. The morning after his sister died, Finn had staggered into the kitchen, the house clammy, claustrophobic, things everywhere, and he'd simply turned, run down the hallway, through the front door and he didn't come back until it was dark.

When he finally returned home, his mum was frantic. She was standing on the front porch keeping watch, Dylan's mum comforting her. She'd clutched him tightly, hurting his body, as his arms hung limply by his sides and when he went into the house everything was back to normal. The party evidence had gone, the cake had disappeared. Finn had demanded to know where the cake was; he looked in the pantry where they often kept leftovers in plastic containers, he looked in the dining room in case it was in there, and then he opened the cupboard beside the sink and found it. In the trash. Smashed to pieces, obliterated, like Mackenzie.

Since that day nobody had said anything about the bee cake that made Mackenzie hug him and tell him how much she loved her big brother, how talented he was. She never said those things to him – it made him blush and feel emotional, and he'd hidden his feelings by smearing her cheek with the spatula of leftover white chocolate. Oh how he wished he'd hugged her back and told her the same.

His dad looked at him. 'I heard you and Mackenzie in the kitchen that day, I heard her tell you she loved you, that she had the best big brother in the world.' His voice caught. 'I heard her talking about bees with you, her fascination for them, her dreams for the future, her admiration for the cake you'd put together with your own two hands. Overhearing that interaction... well, it was one of those moments for a parent, those moments when you know you did something right. You've got two wonderful kids and you feel lucky.'

'It still doesn't explain why you threw the cake in the trash.' Finn dismissed the waitress's attention when she came to see if they wanted more. He was rude but he'd give her an extra tip; this had to be done now, no interruptions.

'I stood staring at it all night after we came home from the hospital,' his dad admitted. 'I stared and stared, the sweet scent wrapping around me so tightly I could barely breathe. I could hear her voice in my head, her young dreams for herself, for you. And I just lost it.'

When his voice faltered it was Beverly who carried on and she covered Andy's hand with her own. 'I found your dad sitting in a ball on the floor crying his eyes out. When he realised I was watching him he tried to hold it together for me but couldn't. We cried together, wailed at the unfairness, and then he threw the cake across the room. He ripped the wrap from the plates of sandwiches and threw those, he smashed every single glass on the table, upended the jugs of lemonade once the lids were slung off, kicked down the gazebo.'

Looking at his dad, Finn struggled to reconcile this timid version of the man who'd always stood tall in his memory. 'So it wasn't just my cake that bore the brunt of your anger.' And it wasn't Finn's talent that Andy had wanted to wreck, to deny, to obliterate. It was his fury at the day that had taken so much away from them.

'No, son, it wasn't. I trashed the entire kitchen. Your mom cleared it all up while I sat there – I couldn't move, I was paralysed with the shock. It was never about the cake. It was a good cake.'

'It was a great cake.' Finn managed to get a bit of a smile in return.

'Do you remember the first birthday of mine after Mackenzie died?' Andy asked. His dad was always big on birthdays, but hadn't been since they lost Mackenzie.

'I remember. I was going to make you a banoffee cake, I knew how much you loved it.' And he'd tried to put the memory of his dad's reaction to his own birthday cake baking aside, he tried to tell himself he was reading too much into the disapproving looks.

'That was the day I told you to man up,' Andy admitted, 'to stop playing about in the kitchen and go do something teenage boys were supposed to.'

'You said it so many times after that.' And Finn never had baked that cake.

'I'm so very sorry. I can't take back what I said or the way I acted, but all I saw when you were cooking was delight on your face.'

'And why was that so wrong?'

'Because it was the same look of delight you and Mackenzie had on her birthday when you finished the cake, when you were laughing in the kitchen, the day we lost her. You and Mackenzie looked so much alike – the same smiles, the same colouring – and every time you were together I felt like the luckiest man alive.' His voice faltered. 'Until I wasn't.'

'We all lost her, Dad.'

'I did wrong, I know that. I was trying to take away my own pain and in doing so, created more for you. It was unforgivable.' He asked for an espresso when the waitress passed by, presumably something to knock him sideways so he could carry on with this conversation. 'I can't repair the damage I did, Finn. But please believe me when I say I am deeply sorry. I reached a point at which I couldn't bear to be where anyone was having a good time. At work, if someone laughed it was as though they were taunting me; if your mom looked happy I got angry at her; if you mentioned baking anything I nearly lost it. My way of controlling was to be an angry, manipulative ass.'

'Pretty apt description,' Finn concluded. The air whipped in and made him shiver when the door to the café opened to let customers out, and then the warmth enveloped their table once again when the door fell shut and the espresso arrived.

'I never meant it to influence your entire life. I thought I knew best.' His dad nursed the espresso, the strong scent filling the space between them.

'It wasn't just the baking and the comments you made.' Finn looked at both of his parents. 'It was the constant fighting, the lack of interest in anything other than yourselves, that had an impact.'

'Your mom did everything she could to try to keep us together,' his dad admitted.

Beverly shook her head. 'It takes two to wreck a marriage, Andy.' They held a look that made Finn feel, for the first time in years, as though he were intruding. 'And I was constantly worried about you, Finn. I knew you sought solace at Dylan's. I was always talking to his mom, finding out things about you – I knew you were okay. She pleaded with me to get some counselling but both your dad and I buried our heads. It's what we do best, I'm sure you'll agree.'

'Grandad did the right thing, engineering all this,' said Finn eventually. 'Maybe we should all be thanking him, and I never thought I'd say that.'

Andy nodded. 'We should've done this a long time ago.'

Finn began to remove his layers until all he had on were his jeans and T-shirt and when Andy looked at him as though he was losing his mind, he rolled up the sleeve to show them his tattoo.

'Is that...?' His mum covered her mouth with her hand, tears in her eyes.

'I got it when I turned twenty-one. I wasn't baking cakes but there isn't a day that goes by when I don't think of Mackenzie. I didn't plan on getting it; I went with a buddy to the tattoo parlour, ended up flipping through the catalogue there and the design leapt out at me.'

'Your sister would love it.' Andy's voice shook as he spoke.

'She'd probably want one herself,' said Finn.

Beverly smiled. 'Not an option if she was living under my roof, let me tell you.'

As his parents examined the design, the marks the ink had permanently left on his skin, Finn suspected the deep running pain for both of them was something they hadn't shared even with each other. Perhaps if they had, they'd still be together now.

But Mackenzie was gone and they couldn't turn back time. The family had split, divided, gone their separate ways. And Finn had no idea where they went to from here.

16

KAISHA

At the Little Knitting Box, Kaisha handed a customer her phone number written on a piece of paper. It seemed her reputation as a talented dressmaker had spread since the school's Christmas pageant and the woman, who taught at the high school, wanted to enlist Kaisha's help for their spring production next year.

After the customer left, Kaisha closed the door to the store. She picked up the broom to sweep away the dirt that had sneaked its way inside with the blustery weather. 'I swear it'll snow today,' she told Cleo, who was busy tidying one of the baskets of yarn. People didn't always drop the same colour back where it should go, or even the correct yarn in its rightful place with the appropriate labelling, and if they didn't stay on top of it as they went along, it would be quite a job by the end of the day.

'Forecast says soon,' Cleo agreed as she finished up by putting the midnight blue in the hutch space next to the lavender rather than in amongst the turquoise. 'I don't mind if it snows on the big day either; it'd be quite romantic, as long as it's not so heavy that it closes roads.'

Time to change the subject before Cleo got too worried and

made up ridiculous disaster scenarios in her head again. 'What did your dad bring you this morning?' Cleo's dad had arrived from England and while Kaisha was talking to the customer about dressmaking, he'd given Cleo a gift bag.

Cleo fetched the bag and pulled out a box, inside which was an ornate, white, sapphire pendant. 'This was Mum's on her wedding day; he gave it to her the day before they got married.'

'Cleo... it's beautiful.'

'We thought it was lost. Years ago we turned the entire house upside down looking for it; I might have even accused my step mum of stealing it at one point. Dad found it when they renovated the bathroom last year – it had slipped into a groove near the base of the tub somehow. He had it cleaned and part of it repaired, but oh... it's as beautiful as ever.' She clutched it against her heart.

'You must be so pleased.'

'I couldn't be happier.'

'What else is in the bag?' Kaisha urged, desperate to know.

With a cheeky grin, Cleo took out a blue garter.

'Also your mum's?' Kaisha wondered.

'No, this was Teresa's when she married my dad, so that covers my borrowed and blue.'

'And what do you have that's new?'

'Some very sexy lingerie that Dylan hasn't seen yet.'

'I don't need the details,' Kaisha giggled.

'Talking of clothing items, I heard the customer earlier asking for your contact information.'

'Oh that,' she dismissed as though it was nothing.

'Are you going to do some work for her?'

'Maybe.'

'You should. You did a brilliant job with the Christmas pageant costumes – you're incredibly talented. I already knew that, of course, but believe me when I say it now, Kaisha.'

'Thanks.'

'It's not the first time you've been approached, is it?'

Momentarily panicked, Kaisha confessed, 'I've done the odd bit of dressmaking. You're not mad, are you? I promise it hasn't impacted on the work I do here.'

'I'm sure it hasn't, and why would I be mad?'

'Because I work here. You know, I love knitting just as much as dressmaking.'

Cleo followed her over to where she was trying to avoid any questions by hiding out near the tree, staring into its beautiful branches. 'I'm going to ask you a straight question and I think you owe me an honest answer.'

'Sure.' Although she really didn't want to have to reply.

'Do you have a desire to move on, from this – this store, the markets – and do something else?'

'No! Well... lately... well, I guess I've been thinking about it.' She reached out to adjust a silver bell on the tree that was almost falling off its branch. 'I didn't want to tell you; it feels like a betrayal. I'm not saying I'm leaving or anything like that, but one day, maybe, I'd like to set up my own business.' She couldn't even look at Cleo now.

'Well, thank the Lord!'

Kaisha's eyebrows arched in surprise. 'What?'

'At last!' Cleo took hold of Kaisha's upper arms, her hands gripping the multicoloured woollen cardigan Kaisha had had since she started working at the Little Knitting Box when it was based in the city. 'It's been a terrible year for you since Cory left and I've been worrying myself silly. I've watched you; I see you're still hardworking and passionate, and your workshops are renowned not only in Inglenook Falls but also in Connecticut. We've had someone book in from Hartford, another from Stamford. But great as it is having you, I know it's time for you to think about moving on. You only get one future – don't stagnate here when there's plenty out there for you.'

'Are you firing me?'

'Of course not, but why don't we sit down in the New Year and talk about it, you can make a plan? I find plans help a lot, show you a way forward.'

'And you wouldn't feel that I'd let you down?'

'How could I? You've been a good friend to me, I love you like a sister, we'll always be close.'

Kaisha's mouth curved into a tentative smile. 'You'll never manage it all on your own, you know.'

'Thanks for the vote of confidence,' Cleo teased in return. 'And that's for Dylan and me to worry about. Perhaps we need to make our own plans, have a think about how many markets I'm doing each year. The kids are getting older and I know I'm missing out on some of the most precious days, so I'll be looking out for another assistant here to replace you.'

'Perhaps we could start asking around.' Rather than feeling afraid, she was full of energy, her secret finally not under wraps.

'That sounds like a good idea.'

'We could ask people who come to the workshops.' Kaisha's enthusiasm mounted. 'Other knitting groups in the surrounding towns. It's the kind of work that's a pleasure to do if knitting is your passion.' She paused. 'And you're really not upset?'

'I promise I'm not.'

'I want to say thank you, for everything you've done for me, you know. You gave me a job, a place to live, and even when I've been off travelling you had me back like I'd never been away. I've loved my time here.'

'You'll have me upset in a minute.' Cleo's eyes sparkled with emotion.

Between them they shared a few happy tears and when their

eyes were dry and they were berating themselves for their senti-mentality, Cleo asked what was going on with Bree.

'We're talking, properly,' Kaisha told her.

'Do you mind me asking what went on between you? I knew something was up but I backed off, I didn't want to pry.'

'And that's why you're such a good friend.'

'May I pry now?'

'Well… I'm going to need a hot chocolate if you want me to tell you anything more.'

'Deal. I'll hold the fort, you go get us a couple of drinks.'

Kaisha was glad of the fresh air blasting at her to tell her things were going to be just fine. In the New Year, with Cleo and Dylan happily settled, she'd make plans of her own and if she could help Cleo find someone else to work in the store she'd feel less like she was abandoning her. Excitement tugged at her insides – this was real, she was going to do this, make the change she'd craved for so long.

Over hot chocolate, Cleo and Kaisha continued their heart-to-heart and Kaisha told Cleo everything that had happened.

'Wow, I can understand why your relationship with Bree is so complicated.' Cleo set her empty cup down. 'I wish you'd told me.'

'I didn't want to admit it to anyone and because I was keeping it from my parents I thought it best to just bury it.'

'Along with your feelings,' Cleo confirmed. 'That's the problem. I've been there, kept things inside when I should've talked about them. You, Darcy, Holly, everyone, have been brilliant friends and haven't let me do that for a long while. You're all there for me, you keep the channels of communication open, but you, my girl, have forgotten that sometimes you need someone yourself.'

'No man is an island, right?'

'Exactly.'

They were seated out back of the Little Knitting Box, hot chocolates long gone and taking the chance to rest before the post-lunch rush that usually came during the week, especially now schools had finished and the markets were full of locals, tourists, and people who'd got wind of Inglenook Falls and wanted to see if it was as special as they'd heard it was.

Realisation suddenly struck. 'I'll have to look for somewhere else to live,' said Kaisha. The apartment upstairs wouldn't be hers by this time next year if she got going with her business.

'Why? You're a good tenant.'

'Let's face it, you could rent it out for a lot more than you're charging me.'

'You're forgetting, the entrance is via my store. I don't think I could trust anyone else to use it.'

'I hadn't thought of it that way.'

Cleo got up when a customer came in looking for a single hank of cerise yarn. She was knitting clothes for Barbie dolls and as they talked it left Kaisha to wonder what the New Year might bring. Getting on track with work, with her passion, would be a really good start. Everything was beginning to come together; even family rifts were beginning to heal.

Cleo appeared out back, a serious look on her face. 'I've got an idea. I don't know why we didn't think of it sooner.'

'Go on...'

'I'm thinking you and I could sit down together and work out a business plan of sorts. Even though you're already getting dress-making work, it isn't much, right?'

'It wouldn't pay the bills, no.' She'd already thought it might take a while before she was able to transition.

'What I'm proposing is – we go into business together. Here.'

'Here? At the store?'

'When Finn goes you'll have the spare room back, yes? Dylan and I can take some of my paraphernalia to our house and store it in the garage. It'll give us a reason to clear it out and get rid of the junk we've been hoarding. You can launch your dressmaking business from the apartment with a bit more space, clients could come in via the Little Knitting Box and go upstairs to you.'

'But the store is crazy busy already.'

Cleo pulled a face. 'Like I said, we need to make a proper plan. But what do you think of the idea, in theory?'

'I'm a little bit excited, in theory,' she said cautiously.

'I haven't completely thought about the logistics yet, but you'd have a good place to advertise here – when people come in they'll see whatever display we have for you and you'll get business that way. There isn't an alteration store in Inglenook Falls either and only last week I heard someone in the café moaning about that.'

'Dylan isn't going to be happy with me. This is going to add to your workload.'

'Dylan thinks the world of you, he'll be happy enough, and I don't think it'll add too much. And sometimes we're here in the store minding it but don't have a heap of customers so perhaps in those lulls I could help out with your dressmaking, even if it's just contacting clients or dealing with accounts, and vice versa if you're quiet, you can turn more to the yarn side of things. It means that I might not need another assistant, at least not full time, if we can manage the bulk of it ourselves. Then, if your business takes off as I'm sure it will, we can reassess arrangements. Go with the flow.'

'Go with the flow,' Kaisha repeated with a confidence she was beginning to really feel.

When Amelia and Nathan rapped on the door, Cleo grabbed her coat. 'There's lots to think about.' She hugged Kaisha tight. 'But do you think you'd be interested? I don't want to push you into anything you're not happy with.'

'Just try and stop me.' Kaisha couldn't believe it; she'd been dreading telling Cleo, and now look what they were doing: talking about going into business together!

'This Christmas is going to be perfect.' Cleo wound her scarf around a second time and flicked out her hair from beneath.

'Starting with your wedding.'

'I'm marrying the man of my dreams.' She twirled on the spot like a kid.

'Go on, don't keep your friends waiting. And Cleo… thank you.'

Cleo gave her one more hug before she tugged open the door to the store. 'I'll see you at my bachelorette party tonight!'

'Can't wait. And I hope you don't mind, but I asked Bree to come along.'

'Then I can't wait to meet her.' She almost bumped into Finn coming through the door and gave him a hug too.

'What was that about?' he grinned when Cleo went on her way. 'She's in a good mood. I thought she wasn't keen on me and now she's hugging me!'

'Long story.' But she didn't get a chance to tell it because Dylan came into the store at the same time as his cell phone emitted a jazzy ringtone. And judging by his face when he answered the call and the staccato speech as he took in information that didn't sound good, she'd have to save her tale for another day. 'Trouble?' she asked Dylan.

'You could say that. That was the wedding cake designer. There was a fire.'

'That's terrible,' said Finn. 'Is she okay?'

'She's fine, everyone got out, but the business – and that includes our wedding cake – has gone.' He swore and then apologised for his language. 'This is all we need. I mean, I'm glad everyone is safe, but the wedding is in two days. Mind if I commandeer the phone out back and call a couple of places? I have to find something.'

'Go for it,' Kaisha told him and ushered him past the cash register to go out back. 'Are you going to tell Cleo?'

Dylan stopped in his tracks. 'She's only just started to believe this will all go without a hitch.'

'She spent so long choosing that cake,' Kaisha murmured when Dylan began calling around and she smiled to a customer who came through the door.

'Did she have her heart set on something special?' Finn wondered when the customer was busy browsing through the selection of knitting patterns.

'I don't know the details, but I imagine so. And I also know that wedding cakes take forever to make.'

'Depends what sort you have, and usually they take ages because the baker has other clients to please as well.'

She shook her head. 'What a total nightmare. I feel terrible not telling her, but perhaps Dylan is right. Maybe she won't care about having no cake once the day arrives and she's married. I'd offer to do it myself, but I'm a terrible cook.'

'You did mention that once,' Finn smiled. 'Mind if I make a suggestion?'

'Anything.'

'Let me do it.'

'You? Are you serious? I'm not sure she'd be hugging you if we let you do it.'

'I have hidden talents, Kaisha.'

'I'm sure you do.'

'Actually, he does.' Dylan came out from the back and caught the tail end of their conversation. 'I've seen what he can do.'

Kaisha began to laugh before she realised Dylan meant it and the look the pair shared said there was more to this than she realised. 'Are you sure you want to do it?' she asked Finn. 'Are you sure it's a good idea to let him?' she directed to Dylan.

Dylan looked so serious Kaisha wondered what the big deal was. She looked from one man to the other and back again.

'I can do it,' Finn reiterated. And when Dylan nodded his assent, he turned to Kaisha. 'And take that look of surprise off your face, have a little faith.'

'If you say so.'

'And let's keep it between us three,' said Dylan. 'That way by the time Cleo sees the cake we'll be married and she probably won't care what it is.'

'Thanks,' Finn joked.

'You know what I mean.' Dylan tapped Finn on the shoulder. 'I owe you big time for this.'

'No you don't.'

'Yes, I really do.'

Kaisha, still bewildered at what was left unsaid between the two men, and still doubtful of her roommate's hidden talents, gave Finn the go-ahead to completely take over the kitchen in the apartment. A quick call to Mitch saw Finn with the rest of the day off and by the time Kaisha finished work at the store and sneaked off up to the apartment without letting on to Cleo, Finn was well underway with his project. Kaisha only hoped he didn't make a mess of it.

'Make yourself useful,' he told her when she appeared in the doorway. 'Tell me where the oven gloves are or the cakes will be burnt.'

She took them out from the tiny shelf below the bottom cupboard that housed the pans. She found an apron on the same shelf and handed it to him.

'You're serious?' he laughed. 'It's pink.'

'You'll get cake mix all over your clothes if you don't put it on.'

He loved it when she got all bossy. 'I'll take my chances.'

The tiny kitchen looked as though a world war might well have taken place with ingredients and utensils littering the surfaces.

Finn's jeans already had flour on them and the milk he'd spilt in the corner was now dripping to the floor.

Kaisha stepped back to give him space to pull out three separate cakes from the oven. And when he was done, puzzled, she observed the sponges sitting on the cooktop. 'They don't look very round to me. Cleo's cake choice was traditional, three layers, all circular, all different – one chocolate, one carrot cake, the other red velvet.'

'Who's cooking here?'

'You, but...'

'No buts, trust me on this. I'm thinking a little differently but I know she'll like it.'

Kaisha wasn't so sure. She watched as he inserted a thin metal rod into each cake, satisfied when it came out clean. 'What can I do?'

'Until it's time to ice, nothing, just make sure she doesn't come up here and if she does, it's your job to send her away quickly.'

'She won't come up, she's busy organising drinks for tonight's party. You still going to Dylan's?'

'Of course. And both Mitch and Holly have shaken off the colds they had so it's a germ-free zone.'

'That's good, in time for the wedding and for Christmas.'

He mopped up the spills, cleaned down the counter, and looked at his watch. 'I hope I make it to the party in time for the strip-pergram.'

'You didn't!'

Grinning, he said, 'No, course not, and nobody else has either. It'll be a sedate night, a few beers, that's all Dylan wants. The guy has four kids to go home to as well as in-laws lurking, he'll be on his best behaviour. Kind of why I led him astray that night at the hotel; it was my only chance.'

'What are you doing now?' He'd gathered up a bag and headed for the living room.

'The cakes need to cool.'

'I might be a rubbish cook but even I know that.'

'Scissors?' he asked, opening the drawers of the bureau.

Kaisha found them for him, plus a knife from the kitchen, and by the time she got back to the table in the living room near the Christmas tree it was as though he was in the middle of a full-on arts and crafts project.

'I hope Cleo doesn't mind me raiding one of the boxes and using her supplies for this.' He picked up a ruler and a pencil.

'I'm sure she won't if you pull this off.' When he gave her a wry grin she asked, 'What exactly are you making?'

'You'll see.' Using the ruler as a guide he drew lines and then cut pieces from tubular polystyrene, other bits from the green, spongy foam usually used for flower arrangements, and after he'd turned each cake out to cool in the kitchen and Kaisha made some coffees, he had a structure of sorts. 'My work for today is done,' he announced.

'That's it? Forgive me for panicking but, on behalf of Cleo, I am.' He didn't look any closer to coming up with something that resembled a wedding cake.

He turned back with a grin as he went to deposit his empty coffee cup in the sink. 'As I said, have a little faith. Now, I've got a bachelor party to get ready for. But how about we meet in this kitchen tomorrow afternoon and I'll finish the masterpiece?'

'You're way too confident. Should I be worried?'

'Not at all.' And when he reached out to give her shoulder a squeeze she got an unexpected jolt of electricity that stayed with her while she got ready to go out herself.

17

FINN

Every swing of the axe hurt his head the next morning but the fresh air of the Christmas tree farm was probably the best thing for a fuggy brain following a late night at the little log cabin. It had been a great occasion with friends, old and new, and Finn was surprised at how much he'd felt a part of it all. And Dylan was more than happy with his plans for the wedding cake, which Cleo still had no idea about.

'How you doing?' Mitch gathered up some of the chopped wood, bagged it, and set it near the kiosk at the top of the fields. There weren't many sales of Christmas trees this close to the big day but with the cold coming in thick and fast over Connecticut, firewood was selling like nobody's business.

'This is the last of what we have so far.' Finn didn't feel the cold much out here, not when he was working so hard, but this morning there'd been a distinct layer of frost across the entire town, snow had fallen as he enjoyed his first coffee of the day, and more was predicted this evening.

'Plenty more to chop if you're up to it.'

'As long as I'm away by midday, happy to.'

Mitch shook his head, the hint of a smile. 'I thought Dylan was winding me up last night when he said you were saving the day by making a wedding cake.'

When Mitch went off to fetch more wood for chopping, Finn looked out across the fields. This place would be amazing under several feet of snow. He loved the city vibe, the glory of travelling, but in its own unique way Inglenook Falls appeared to be a little slice of heaven.

By midday he was free to go and acted as casual as he could when he passed through the Little Knitting Box to get to the apartment. He'd learnt to bang off his shoes in the gutter on the street outside so he didn't traipse through dirt, and Kaisha gave him a knowing look when he arrived back. She was only doing a half day before she shut the store, which was quiet already. Cleo was looking forward to going home early too, to do last-minute preparations with only one day more before her big day.

'This time tomorrow I'll be at the Corbridge Hotel spa being pampered,' Cleo announced to them both.

'Sounds all right to me.' Maybe the fact Dylan had remained intact following the bachelor party had lowered her guard some more when it came to his wayward friend who she'd been wary of before. 'You're all set for the big day?'

'I am. And, Finn, I want to say thank you. For being here for Dylan. It means the world to him to have you as his best man and I know you aren't always keen to stay in one place for too long.'

'I don't know, Inglenook Falls has a way of growing on you, doesn't it?'

'It sure does.' Before he walked through the back room she called after him again, 'I hope we'll be seeing more of you in the New Year.'

He smiled back at her. 'I guess we'll have to see.' It had been a long time since he'd settled in the one place, a while since he'd been so close to the town where he grew up, but slowly pieces were falling into place.

Upstairs he got organised in the kitchen and it wasn't long before Kaisha joined him and pulled on the pink apron she'd tried to have him wear yesterday.

'Suits you way better than me,' he concluded. 'Now keep watch and make sure Cleo doesn't come up here. I don't want to spoil the surprise.'

'I want to help, give me a job to do.'

'You can mix the buttercream, once I've started it off.' He concentrated, cutting the red velvet sponges into the shapes he needed: a rectangular base; a longer, thinner rectangle at the top; smaller wedges to build up one side of the structure.

'I'm still curious as to what you're making. What's with all the bits of polystyrene and foam? I'm pretty sure Cleo had a summer flower arrangement in the store last year using the same stuff, so I don't know if she'd be happy with it being used for her wedding cake.'

'You're not very patient.' He had all the pieces he needed. Time for assembly, although he was kind of enjoying the attention, her desperation to know more. Or maybe for Kaisha it was more the worry of whether he'd make a mess of this and ruin Cleo's day. He took the room-temperature butter and put it in a bowl.

'Where did you find the electric whisk?'

'I borrowed it from Enid at the café.'

'I didn't know you were friends.'

'I used my charms, what can I say?' He put the whisk onto the butter, holding the body of the equipment. 'You want to make a start?'

'Can I?'

'Of course. Just don't mess it up.' Their hands touched for a brief moment as she took hold of the whisk from him and he stood to the side, but not too far; he needed to make sure every element of this cake was spot on.

'How long do we do this for?' she asked over the sound of the whirring implement.

He remembered Mackenzie using the electric whisk too, giggling away when she accidentally lifted it out when it was on and sprayed mixture everywhere. Lost in his reverie, he didn't answer Kaisha's question until she repeated it. 'Five minutes,' he told her. 'It'll make it light and airy, much nicer.' He made her pause on a couple of occasions so he could scrape down the bowl to ensure everything was beaten evenly.

Once the butter looked as though it had reached the desired colour and texture, they added the sifted icing sugar gradually, combining each time, added a little milk but not too much as he wanted this thick so it would stick the pieces together and be a good base for the fondant.

As he put pieces of sponge onto the shape he'd constructed, pressing them together with buttercream between, Kaisha watched him. 'Know what it is yet?' She'd been observing closely as his arm skilfully moved along with a hand that worked more delicately, using the red velvet sponge, the polystyrene, the green, spongy foam.

She screwed up her nose. 'Honestly? It looks a bit of a mess.'

He laughed hard. 'There's a way to go yet, believe me.' He fashioned another piece of the sponge along the top of a section of cardboard and then began to cover the entire shape in buttercream.

'Wait a minute. Are you... are you making a sewing machine?'

'Took you long enough to get it.'

'That's...' She seemed lost for words. 'Well, I'm impressed, that's all.'

He leaned over the cake structure to cover the other side in buttercream. She was hovering behind him and he wondered what it would be like to turn round right now, so close. She'd be unable to move because she'd be sandwiched between him and the cupboard at the end of the room.

He got his focus back. 'Could you open the fridge for me?' She did the honours and he slotted the structure inside, on the top shelf he'd already cleared.

'What happens now? It's the shape of a sewing machine but it doesn't really look like one. I mean, it's the wrong colour for a start.'

'You just said you were impressed.'

She pulled a face.

He scraped the very edges of the bowl to get the remains of the buttercream as they stood there. 'The buttercream will allow a fondant layer to sit smoothly on top and it'll help it stick. But for now, the buttercream has to set a little. So we get to enjoy this...' He held out the spatula for her to take some of the buttercream off and with the bowl in her hands she had no choice but to lean closer and open her mouth. Her eyes rolled at the heavenly taste and she cradled the bowl in the crook of her arm so she could take the spatula herself to enjoy the rest.

He did his best not to watch her lips as she tasted more of the creamy mixture from the spatula and wiped down the counter, ready for the next stage.

She leaned against the kitchen counter after dropping the spatula into the sink. 'That was amazing, you've got quite a talent.'

'You haven't seen the finished product yet.'

'I'm looking forward to it. How long do we need to leave the cake for?'

'A couple of hours.'

'I'd better go down to the store for a while, make sure Cleo doesn't come up.'

'Of course.' If he didn't know better, he'd say she was trying to get away from him, but for once he suspected it wasn't because she didn't like him, but rather that she did. Or was he being too cocky? Too much like his former self? 'If you come up in a couple of hours you can watch me finish, check out the fondant pincushion I'm making, the lettering, the reel of cotton.'

'If you'd told me when you first arrived that you were a master baker, I'd have laughed at you.'

'And now?' He leaned on the door jamb of the kitchen as she opened the door to the apartment ready to take the stairs back down into the store.

But she just smiled and went on her way, leaving him to wonder whether, without knowing it, he'd stumbled upon something or someone that made staying in this town or New York for a while worth it after all.

* * *

True to her word, Kaisha was back again a couple of hours later as he was adding food dye to the fondant for the main cake. He wanted to replicate the sewing machine Cleo had in the store downstairs as closely as possible so the main body of the machine would be black, and he'd already set aside other portions of the fondant to make a few accessories.

'Not very wedding-y,' Kaisha commented of the colour. 'Unless Cleo was a goth, of course.'

'What colour is the Singer sewing machine in the store?'

'Okay, I see your point. How will you do the gold writing and design?'

He indicated the jar of gold leaf and a thin brush he'd use to do the embossed writing and design details.

At last she seemed to feel confident in his abilities. 'I really think she's going to love it.' Her voice caught and he looked up as the fondant showed no signs of having any white remaining.

'I thought it would be meaningful. That's why I chose this design.'

'It's so much better than a traditional wedding cake. I don't think she ever thought of having anything different. But this is special, unique to her.'

'It's part of what I love about baking. The element of surprise, making something for someone that represents who they really are.'

'Can I ask you a question?'

'Shoot.'

'What's with the bumblebee tattoo?' It was poking out from the sleeve of his T-shirt, moving every time his muscles tensed and relaxed as he worked.

'My sister, Mackenzie.'

'She loved bumblebees?'

'Totally. She was obsessed by them, never understood it myself. I made her a bumblebee cake for her birthday.'

'Special and unique for her.' She'd read his mind.

'I haven't done much baking since.'

He worked in near silence as he rolled out the fondant and then laid it carefully over the top of the cake before trimming it, folding it and smoothing it down in all the right places. Baking since they'd lost Mackenzie had been too painful and maybe one day he'd share his feelings with Kaisha, but not right now; he didn't want to scare her off, not when he was only just processing his emotions himself. He'd thought making this cake now might have been too much, brought back too many painful memories, but it hadn't. In fact, it had worked the opposite way as he'd lost himself in the task, buzzed on the thrill of it for the first time in far too long. Dylan knew what a big ask this was and Finn couldn't wait to tell his buddy that rather than being a chore, this had been an absolute pleasure.

'I'm glad you told me,' said Kaisha. 'About Mackenzie.'

He exchanged a smile with her, washed his hands, and stopped Kaisha before she put the cake in the fridge. 'Not now it has the fondant. On the table in the living room will do, it's cool in there – as long as you don't put it near the heater.'

She obliged and he picked up more of the fondant when she returned. 'Time to make the accessories. This piece' – he held up a ball – 'will be a pincushion.' He held up another. 'This is going to be a square of material to go beneath the needle.' He held up a third piece. 'And this will be the cotton reel.'

She watched him work, explanations accompanying hands that toyed with the edible models, added colour appropriately, and before long they had one pincushion and one square of blue and pink material to go beneath the needle. 'Now for the reel of cotton.' He used one colour for the plastic reel and Kaisha had fun rolling out the red line of cotton, getting the fondant so thin it broke off more than once. 'Shove it back together and carry on,' he advised.

'How professional,' she joked, and before long her cotton thread made of fondant went all the way from one end of the counter to the other.

'You want to wind it round the reel I've made?'

'You know, this is more art than cooking, so no wonder I haven't messed it up,' she said as she focused on getting the red cotton around the reel.

He leaned closer to ensure it was looking the same as he expected. 'You make a good assistant.' When she looked at him briefly, her smile faded. He could see the shimmer in her eyes where the lights shone down and caught the rich hazel of them that had once been wary but now seemed open and trusting. He was so close all he had to do was reach out, put his hand beneath her chin, tilt her mouth upwards, kiss her.

But a knock at the door changed all that.

'Quick, it might be Cleo,' Finn instructed, panicking the surprise would be spoiled.

'Relax, she won't come in uninvited.' She closed the kitchen door behind her but peeked around it less than a minute later. 'You were right, it *was* Cleo. She's gone downstairs again, but I need to go help out.'

'I'll finish up. I'll cover this in the living room on the table before I head to the city.'

'You're out tonight?'

'Grandad has us all meeting at his apartment in the morning, early, so I'll head to Manhattan and stay the night with him. Don't worry,' he smiled, 'the cake will be done.'

'I was thinking more about whether you'll be back in time for the wedding.'

'Don't stress.' He positioned the reel of cotton on top of the spool he'd made out of plastic dowel and trimmed to size. 'I'll be on time.'

'The snow's coming down.' She moved to the kitchen window, a tiny pane of glass that gave just enough light from that direction. 'No wonder Cleo's in a flap. It's not often she's so busy she calls on me so easily. I thought she'd have gone home by now. I'd better get down there.'

'There's no snow forecast after midnight, so I'm sure it won't be a problem.'

Kaisha looked at the cake again. 'It's really special, Finn. It'll mean the world to Cleo, and to her gramps when he sees it. I can't wait to see her reaction. You've saved the day in a big way.'

'Time to focus.' He picked up the jar of gold leaf and the brush. Time to stop thinking about what he'd like to do with Kaisha, anyway. He wanted to wrap his arms around her, kiss her... and, well, a whole lot more that wouldn't help finish a wedding cake.

* * *

The next morning dawned and Finn had forgotten how uncomfortable it was sleeping on the floor at his grandad's apartment, but for once, without quite so much stress at the thought of seeing his parents now they were at least making a start at pushing through to the other side of their grief by talking for once in their lives, it didn't seem so bad.

Grandad was already up and about. Finn had woken to the sound of the coffee machine and the smell of the grounds infiltrating the apartment. His feet poked out from beneath the blankets and it reminded him of his childhood, the excitement Christmas brought with it, him and Mackenzie whispering to each other late at night about what Santa was going to bring them, their parents calling up the stairs to tell them to go to sleep. Of course he'd long known the big dude wasn't real, but he'd loved every second of going back to the days when he still believed, carrying it on for his kid sister that little while longer.

He turned onto his back the best he could, hands clasped behind his head as Grandad pottered in the kitchen. He looked up at the ceiling. Mackenzie was gone. But his family were gradually coming back to him. And although the same magic no longer existed in the holiday season, he felt closeness for the first time in years and the promise of more. He checked the time on his watch. Dylan's wedding was still another eight hours away, which meant he had plenty of time for family before he had to get the train back to Inglenook Falls, pick up the rings from the back of the wardrobe where he'd hidden them, get dressed, and be best man to a buddy who'd always been there for him even though he'd kept him at a distance over the years. When they'd lost Mackenzie, Finn hadn't seen that the whole neighbourhood suffered an unimaginable pain too but last night he'd talked to his grandad about it. They'd recalled names of other families living in the same street, Grandad had told him of the condolences that came their way, the tears others shed, the help that had rallied around the family. The neighbourhood kids had played together a lot, outside in the street, kicking the football, taking turns to keep watch for cars as they practised their baseball pitching and batting. They'd all run to the ice-cream truck when it cruised the neighbourhood, all gathered to see the Christmas lights every year, and Finn had never really allowed himself to see anyone else's grief apart from his own, and that included his parents'.

He staggered into the kitchen area rubbing his arms as the apartment did its best to warm up. 'You should've stayed in bed a bit longer, Grandad, it's early.'

Grandad was standing at the window, right up close to the glass, looking up at the patch of sky beyond the height of the buildings. He looked tired, yet somehow content. But Finn was still worried he was overdoing things. 'I love this city in the early hours when it's quiet and still dark.'

Finn retrieved his phone from the counter and scrolled through the photos on there. 'I wanted to show you something, didn't get a chance last night after our chat.'

Grandad's hand shook but he took the phone to see pictures of Cleo's wedding cake. 'Did you do this?' A slow grin spread across his face.

'I did.'

'Oh, where have they gone?' He handed the device back.

The phone had died, the screen was black. 'Should've charged it last night,' Finn cursed.

'I'm impressed, Finn. Your talents are still there.'

'First time I've made anything like that in years.'

'And now I know.'

'Know what?'

He reached out and touched a cold hand to Finn's cheek. 'That's how I know that you, your mom, and your dad are all telling the truth. I know you've all spent a good amount of time with one another because how else would you have finally processed your grief and moved forwards? That cake is what tells me.'

'We all thought it a crazy idea of yours at first.'

'Of course you did. But you were all in a bad place. I couldn't stand by and let that happen any more.'

'It was wrong to blame Dad and his attitude for everything, it was as much my choice to stop baking as it was his remarks.'

'You need to tell him so.'

'Maybe later, not this morning. I don't want to get into any arguments.'

Grandad nodded. 'They've been meeting up, you know.'

'Who?' Finn poured the coffee. 'Mom and Dad?' Grandad looked like he had more to say. 'What aren't you telling me?'

'I won't gossip but let's just say Byron is no longer on the scene.'

Finn wasn't sorry. 'Mom can do better.'

'Paige has been having an affair.'

'No way.' The coffee jug paused mid-air as Finn shook his head. 'How's Dad?'

'Less bothered than you would expect.'

They shared a conspiratorial look of relief. Neither Byron nor Paige had been a welcome addition to the clan, neither ever seemed to quite fit, even in the mess that was their family. Finn handed Grandad his coffee. 'Drink up before Mom and Dad get here and tell you you can't have it.' Finn looked through his things to find a charger and cursed when he couldn't find it – he must have left it in Inglenook Falls. It turned out Grandad didn't have the same cable so Finn had him message his dad to bring his along this morning, picked up his coffee, and headed for the shower.

'Finn...' Grandad had lowered himself into his favourite chair.

'Yep?'

'I've given my solicitor instructions, the will is back as it should be.'

'I was never worried about that anyway.'

His eyes met Finn's. 'Funny, that's what your dad said. All he was worried about was you.'

Finn swallowed hard. He'd misjudged his dad over the years when they both should've faced up to their problems and worked through them together. He'd be eternally grateful to Grandad for stepping in before it was too late and they pushed each other so far away they could never be a family again.

'Do me a favour?' Grandad leaned his head back against the chair. 'Put the music on that's in the CD player.'

He left his grandad with the sounds of Chopin. The first track, according to the CD case beside the player, was 'Winter Wind' and when Finn glanced in after his shower his Grandad had already shut his eyes, perhaps thinking about today, about Christmas, about his family once again bonding together in a way they hadn't in years.

Finn dressed in jeans and an ink-coloured sweater and took his empty coffee cup through to the kitchen. He'd come back in a couple of days and give the whole place a clean. Beryl was doing her bit but what they needed to do was pull out cabinets, go through Grandad's old things, and give it an early spring clean. Usually when he'd been somewhere this long, Finn was already thinking about moving on, but this time his mind was in a whole new place.

'Grandad.' Finn touched his shoulder lightly. 'You're tired, why don't you go back to bed?' His cup of coffee remained untouched on the side table and Grandad groaned, he was pretty much asleep in the chair anyway. 'Let me take you there, we've got plans later, remember? I'll wake you in time for breakfast. We can make it more of a brunch.'

His grandad smiled up at him. 'I was looking out at the snow. Only a light fall, but enough, don't you think?'

When had that started? 'It's beautiful.' And oddly enough he meant it this morning.

'Mackenzie would've loved it.'

'That she would.' He helped him towards the bedroom.

'You're a good kid, Finn.' Once the tall man, the sprightly grandad who'd always taken the stairs up to the apartment two at a time when Finn's legs weren't long enough to do it himself, he seemed tiny now. Finn and Mackenzie had looked up to him as kids, they'd taken his hand as they walked down the street, but now it was as though the roles were reversed.

'Don't go getting all emotional now,' Finn joked, helping him off with his slippers before he lay back on the bed. 'We'll keep the noise down when Mom and Dad get here, I'll wake you to eat.'

'And then we'll go out to Central Park.'

'Of course.' Although he wasn't sure it was a good idea with the plummeting temperatures.

Grandad had wanted them all together for this one meal. When Finn's parents arrived, they talked in the living room to give Grandad a chance to sleep, and then, when it was time, worked together in the tiny kitchen. They pulled together ingredients for French toast, they baked apple turnovers, the waffle iron his dad brought with him was at the ready, fruit and syrup toppings lining the table that his mum had dressed in red and gold with the box full of accessories she'd found. She'd used the silver cutlery Grandad still had in a box but which rarely saw the light of day, and when Finn woke his grandad from slumber, he didn't miss the look on his face at the perfect Christmas room in his pre-war apartment, all there for him with every person he loved.

'Do you like it?' Beverly took Grandad's hands. 'I hope I didn't overstep too much and go over the top.'

'You wouldn't be you if you didn't, Beverly.' And when he spoke there was no resentment, just pleasure at the company of family. 'Tell me one thing… do I get first dibs on the waffles?'

She wrapped her arms around him. 'You sure do. Finn, wait your turn,' she said pre-empting his remark.

'Do you have your cell phone charger?' Finn asked his dad.

'In my coat pocket.'

Finn retrieved it, set his cell onto charge, and joined in the family banter. The late breakfast was filled with chatter and laughter and so much food Finn was glad he wouldn't have to sit down to Christmas dinner today – having the wedding much later on would be a welcome relief to his stomach. Grandad hadn't eaten all that much apart from one waffle and some fresh fruit, along with a small glass of juice and another of water, but still the food had dwindled before them. They'd played a few games of cards, clearing the breakfast debris to one end of the table, Finn and his mum had washed everything up, and by the time they came back into the living room, Grandad was ordering Andy to find his coat, scarf, and gloves.

'It's freezing out there,' said Finn. 'Are you really sure about going?'

'I've been a New Yorker longer than you've been alive, don't tell me about winter. I could tell you a few stories about winters that would make your toes curl.'

Finn supposed it was a good sign that Grandad wanted to get out because he hadn't in days. Beverly fussed over whether he had enough layers on, Andy was still debating whether this was a good idea, but all three of them knew it was no good arguing. Grandad had a taxi booked already and as they bundled inside and made the short journey to Central Park, Grandad told them about the worst blizzard he'd ever experienced, making even the taxi driver gasp in shock.

'It paralyzed the city, the whole place shut down. It was just me and your mom in the apartment,' he told Andy, patting his hand and then keeping a hold of it. 'She was carrying you at the time; I waited on her hand and foot, terrified you'd come early and we wouldn't be able to get any help. She calmed me down, told me we had each other, we'd cope with whatever came our way. That's what families do.

'Your mom and I came here in winter as much as we could,' Grandad continued as they reached the park, left the taxi, and made their way inside. 'It was her favourite place as much as mine. When she died, I never stopped coming; it made me feel close to her. That's why I needed to be here today.'

In such a sombre moment nobody said much more as they walked, taking in the beauty of the park that never ceased to amaze Finn. He patted his pockets about to take a few photos with his cell phone when he realised he'd left it on charge back at Grandad's. He checked his watch. Still plenty of time to make the trip to Inglenook Falls, get those rings, change his clothes, and make it to the wedding out in Bampton. The main roads were all fine, he'd checked on Grandad's iPad twice already.

'Let me take some pictures,' said Beverly, jostling them all together, three generations of Thompson men, snow falling in the background.

'You need to be in it too, Beverly.' Grandad coughed and Andy found a drink from the bag he'd brought with him. 'What is it you kids call them?' he asked Finn when he'd recovered. 'Where you're all in the photograph, someone holds the phone.'

'A selfie,' Finn grinned.

They had a laugh trying to all squeeze together but Finn got it on the first take. The beauty of the lake behind them, four faces close to the lens grinning as though everything in their world was right at last.

'I love this place,' his mum declared, taking a deep breath in of the freezing New York air, letting it out just as slowly, as she and Finn walked on from the others. 'He looks worn out,' she said of Grandad, who stood with Finn's dad a short distance away not wanting to go any further. Grandad's arm was linked with his son's as they looked out over the lake, an oasis of calm in the warmer months and no less remarkable now. 'He's putting on a good front but we're not fools.'

'We're not,' Finn agreed. 'I've been worried about him too, but you try telling him to stay indoors.'

She laughed. 'I wouldn't even waste my breath.'

They walked around the curved edge of the lake to look out over the water from their position too. 'I'm glad he forced us all to spend time together.'

'It wasn't your grandad.'

'What are you talking about?'

'It was all your dad's idea. He enlisted your grandad's help because he thought it was the only way you'd agree to it. He told me a few days ago – he probably knew that I wouldn't go along with it either if I thought it came from him.'

'Wow.' Finn stared at the water, not frozen over, not completely, but cold enough that if you touched the surface its temperature would bite, if you tried to stand on the frozen parts of its surface there was a chance you'd fall through.

'Your dad and I, we've both been guilty of letting things get so bad. But losing a child… well, it broke us.'

Finn didn't say anything; how could he? He wasn't a parent, he had no idea how it felt. Children were supposed to outlive their parents by decades. Mackenzie had been robbed of so much. They all had.

'We weren't good parents after Mackenzie died. We weren't good at anything much apart from fighting. Bickering, disagreeing, shouting, it all masked our pain and we shouldn't have let it. Your dad and grandad put together the plan – you'd do anything for your grandad and they both knew it.'

'They're not wrong there.'

'Please tell me you're not upset they did this.'

'I might have been had I known earlier,' Finn admitted. 'I might have felt manipulated, I probably would've walked away from the lot of you. But I'm glad I didn't.' He put an arm around his mum's shoulders. When had he last done that? And as she finally relaxed against him, he looked over at his dad. The man he'd despised for years for making a mess of the family. He hadn't been able to see the hurt his dad had felt himself, hadn't recognised that just like him, his dad hid the pain from anyone who cared. They were very similar in that regard. But now, he was proud. Proud his parents, particularly his dad, had turned this around.

'We love you very much, Finn,' said his mum as she stood back. She let a low laugh escape. 'I thought these so-called bonding experiences would be the end of all of us.'

'Me too, especially the ice-skating.'

'And that turned out to be the best thing we've done together in a very long time.' She was looking at him now, full of hope and the joy of the season. 'Your dad and I let you down, we let each other down.'

'What's going on with you two? You seem to be closer after all of this.' He'd noticed the odd look pass between them, the occasional tentative touch as though it were the two of them in a bubble separated from anyone else.

She shrugged. 'I don't really know, but at least we can be in a room together without arguing.'

'A room? I'm just happy you can both be within ten blocks of each other without a fight breaking out.'

'You always did like to exaggerate, Finn,' she smiled in good humour.

His dad came over with Grandad and slowly they made their way back to where the taxi was waiting for them. Grandad had swatted away any attempts to pay, he said he'd already dealt with that, including recompensing the driver for hanging around.

'Hot chocolates?' Beverly asked the second they bundled inside the apartment.

Grandad took his layers off with Finn's help and looked at Beverly. 'We're not three years old.'

'Mackenzie said it wasn't Christmas without hot chocolate,' said Andy.

'She always did say that,' Finn confirmed, sharing a look with his dad that conveyed respect, a fresh start.

'And marshmallows,' Grandad remembered fondly. 'Right then, hot chocolate it is.'

'Made from scratch, might I add?' said Andy.

'Do we have everything we need?' Finn wasn't sure he'd seen any supplies but when his mum brandished another bag filled with ingredients that would meet Mackenzie's approval, he grinned.

Grandad was already in his favourite chair and the three of them set about organising the hot chocolates. Milk was measured out, they found some cream to dollop on the top, Andy laid out marshmallows onto plates, and they chatted about some of their favourite Christmases over the years, making sure Mackenzie was a part of their banter, gone but never ever forgotten. Always a part of them.

And with mugs filled to the brim with chocolate mixture, they'd remember her again as they sat with Grandad in the time-worn apartment he so cherished. In the apartment that today had so much love inside that Finn no longer felt the urge to keep running from anything.

18

KAISHA

Kaisha had woken this morning with excitement in the pit of her stomach. She always did on Christmas Eve but with it being Cleo's wedding day too, she had an energy she couldn't describe. She'd slept really well after a bubble bath, an early night, and now she thought of that beautiful cake Finn had skilfully put together, a man she'd misjudged as someone arrogant, selfish, and who did little to invest in relationships at all.

She stayed in bed revelling in the bright day it must be outside with sun streaming through the gap where the drapes didn't quite meet. She thought about Finn, she remembered talking to Cleo about their potential business venture, and best of all, she and Bree had at last begun to make headway.

She switched on her phone to text the excited bride-to-be, but anxiety mounted when she saw four missed calls from Cleo.

This couldn't be good.

As she dialled her back she ran through all the potential disaster scenarios in her head – ripped wedding dress? A bad case of the jitters? Ruby playing up and refusing to go to the wedding?

Perhaps this was just a pre-wedding panic that not everything would go smoothly.

But it was nothing so simple.

Dylan had managed to hide the cake debacle from his soon-to-be wife by telling a white lie – that it had arrived at Bampton Lodge. He'd insisted he be the one to go check everything there was as it should be and Cleo had let him. The cake was still safely here upstairs in the apartment. Finn hadn't wanted to let it out of his sight, insisting on taking it to the venue himself.

But they couldn't hide this latest problem from anyone.

Kaisha looked out of the window in the living room as she spoke to Cleo. Inglenook Falls was picture perfect this morning. The markets across the fields were still visible but would likely be shut today given the conditions, the bandstand and tree on the green were still lit up but white powder had blasted both and even local kids weren't out yet. There were no footprints anywhere, Main Street looked gorgeous with stores' windows having a lining of snow that felt like Christmas all wrapped up in one beautiful package.

But picture perfect didn't make for good travel news. The main roads were fine from here to Bampton Lodge, but it was the long track leading directly to the venue that had issues.

'Heavy snow has caused a landslide, partially blocking the road,' Cleo told her. Her voice was calm at first, matter-of-fact, but as she continued, with each word she became more and more wound up. 'On top of that there was a leak in the reception room, which means the ceremony would have to be held in another part of the lodge, and the caterer coming from the other side of Bampton has no way of getting through. The lodge had suggestions for catering, they had ideas for the alternative reception room,' she garbled, 'but it would still be a risk for anyone coming to the venue from Inglenook Falls.'

'First things first,' said Kaisha. 'Deep breath.' She heard Cleo trying to do just that. 'Now, stop panicking.'

'How can you say that? I've been calling around, and nobody can fit us in. I tried the Corbridge Hotel but they have a function today, Darcy's offered the Inglenook Lodge, perhaps on the porch. I guess that might work. But then there's food… oh my God, the cake too!'

Kaisha couldn't let on about the cake, not yet. But her mind was ticking over and as Cleo's hopes of the perfect day continued to fade while she ranted, a plan to salvage their wedding day and give Cleo and Dylan the Happy Ever After that they deserved boiled to the surface. 'Can you put Dylan on the phone?'

'Why?'

'Just do it, I've got an idea.'

'And you won't tell me?'

'No chance. You know you have to let people help out more, so consider this one of those times. Dylan and I will deal with it. All you need to focus on is being pampered at the Inglenook Lodge as planned and we'll update your dad on where to bring you. Think of this as good practice if you and I go into business together, you'll have to trust me then.'

When Dylan came on the phone eventually after Cleo relinquished control, Kaisha told him what she had in mind.

'You know what, I think it'll work,' he said. Cleo was in the background organising the kids. 'I'll pack Cleo off to the Inglenook Lodge to be pampered – they've got hair and make-up going on there anyway, they'll all get dressed, and you and I will put this plan into action.'

'Are we really not going to tell her?' Suddenly she wasn't so sure.

'This is more fun. Kidding,' he added, as this really wasn't a time to joke. 'But it'll prove to her that she can trust other people, she always needs reminding of that, and I want her to be surprised. It's going to be incredible.'

Cleo's pleading in the background continued and Dylan was right, this was actually fun. And if the plan worked, it would be perfect.

Ever since seeing the cake Finn had pulled together, Kaisha should've known this was going to be a wedding to remember. She thought about it now, tried to imagine the look on Cleo's face when she saw it. Finn had added the gold leaf and it did indeed look spectacular. The Singer design and name was branded against the black fondant, Cleo and Dylan's names were etched on the board, a love heart with their initials had been drawn on the fondant material passing beneath the needle of the machine.

Cleo deserved this special day and perhaps the treacherous conditions leading up to Bampton Lodge would end up being a blessing for them all rather than a curse.

At least that's what she hoped.

* * *

'Let's do this.' Dylan had rallied together some helpers. Mitch was there at the ready, Nathan had left Amelia with the girls to come help and if Finn showed up soon, it would be all hands on deck. They'd put the time of the wedding back an hour to allow them time to get this all sorted. Cleo would, right now, be having a massage, getting a manicure, and relaxing as much as she could on her big day, trusting in those who loved her most.

At the Little Knitting Box it was all systems go. Kaisha had fired off another text to Finn telling him there was a change of plan but she'd had no response. She didn't suppose it mattered anyway, he'd be here in Inglenook Falls before long and they'd update him then.

Mitch, Nathan, and Dylan got started with snow shovels,

clearing the sidewalk outside the store. Luckily, with the snow being fresh it was loose enough that it didn't take too much to get rid of it. They went all the way along and then cleared the road, piling the white powder up the other side on the edge of the field. The markets, as predicted, were closed for the day and unlikely to get any visitors heading in this direction anyway. They cleared all the way along and around the corner and with no further adverse weather conditions predicted until much later – Kaisha only hoped that this time the report was correct – it should stay clear until they got this ceremony under way.

Kaisha, meanwhile, was in charge of the store. It wasn't a huge space but they'd make do. She took all the baskets of yarn upstairs to the apartment and dumped them in the living room. She left the wall ladders, she cleared all the sections in the hutches using empty boxes to transport yarns upstairs and she took everything off the shelves except for the Singer sewing machine because she knew Cleo would love it to be there for the ceremony. The cash register was a little more difficult to shift so Mitch helped her with that and when Holly stopped by with a whole heap of flowers in buckets, they left all of those in the store while they cleared the back room. They took up the table, the chairs, the boxes of paraphernalia, and Kaisha made a note to talk to Cleo when she returned from her honeymoon and persuade her they really needed to have a clear out. Probably not a bad idea if this business idea of hers was going to work as they'd need to encompass dressmaking in some capacity. She'd thought perhaps they could even add a mannequin in the store front with one of her own designs on it so people could see first-hand what her work was like.

Her mind back to the present, Kaisha was delighted to see so many people pitching in to help out today. Holly had sourced several outdoor heaters they could stand on the streets, Enid from the café had delivered a bucketful of mistletoe cuttings, Mitch had his helper Jude load in the remaining Christmas trees that had been felled but hadn't yet sold and now they lined the street beside the sidewalk to make an aisle for Cleo to walk down. Darcy had lent them extra twinkle lights, Mitch had taken down the sets he had lining the kiosk at the Christmas tree farm and of course they already had plenty in the Little Knitting Box, which was all decked out for Christmas.

At last the trees lining the aisle glowed with the soft white lighting against the pure green needles, the doorway to the store and the doorway leading out back were framed with lights, and the plan really was coming together.

'I still can't get hold of Finn.' It was Dylan, who came over when he saw Kaisha taking in their progress so far. 'He should be back by now.'

'Plenty of time, don't panic.' But Kaisha was worried too. Time had marched on as they began their preparations, and she was beginning to get a bad feeling.

But she couldn't let that stop them and she feigned nonchalance to keep Dylan calm.

White roses, lilies, and blue delphiniums were held together with silver mesh ribbon in bouquets dotted around the store. 'They're gorgeous,' she told Holly, who'd been the one to bring them all here. 'How did you manage to find them, with vases?'

'Darcy gave them to me.'

'I thought they looked familiar. The lodge looked so beautiful with them.'

'She was happy to donate them for the cause.'

'We'll get them back to her tonight. It'll be a champagne toast here once the happy couple are married, then time for everyone to warm up. She's holding the main reception at the Inglenook Lodge.'

'How are you for catering? Have you got it sorted?' Holly wondered.

Kaisha was pleased to share this snippet of news. 'My sister, Bree, is lending a hand. I called her in a flap. She's always been popular, always known a person who knows another person if you know what I mean. But then she reminded me of the jobs she's had helping out in kitchens over the years, the way she'd put on dinner parties when we were kids, and she's got the catering sorted. It's canapé style for the wedding for twenty-eight guests and she's promised a smorgasbord of treats – tempura prawns, camembert and cranberry twists, egg rolls...' She thought hard about all the items Bree had reeled off. '...mini fruit tartlets, mini turkey and cranberry pies, and something called mint-chocolate bites and a few other items I really can't remember.'

'You're smiling,' said Holly.

'I think this wedding is going to be fun, the food certainly sounds it. No input from the bride and groom, I just told Bree to go for it.'

'You trust her?'

Kaisha took a deep breath. 'She won't let me down.' And this time she said it with confidence as, true to form, a text message buzzed through as Holly and Kaisha were threading a few loose flowers up the wall ladders among the fairy lights already there. Kaisha showed Holly Bree's message attaching photos of all the food, made and ready to be boxed and brought up here.

'Your sister did good,' Holly smiled.

'She sure did,' Kaisha beamed, and so as not to get too senti-mental, added, 'The main roads are fine. Bree will deliver the food to the lodge soon and she and Darcy will get everything set up, discreetly while Cleo is having her hair and make-up done in one of the bedrooms.'

'You know, I've never heard much about your sister before,' said Holly, puzzled. 'It was lovely to meet her at the bachelorette party.'

'There are things that happened a while back. I won't bore you with the details, but we're moving past that.'

'I'm glad you're working on it,' said Holly. 'Family is important.' She reached out and rubbed the top of Kaisha's arm reassuringly. 'And so are friends. What you're doing for Cleo, it's nothing short of amazing.'

'She's been so good to me. It's the least I can do. I wonder if, once she's married, she'll stop stressing so much.' They shared a look. 'Maybe that's too hopeful; it's the way she's wired.'

Holly waved to Mitch, who was repositioning some of the trees so no branches protruded too much onto the sidewalk. They wouldn't want Cleo's dress to get caught up in them. 'How long do we have until the ceremony?'

'Two hours to go. And more snow is scheduled to fall around 9 p.m. – weather report says it's a one hundred per cent chance – for the rest of the night and well into Christmas Day. So everyone can get here, we'll have the reception over at the lodge, and by the time the snow starts anyone who isn't local will still be good to get home.'

'You've planned it well. And then tomorrow, as Mitch always says, he doesn't care if we're all snowed in.'

'Exactly.'

For the next couple of hours, Holly and Kaisha fine-tuned the decorations in the store where guests would stand. Cleo and Dylan would exchange vows beneath the doorway leading out back and glasses were lined up on a shelf, bottles of champagne were already in the fridge upstairs with ice buckets all ready to go. Once the ceremony was over, Darcy would head back to the Inglenook Lodge and get things ready and they'd shut the door to the Little Knitting Box, the snow could lightly fall and the happy party would be cocooned in a winter wonderland for a while.

Holly and Kaisha added some finishing touches: pine cones in all sizes, Mason jars filled with vibrant-red winter berries, silver twigs arranged in slender vases, a good cluster of mistletoe above the spot where Cleo and Dylan would stand, more dotted in jars around the store. Finn would be by Dylan's side soon enough, she hoped. She thought about how handsome he'd look and as she looked around the space, the magical wedding venue they'd created, her eyes misted with tears at the knowledge they'd almost pulled it off for two people who couldn't be more deserving.

She caught sight of Bree at the door to the store, her hand hovering tentatively on the glass ready to knock. Kaisha beckoned her in.

'It's all ready, the food is at the lodge,' Bree gushed straight away.

'Lovely to see you again, Bree.' Holly stepped off the stool after perfecting the mistletoe arrangement and moved on to busying herself sweeping out back where bits had fallen from twigs, scraps of ribbon they'd trimmed lay about.

Kaisha stood with her sister by the window to the store as the men brought the street and sidewalk to life.

'This is going to be a wedding to remember,' Bree smiled.

'Thank you. For saving the day with the food.'

'What are sisters for?' she smiled cautiously. 'And, I made some marshmallow penguins and snowman cookies.'

Kaisha grinned, remembering those from their childhood. 'You did?'

'Hey, strictly for the kids.' But she took out a container from her bag and when she opened up the lid, inside were two of each. 'If you can take a break for a minute, we could eat these before I head off?'

'Sounds good to me.' Kaisha went for the snowman cookie first. 'You always were the better cook.' She caught the crumbs from the cookie in her palm held beneath.

'Whereas you were shocking.'

'I wasn't that bad.' She paused before she popped the last of it in her mouth. 'Okay, I really was.'

When they'd finished the cookies, Bree put the container back in her bag. 'I'd better leave you to it, but all I can say is, wow. You might not be able to cook, but you've got the creative genes for sure.'

'Hey, why don't you hang around?'

'No, you're busy, you'll need to get ready soon, I assume. Have you bought something really special?'

'I've made something.'

'No way! Send me a photo?'

'Of course I will.'

Bree pulled open the door to the store. 'I'm sorry about the dress.' To Kaisha's puzzled look she added, 'The dress you made me and I sold on eBay. It was a terrible thing to do and very wrong of me, I should never have done it.'

'Bree...' Kaisha stopped her before she disappeared. 'I was wondering, what are you doing on New Year's?'

'No plans yet.'

'Want to do something together?'

'I'd love to.'

Kaisha made the first move and enveloped her sister in a hug. 'Merry Christmas, Bree.'

'Merry Christmas, Kaisha.'

When Bree went on her way, Kaisha recovered from the sentimentality as Holly came to join her.

'I've just thought, what about a wedding cake?' Holly wondered. 'Mitch said something about Finn saving the day at the last minute, but that can't be right. Did Bree make something?'

'No, Mitch got it right. But the cake is top secret for now, although I can assure you there is one and it's absolutely perfect.'

'I'm intrigued. About the cake… and Finn.'

'I don't know what you're talking about,' Kaisha grinned.

They stood back to look at the store and turned off the main lights. The whole space twinkled with magic, with promise, with happiness.

But when Kaisha caught sight of the Singer sewing machine sitting proudly on the shelf, she checked her watch.

Talking of Finn, where was he?

He should be here by now. But she had a terrible feeling he was going to let them down, and she really didn't want to be proved right.

19

KAISHA

Kaisha tried yet again to text Finn but got no answer.

She was getting frantic. She was ready, given the ceremony started in less than an hour, but where was he?

She thought of him as she carefully transported the cake downstairs to display in the back room before it would later be taken to the lodge, unless they decided to have cake with champagne here. It was, after all, a thrown-together, completely unconventional yet brilliantly special wedding.

Thinking about Finn, she swung from being worried to being furious and then back again. It would break Dylan's heart to not have his best man by his side, not to mention they had no rings for the ceremony.

A knock at the door to her apartment told her it was probably Dylan back again and she was right. 'Any news?' she asked.

'Not a thing. I've sent far too many texts, I feel like a stalker.'

She took a moment to smile. 'Dylan, you look so handsome.' Dressed in a well-tailored dark suit with a silver swirl leaf cravat, he didn't look at all nervous, just concerned.

'Why thank you. You, as always, look beautiful too.'

But the sentimentality didn't last. 'Where is he, Dylan?'

'I've no idea. I've texted, I've called, he just isn't replying. The trains are all running on time, there's no reason for him to be late.'

'Have you any idea where he put the rings? You know, in case he doesn't show?'

Dylan sighed. 'No idea. I was rather hoping you might.'

'Will we wait for him? Should we, do you think?'

'We can't. People are going to be outside for a while, it wouldn't be fair. Cleo's Grandpa Joe, for one, is too old to be doing that; even I don't want to linger that long in the cold.'

'You'll be waiting at the altar,' Kaisha pointed out. 'Warm and inside.'

'Good point. My head's all over the place.'

And the only person to blame for that now was Finn.

She was about to try his phone one more time when the door flew open.

'I'm here, I'm ready… well, almost,' came Finn's flamboyant announcement. 'Sorry, got held up. No need to panic.'

'Where the hell have you been?' Dylan scraped a hand through his hair. 'Are you all right?'

'All good, I assure you. Logistics, that's all.'

He smiled Kaisha's way but she couldn't return the gesture. It seemed all he'd done was lose track of the time, thinking of only himself yet again. 'What happened, why are you late?'

'Take your hands off your hips, doesn't suit you in that beautiful dress. Your talents are quite something,' he added, looking again at the garment she'd made and hidden away until now. In a midnight blue, a bustier-style bodice flowed into a billowy skirt. Satin spaghetti straps ran over her shoulders and crossed at the back, and embroidered onto the material were hundreds of tiny flowers in colours from pear green and holly-berry red to delicate white and pale yellow. It was elegant, intricate, and most of all colourful.

'Don't think you can sweet-talk me,' she snapped. God, he was cocky – and today of all days. 'We thought we were going to have to turn your room upside down for the rings.'

'Is the family okay?' Dylan asked, with more patience than she had right now.

'They are.' Finn patted Dylan's shoulder. 'How are you holding up? Any last-minute nerves? Second thoughts? I can help you escape if necessary.'

'Not a chance,' said Dylan confidently, much more at ease now his useless friend was here.

Finn went into his bedroom and soon returned with the rings. 'Here they are, I wouldn't let you down. Never, Dylan.'

'Appreciate it, buddy.'

'You guys had better get ready,' Kaisha urged. There was no time to call Finn out on his behaviour this time, or ever for that matter. She'd been right about him all along. He'd been in the city, must've got carried away with whatever he was up to and lost track of time, and although she knew of the problems in his family and how much he needed to fix them, this was their friends' day. Cleo and Dylan came first.

Finn disappeared into the bathroom and it wasn't long before they heard the water for the shower. 'You wait here,' she said to Dylan. 'I'll go downstairs and ensure we're ready when you both are. And I'll message Darcy, let her know we'll be good to go soon.'

'Kaisha.' He put a hand on her arm. 'Thank you for all your help. You're a good friend, you're like family, to both of us.' He kissed her on her cheek.

'It was my absolute pleasure,' she smiled back.

* * *

Kaisha felt more nervous than a bride herself. Everything was in place and she knew that Cleo was on her way from the Inglenook Lodge. It was a ten-minute walk at the slowest of paces but still Mitch had insisted they use the cars they'd hired to take her out to Bampton Lodge and instead collect her from the Inglenook Lodge and drop her on the corner of Main Street to see what they'd come up with as an alternative.

The sun had set already and the town was blanketed in darkness, which meant the aisle they'd manufactured looked spectacular, especially now the moon had come out to cast its glow through the trees along the sidewalk.

'You ready?' It was Finn behind her as she stood near the entrance to the store waiting to watch her very close friend on one of the happiest days of her life.

'I've been ready for a while.'

'You don't miss a chance to tell me off, do you?'

When she glanced at him, he looked far too good in his suit, the same colour as Dylan's, tailored to show off his physique. He had a hint of stubble on his jaw and a tiny nick that was inconspicuous unless you were as close as she was. A waft of the aftershave he often wore when he wasn't working at the Christmas tree farm came her way, threatening to distract her from the fact he was no good. She'd known it at the start and his antics today should serve as a reminder.

'This place looks amazing,' he went on as though he hadn't been responsible for a lot of added stress. 'I hear it was your idea. Dylan texted me the details and I wondered how you'd pull it off, but the whole space looks great.' His body hovered so close she shivered even in the wrap that covered her upper body and arms.

'You didn't think to reply to his texts?' She shook her head, she needed to let it go. 'And it was worth all the effort to do this, believe me.'

When the black car drew up at the end of the street, Kaisha took her place beside the pine trees opposite the entrance to the store and without another word to Finn, she watched as the wedding party assembled on the street. With four kids, Cleo had decided they had all the extras they needed and so it really was the perfect family affair with Ruby a jubilant chief bridesmaid, Emily and Tabitha as flower girls, and Jacob as proud as could be looking like a mini version of Dylan.

Ruby led the procession, then came Emily and Tabitha holding hands. All the girls had matching outfits – midnight-blue dresses, just visible beneath white faux-fur coats – and carried miniature bouquets, a mixture of pansies and winter jasmine. Jacob came next, wearing a suit in the same colour as his dad's, complete with a cravat. He walked slowly; Kaisha could see he was nervous, but all four of them looked excited. Kaisha wondered whether the change of venue had something to do with it – this was, after all, completely different to what anyone had expected.

All eyes turned at long last, because here came the bride.

Cleo, dressed in an almost-to-the-floor gown, dazzled everyone. Locals, close family, and friends lined the street and watched as she made her way along beneath the lit-up trees, her ivory gown filled with enough sequins to rival the Christmas lights. The tiara pinned in front of her veil sparkled in the moonlight and was as bright as her smile that stretched so far Kaisha suspected by the end of the day she'd have an aching jaw.

Kaisha turned to see Finn not watching Cleo but watching her, with a hint of sadness on his face. She smiled at him. She couldn't be angry, not at a wedding between two people who meant so much, to both of them. But neither would she be fooled. She wasn't going to be taken advantage of or messed around. Never again; she didn't deserve that.

Cleo looked her way as she reached the door to the store on her dad's arm. She mouthed 'Thank you' to Kaisha and Kaisha smiled but motioned for her to get inside before she got cold. Or, more likely, before she herself ended up blubbering away with the emotion of it all.

Cleo made her way through the decorated store and when she reached Dylan standing under the arch that separated the store from the back room, everyone crowded in the best they could, the doors remaining open so nobody missed out on the event the town seemed to have been waiting for for a very long time.

Kaisha had been pulled up to the front by Darcy and Holly and the women stood side by side as they watched their friends take their vows. And Kaisha only exchanged a look with Finn once during the ceremony itself. He looked right at her, his stare penetrating so intently she got flustered and had to refocus. But not so much as he did when Dylan had to gesture a second time for him to hand over the rings. It had made onlookers laugh, but Kaisha wasn't ready to be amused by him at all. He wasn't the man she thought she'd got to know and her heart broke at the thought she'd almost dared to hope.

When Judge Ramsey pronounced them husband and wife, Dylan and Cleo kissed beneath the mistletoe and the Little Knitting Box erupted with cries of joy, whoops of happiness, the magic of a wedding at Christmas. Champagne glasses were filled, people filtered into the back room to make more space in the store, and the doors to the outside were shut firmly to keep the cold out.

'Are we going to show off the cake soon?' Darcy asked Kaisha. She'd been told the cake unveiling would happen here rather than at the lodge purely because Kaisha felt it fitted more with the store and the special memories, and seeing the real sewing machine standing tall and proud on the shelf, knowing her friend had glanced at it during the ceremony as though it were a tiny piece of her grandma Eliza watching over her, she felt sure it was the right thing to do.

'I'll get Finn. It was his masterpiece.' She went to look for him but couldn't spot him in the crowds until she saw him through the window, outside talking on his cell phone.

Who went on their phone during wedding celebrations?

But she bit her lip. This was no time to be furious, to berate him.

She went outside, a stern look on her face, her bare arms feeling the snap of cold straight away. 'If you've finished, we need you for the cake.' She turned on her heel but his hand pulled her back – inside the store everyone was having a magical time; outside they were enveloped in a bitterly cold winter.

'Kaisha, have I done something to you?'

She sighed. 'Not really, but let's just say I was right the first time. About you.'

'I thought we'd moved past that.'

'That was before you turned up late, got Dylan all worried about you and having no idea whether you'd turn up on one of the most important days of his life. And now, on the phone during a wedding, really?'

She turned to go again but his voice stopped her.

'My grandad passed away at 1:42 p.m. today.'

She froze on the spot from the shock rather than the cold. 'Finn…'

'He went peacefully, in his favourite chair.' His voice caught and his sad features in the moonlight made her want to burst into tears. He'd kept it together for his friend, for the big day, when he was surely breaking inside.

'Finn… I'm so sorry.'

'We'd had a family meal, taken him to Central Park, then he just…'

She put her hand out to reach his but the door to the store opened and it was Darcy.

'Not a word, okay?' Finn walked past, into the store and she followed on. And after tapping on the edge of a champagne glass to get everyone's attention, it was time.

'What's all this?' Cleo smiled, relaxed now she was finally married.

Kaisha knew she had to hold any emotions in, just as Finn had done. 'Cleo… today might not have gone as planned,' she began, 'but the venue wasn't the only problem we had today.' Even though her voice was shaking in sympathy at Finn's revelation, she pulled herself together and recounted the story about the cake, the fire, the disaster they hadn't told her about.

'You know what,' said Cleo. 'You lot all think I'm too delicate to share these things with but you're wrong. And not having a cake… well, it doesn't matter. I have everything I want and need right here and now.' She leaned towards Dylan and he dipped his head to kiss her. With a gentle touch to Ruby's cheek, a smile at Jacob, and a wink at Tabitha then Emily, she really did have everything, but Kaisha knew they were about to go one step further.

'Ever since I've known you, Cleo, you've been a solid friend. From the moment I walked into the Little Knitting Box in the West Village, before your husband put you out of business,' she announced before getting a few laughs, 'you've been a constant for me and a friend I couldn't do without. When we heard about the cake disaster, I couldn't possibly make you one; you'd never have forgiven me.' She gestured over to Finn to take the lead.

He cleared his throat. 'I haven't known you long, Cleo, but as soon as I met you, I knew you'd never hurt Dylan and that was enough for me. You will love him, protect him, be by his side, and he'd do anything for you. But don't worry, he didn't make the cake either.' He got as many laughs as Kaisha, who wanted to cry knowing how much he must be hurting right now. 'I took on the responsibility and made the cake myself.'

Cleo's eyebrows weren't the only set to shoot up in surprise.

Finn went out back and brought through the board with the cake on it, hidden beneath a cloche. 'This cake is a reminder of the conversation you and I had about family, in particular grandparents and the role they play in our lives.' His voice wobbled but he pulled himself together again. 'It's also a thank you for giving me a roof over my head for a while, for welcoming me to town without question. I know you had your doubts, but I hope this goes some way towards showing my gratitude.' He took a deep breath. 'Now, it's not your classic wedding cake but it *is* something special and unique to you, this store, your memories, and a tribute to the people who can't be here today to share it with you.'

'Go on, show me!' She was laughing though, probably with nerves more than anything else, but when he lifted off the cloche, she gasped.

Cleo stood staring at the replica of her grandma's sewing machine. Tears sprung to her eyes before she began flapping her fingers. 'I don't want to cry, it'll ruin my make-up,' she giggled, but had no qualms about rushing towards Finn and giving him the biggest hug.

The Singer sewing machine cake sat there proudly, the gold lustre dust perfecting its beauty, everyone admiring it. Cleo's Grandpa Joe dabbed at a tear too; in fact, there weren't many dry eyes in the house by now.

'Finn, I don't know how to thank you,' Cleo told him.

'You haven't tasted it yet,' he joked, masking any of his own pain.

Cleo addressed the crowd. 'As I'm sure you all know, the sewing machine up there,' she said pointing to the real one that had been in their family for years, 'once belonged to my Grandma Eliza. It is from her that I got my love of knitting.' She smiled her grandad's way and he winked back at her. 'And, Finn, you brought her to my wedding in a way I never could've imagined. I really don't know quite how to thank you.' She hugged him yet again.

'Steady on,' said Dylan. 'I'm the groom, she hasn't hugged me that much yet!' He mock-punched Finn in the arm before thanking him just as much for what he'd done.

Champagne was well and truly flowing and all around them friends and family embraced the day, the excitement, and the promise of things yet to come. Nathan and Amelia told everyone how they'd be spending New Year's in New York City. 'Times Square,' Amelia announced, 'no matter how cold and busy it is.' She winked at Nathan, who seemed less keen at the idea but completely on board with anything his other half wanted.

Myles and Darcy sipped champagne and Kaisha asked them all about the Inglenook Lodge, the guests they'd had so far, and whether Myles ever regretted leaving his job in the city. His reply had been along the lines of only when Darcy gets too bossy shortly before Darcy had shuffled him out the door so they could go get the lodge ready to receive all these guests for the next phase of the wedding.

Kaisha hovered at the edge of the store watching Holly and Mitch, an unlikely couple for a while until they'd both realised how suited they were. And now they lived in a little log cabin in the woods, where Mitch ran a Christmas tree farm. Could there be anything more romantic?

Kaisha sighed. Weddings brought on a certain melancholy if you were on your own, no matter how happy you were for the couple who'd just exchanged vows. She mingled with more guests, the store so warm now it was filled with bodies. She noticed Finn doing the same, nobody any the wiser about his pain. And when she saw him sneak outside, she picked up her wrap, draped it around her shoulders, and followed.

'I don't know how you're managing to hold it together in there,' she said softly. 'I'd be in pieces.'

'Easy: this is Dylan's day, not mine.' He finally looked at her, hands in pockets, determination set in. 'Grandad passed peacefully, that's all I ever wanted. And he got his last Christmas wish, for us to be a proper family again. That and seeing the beauty of Central Park as the snow fell.' He rested against the glass exhaling into the cold, both of them surrounded by the pine trees of the aisle as snow began to fall lightly once again.

'Making amends is good. I'm pleased you did it.'

'I hear Bree did the catering. Dylan told me.' He grinned. 'He warned me off you at first but now… maybe it's after he saw the cake, or else he's so full of love that he can't see straight, but he told me to go for it with you.'

'He said that?'

'Actually, it could've been the champagne. How many bottles did you get?'

She put a hand out to catch a falling snowflake, trying to ignore the implication of what he'd just said. 'Too many but I'd have hated to not have enough.'

He turned to look through the window of the Little Knitting Box. 'They really are happy, aren't they?'

'Finally. Some of us thought it would never happen.'

'People say I'll never settle down.'

'And what do you tell them?'

'Before I came back I would've said they were right. I would've been here for the wedding and moved on in a few days.'

'You're still planning to leave?' Her insides plummeted.

'That depends.' He still hadn't looked at her; they were both watching the happy crowds inside the store. 'It depends on whether there's anything here for me in Inglenook Falls.'

'Well, Dylan and Cleo are around, you've made friends with Mitch, Myles... and there's work year-round at the tree farm.'

'All true. I'm wondering if there's another reason to hang around, perhaps.'

Was he talking about her? 'I jumped to conclusions again today.'

'Is that another apology?' he asked.

'Yes, I'm very sorry.'

'I can see you'll keep me on my toes.' He wasn't wrong there. 'I've got a job at a bakery in Manhattan.'

'Finn, that's great.'

'Grandad used his contacts and they've been waiting for my call for months as a favour to him. I went in there yesterday as soon as I got to the city. They called earlier after we got back from Central Park. Grandad was over the moon.'

'You and he had a special relationship; you're lucky to have had him in your life.'

'We all were.' He sniffed back the prickle of tears. 'Sorry.'

'Don't apologise.'

When he gathered himself, he pinched the bridge of his nose to stop any more tears. 'I expect I'll start the job sweeping up floors for a good few months before the bakery trust me to do much else, but it's a start.'

'It's the best news, it really is,' she assured him. 'I'm so pleased for you.'

'I wish you could've met Grandad.'

'Me too.' She leaned her head on his arm.

'You know, he once said that when he met my grandmother all those years ago the only mistake he ever made was not to kiss her within five minutes of meeting her. He'd been too worried he'd get a slap in return, but he'd almost missed out when someone else came along and nearly stole her away.' He turned so their bodies were almost pressed together. 'I don't intend to make that mistake.' He wrestled something from his pocket and showed it to her. 'Enid saw me pinch this, gave me a wink.'

Kaisha looked up at the sprig of mistletoe clutched in his hand that he was now holding high up above them both. And before she had a chance to say anything else, his arms wrapped around her waist as the snow fell, delicate white flakes illuminated in the moonlight, and he kissed her.

Inside the store someone may have cheered but neither of them cared. Because tonight was a night filled with magic, new beginnings, and happy ever afters.

EPILOGUE
SIX MONTHS LATER

Kaisha and Finn

Kaisha ran the last few metres to Finn when she saw him in Madison Square Park. 'I've missed you!' She wrapped her arms around his neck as his hug lifted her off her feet. The sun was shining on a brilliant June day in New York City and after a fortnight in the Napa Valley with Bree enjoying sister time the way it should be, Kaisha was glad to be with her boyfriend again. Two weeks was too long to be apart.

Losing his grandad had, of course, had an effect on Finn and even though Kaisha had never been lucky enough to meet him, his grandad's spirit lived on in his grandson, who had no intention of moving on anywhere these days. He had a job with a bakery who were more than impressed with him and who had already involved him in the design side whenever they could.

Finn and Kaisha walked hand in hand towards East 74th Street. 'I can't wait to get back to work after my holiday. Is that bad?' She pulled a face.

'Not when you love it... I get that.'

Of course he did. Finally, he was doing what he loved and instead of it bringing painful reminders of his younger sister, it gave him great joy and he remembered the happy moments rather than the sad times that followed. 'I resisted checking my emails while I was away too. Cleo told me to take a real break and she'd keep an eye on any new orders or queries that came in.'

'You two do make a great team.'

Kaisha had also managed Cleo's email while she was away on honeymoon and, for now, they were working well together. The Little Knitting Box store was largely the same except for the mannequin that displayed garments Kaisha had made, alternating them with the seasons. There were business cards at the front desk too and Cleo was sure to sell the dressmaking side to any customers, popping a card into the bag along with their purchases. Most locals knew about the dressmaking but Kaisha had also attracted tourists with emergency clothing repairs – broken zips, hems coming down – as well as a school in Bampton who'd heard about Kaisha's Christmas pageant costumes and signed her up to do theirs this year. She'd already started work on them given they needed forty costumes.

'I only have one problem with that dress you're wearing now,' he said of the piece she'd made a few weeks before going away. Navy and white patchworked material with a halter neck was perfect for the summer and she'd made Bree one in the same design except in reds.

'And what might that be?'

'I'm not sure I can work the knot at the back.'

'Cheeky,' she grinned.

'Did Bree like hers?'

Kaisha hadn't shown her sister until they arrived in the Napa Valley and she pulled it from her suitcase as a surprise. 'She laughed and told me that we weren't little girls any more, she suggested we wear them on alternate days.' With a smile she added, 'I told her there was no chance of that, it was a sisterhood ritual. And it was payback for selling that dress on eBay. She laughed, said I'd guilted her into it, and put the dress on. We did get a few odd looks.'

'You two had a good holiday?'

'We had an amazing time, just the two of us.'

'Your parents must be pretty happy.'

'They are, and Dad looks more relaxed these days. Even though neither of us had ever told them what happened, I get the impression they knew there was something going on. But now, retirement and family getting on is good for everyone.'

'Amen to that.'

'Are you looking forward to seeing your parents today?' They were coming over for lunch to celebrate his dad's birthday.

Finn slung an arm across her shoulders, pulling her closer as they turned onto his street. 'I'm happy to say that I really am. Never thought those words would pass my lips.' They reached the stoop leading up to what had once been his grandad's home and was now his.

'I can't wait to see what you've done with the apartment.'

But Finn didn't let her go past yet. Instead he took her in his arms again, kissed her as though nobody was watching, and then took her by the hand, greeting his new neighbours flamboyantly on their way past.

Inside the apartment she took in the antique-white walls. 'You really have been working hard while I've been away.' It looked fresh now that the chipped paint had been replaced, making the whole place brighter.

After New Year's, Finn had moved his things out of the apartment above the Little Knitting Box and to Manhattan to give his relationship with Kaisha a good chance of lasting. They didn't want to start living together now they were a couple; they wanted the excitement of the early stages of a relationship, a chance to get to know one another properly. And he had the job in the city, she had a new business to focus on, so it made sense.

The apartment had been left to Andy but he and Beverly had agreed it wouldn't be sold, it would stay in the family, and Finn was living there while he sorted the place out. He'd insisted on paying rent, although it was a steal compared to other places in Manhattan, and everyone seemed happy with the arrangement for now.

Sorting out Grandad's apartment had been Finn's project with the unexpected help of both his parents, who'd come over together many times. Kaisha suspected it had been cathartic for all of them to process their memories, address their grief for Grandad and Mackenzie, lean on one another rather than push each other away.

'Can I take a peek?' Kaisha spotted the cloche covering up the cake Finn had made for his dad's birthday lunch today. The kitchen was the only room untouched as yet, but in time, when Finn saved enough money, he'd tackle it.

'Go for it.'

She raised the cloche and although she knew she was about to be wowed, she hadn't expected such intricacy. The cake was the same beehive construction he'd made once for his little sister. This year, his dad would celebrate his birthday with pride and thanks for everything he had in his life, and they'd all stop hiding away from talking about Mackenzie. But this cake wasn't a surprise. Finn had asked both of his parents and they'd been delighted with the idea. Kaisha had been there at the time and had seen a family reunited, parents who clearly loved their son and may even have some love left over for each other. Finn was waiting for news on that one.

Finn showed her the bathroom that she'd already seen refitted but not painted. And when he showed her the bedroom, the room with the colour that had taken forever to decide upon, she knew they'd chosen right. A barley colour gave it a lift but left a warmth to it, especially with the sun creeping across the sky and sneaking in through the sheer drapes that stayed there all day for privacy and were covered by thicker material at night.

'I'm kind of hoping you move in eventually,' he told her, taking her in his arms.

'All in good time, you know that.' To be here, back in Manhattan, was what she really wanted long-term. She still had to pinch herself that she'd get the whole dream – the city, the man, the job she loved. She was happier than she'd been in years and Finn had a lot to do with that. She'd never been so at ease or had this kind of confidence with a man, knowing he'd be right by her side. He'd put her through her paces at first, but she kind of hoped he'd continue to do so.

'What does a man have to do?' He looked heavenwards.

When the buzzer to the apartment went, Kaisha grinned. 'Answer the door, that's what you need to do.'

'You'll keep,' he told her, sweeping her into his arms and planting a kiss on his lips. 'And later, I'll show you the bedroom properly.'

'I look forward to it, but we'll be straight out to Inglenook Falls by early evening so I don't think we'll have time for much else.'

'Kaisha,' he said, ignoring the buzzer. 'We have all the time in the world.' And with his kiss he left a promise that had her knowing he'd never ever let her down.

ACKNOWLEDGMENTS

A huge, huge thank you to every single one of my readers who have picked up this story and fallen in love with the *New York Ever After* series. I have loved spending time with these characters and adding another book to the collection is always a thrill.

Thank you so much to Katharine Walkden for her superior editing skills in the early stages of this book and to the team at Boldwood Books for continuing the process so that we can deliver the best possible story to readers. And thank you Team Boldwood for a sixth stunning cover in the *New York Ever After* series!

A huge thank you as always to my husband and children who never doubt me and are always on hand to listen to my woes or tell me to get on and finish the book! I love you all.

Helen x

MORE FROM HELEN ROLFE

We hope you enjoyed reading *Moonlight and Mistletoe at the Christmas Wedding*. If you did, please leave a review.

If you'd like to gift a copy, this book is also available as an ebook, digital audio download and audiobook CD.

Sign up to Helen Rolfe's mailing list for news, competitions and updates on future books.

https://bit.ly/HelenRolfeNews

You can now order the first book in Helen Rolfe's heart-warming *Heritage Cove* series.

ABOUT THE AUTHOR

Helen Rolfe is the author of many bestselling contemporary women's fiction titles, set in different locations from the Cotswolds to New York. Most recently published by Orion, she is bringing sixteen titles to Boldwood - a mixture of new series and well-established backlist. She lives in Hertfordshire with her husband and children.

Follow Helen on social media:

 twitter.com/hjrolfe

 facebook.com/helenjrolfewriter

 instagram.com/helen_j_rolfe

Boldwᴏᴏd

Boldwood Books is an award-winning fiction
publishing company seeking out the best
stories from around the world.

Find out more at www.boldwoodbooks.com

Join our reader community for brilliant books,
competitions and offers!

Follow us
@BoldwoodBooks
@BookandTonic

Sign up to our weekly
deals newsletter

https://bit.ly/BoldwoodBNewsletter

Printed in Great Britain
by Amazon

23334265R00155